BROTHERS
★ IN ARMS ★
HELL'S HIGHWAY

Also by John Antal

Armor Attacks
Infantry Combat
Combat Team
Proud Legions
TALON Force
City Fights
Forest of Steel

BROTHERS ★IN ARMS™★

HELL'S HIGHWAY

A BROTHERS IN ARMS NOVEL

J O H N   A N T A L

PRESIDIO PRESS

BALLANTINE BOOKS • NEW YORK

A Presidio Press Mass Market Original

Copyright © 2008 by Gearbox Software, LLC & ® or ™ where indicated.

All Rights Reserved. Used under authorization.

Published in the United States by Presidio Press, an imprint of The Random House Publishing Group, a division of Random House, Inc., New York.

PRESIDIO PRESS and colophon are trademarks of Random House, Inc.

Operation Market Garden Plan map copyright © by 2006 *Armchair General* magazine. All rights reserved. Used by permission of *Armchair General* magazine.
101st Helmet Markings chart copyright © by 2005 *Armchair General*. All rights reserved. Used by permission of *Armchair General* magazine.

ISBN 978-0-345-50337-4

Illustrations © 2008 by Don Moore
dmoore@donmooreillustrator.com

Printed in the United States of America

www.brothersinarmsgame.com
www.presidiopress.com

OPM   9 8 7 6 5 4 3 2 1

With gratitude and thankfulness for those who came before us, and remembering those who created our today, this book is dedicated to all those who serve and do their part to save the world from darkness and tyranny.

Thanks

Writing a novel is difficult work. It is easier, however,
when you have the support of someone special.
In my case, this support is never-ending and comes
from my wonderful wife and partner, Uncha.
To her, I owe my inspiration, my fire, and all my love.

Special thanks also to my sister-in-law, Beth Antal, and
to Carolyn Petracca
for help in editing the manuscript.

I also want to thank Randy Pitchford, Brian Martel,
Stephen Bahl, and P. J. Putnam at Gearbox Software.

The Minstrel Boy to the war is gone,
In the ranks of death you'll find him;
His father's sword he hath girded on,
And his wild harp slung behind him;
"Land of Song!" said the warrior bard,
"Tho' all the world betrays thee,
One sword, at least, thy rights shall guard,
One faithful harp shall praise thee!"

—Verse from "The Minstrel Boy"

The darkest places in hell are reserved for those who
maintain their neutrality in times of moral crisis.

—Dante

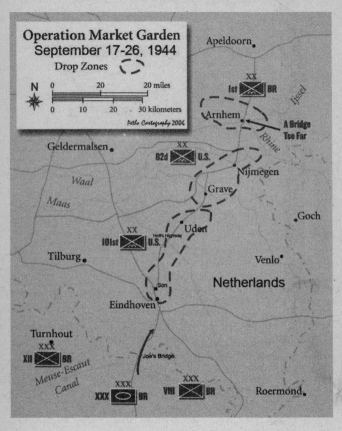

Map of the Overall Market Garden Plan
(Originally published in *Armchair General* magazine)

Hell's Highway

Map of the 101st Airborne Division Area of Operations

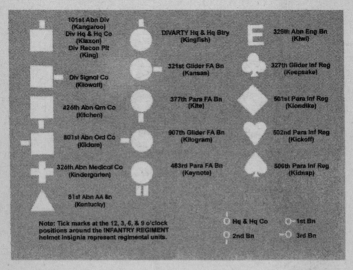

The helmet markings of the various units of the 101st Airborne Division. Not shown is the "R" that marked the sides of the helmet of soldiers assigned to the 101st Airborne Division Reconnaissance Platoon. (Originally published in *Armchair General* magazine)

HELL'S HIGHWAY

Staff Sergeant Mathew Baker

1: THE CANAL

Out of every 100 men, ten shouldn't even be there. / Eighty are just targets. / Nine are the real fighters, and we are lucky to have them, for they make the battle. / Ah, but the one, / One is a warrior, / And he will bring the others back.
— HERACLITUS, circa 500 BC

Monday, 0140 hours, September 25, 1944.

Cold, wet, tired, and scared. Why, Baker thought, is war always this way?

The air was heavy with moisture, and a thick fog blanketed the flat, marshy land.

"Let's get on with it," Staff Sergeant Matt Baker announced with a grim smile that was more a measure of determination than anything else. Baker stood five feet, eleven inches with the build of a Notre Dame linebacker. His closely cropped brown hair and blue eyes made him look older than his twenty-one years. His youth and confidence belied the fact that he was a veteran of many skirmishes and battles. Now, he was the leader of a small, forlorn group of soldiers facing an impossible task.

"A helluva way to fight a war," Corporal Tom Zanovitch answered. "But you'll do okay. Both of you. I know you will."

Baker took off his helmet and handed it to Zanovitch. The helmet was emblazoned with a white "R" painted on both sides, designating that Baker was a member of the elite Reconnaissance Platoon of the 101st Airborne Division, the Screaming Eagles.

The rumble of distant artillery interrupted the moment, reminding everyone that there was a bigger war going on than just their personal battle in this small section of Holland.

"We'll only need our pistols for this mission," Baker added, and gave his submachine gun to Zanovitch.

Zanovitch took Baker's helmet and weapon and placed them in the jeep. At the same time, Private First Class Johnny Swanson, a tough New Yorker from the 326th Airborne Engineer Battalion, took off his helmet and weapon and laid them in the jeep.

War changes you, Baker thought as he reflected on his short twenty-one years of existence. It compresses time and experience.

Two years ago, he was a civilian. A year ago he was a recruit. A little more than three months ago he was a rookie soldier, jumping into the dark night on D-day. As a squad leader he fought his way across the Normandy hedgerows to Carentan, leading his paratroopers with distinction but unable to save them all. He had earned a Bronze Star for valor for his leadership in the Normandy operation and lost some good friends. He had aged a lifetime in the process.

Baker drew a .45 caliber pistol from the brown leather holster at his side. He carefully looked at the pistol for a moment, read the inscription on its side, and then pulled back the slide and let it jump forward. A .45 caliber round was now loaded in the chamber.

"That pistol has come a long way. The colonel would be proud. Honor and courage," Zanovitch offered.

Baker looked at Corporal Zanovitch for one protracted moment, searching the eyes of his fellow soldier, looking for a meaning behind the comment. Like a flare in the night, Baker's glance seemed to say: "Not now—don't burden me with this now."

"Well, in any case, good luck," Zanovitch offered, looking straight at his sergeant's face. "If it can be done, you and Swanson can do it."

Baker didn't answer. He pushed the thumb safety up on the pistol, holstered the weapon, then turned to Private Swanson. "Let's move out."

"I'm ready," Swanson answered.

Swanson, also armed only with a pistol, slung two satchel charges over his left shoulder as he handed two demolition packs to Baker.

Baker took the charges, nodded to Zanovitch. "Be ready with your bazooka, just in case."

Zanovitch smiled. "No problem. You know I never miss."

The two men walked away in the dense fog. They moved silently through the cobblestone streets of the village to the fields. The ground was soggy and the movement cross-country was difficult as the mud clung to their boots. They headed east toward the canal.

Baker looked back to see that Swanson was behind him, then stopped to check his compass. He identified an east-southeast heading and quietly moved out on that bearing, hoping they would not accidentally stumble into a German outpost.

The boom of shells, detonating somewhere far to the north, was testimony that the battle for Hell's Highway was still under way. Maybe there was still a chance for the beleaguered British 1st Airborne and the Polish Brigade at Arnhem? The British 1st Airborne, the Red Devils, had been told to seize the bridge at Arnhem and hold on for two days—three at the most. Now it was already nine days and the tanks of the British XXX Corps had yet to reach them.

It seemed hard to believe that only nine days ago Baker and his men had been safe in England. More poignantly, only a few days ago, all those who had died in battle in the past few days in the towns and fields near Son, Eindhoven, St. Oedenrode, and Veghel were still alive.

Only nine days ago.

That was the funny thing about time, he thought. Whether it was nine days or ninety years, dead was dead.

It began nine days ago. September 17, 1944, was the 101st Airborne Division's second D-Day, and Baker was a part of it. The greatest airborne fleet ever massed for an operation, 35,000 Allied paratroopers, roared across the skies from the United Kingdom and spanned the Channel waters in what was being called Operation Market Garden. The air armada was so large that while the first planes were spewing forth parachutists on drop zones (DZs) and gliders were crash-landing on landing zones (LZs), planes and gliders transporting the division were still taking off from British airfields.

Some genius had decided that this airborne assault would occur in broad daylight, and the German antiaircraft gunners had a field day. German flak, a term derived from the German acronym for antiaircraft cannon, met the invaders en route, hot and heavy, bursting in bright flashes of orange and red and remaining as black puffs in the sky, but the huge armada droned steadily on. Formations of slow-flying, two-engined C-47 Skytrain aircraft held firm despite the enemy's fire. Pilots of burning planes struggled with controls as they flew to their designated DZs, but stayed on course as paratroopers jumped from the aircraft and plummeted earthward.

The invasion of Holland had begun with the Screaming Eagles dropped behind German lines as the base of the airborne penetration. Surprise was complete and the Germans were initially caught off-guard. Allied aircraft, parachutes, and gliders filled the skies. On the first day, there was little opposition from the Germans, and Baker began to believe that the intelligence reports might be correct—that they would only be up against old men and Hitler youth. The veteran paratroopers of the Screaming Eagles quickly assembled and marched on their objectives. They had eleven bridges to take in their portion of the Market Garden plan, and the men of the 101st Airborne always took their objectives.

The mission of the 101st Airborne Division was to capture Eindhoven and to seize the bridges over canals and rivers at Veghel, St. Oedenrode, and Son. To attain these objectives the paratroopers of the Screaming Eagles had to seize and hold a portion of the main highway extending over a twenty-five-mile area. Commanders realized that their units would be strung out on both sides of the single road that ran from Veghel to Eindhoven. In-depth security would be sacrificed, and the paratroopers would have to march and countermarch to stop the Germans from blocking the route.

At the same time, the British XXX Corps was charging forward with tanks and infantry along a single, narrow road to link up with the paratroopers. XXX Corps's goal was to make sixty miles in forty-eight hours, pass through the U.S. 101st Airborne at the base of the airborne carpet from Eindhoven to Uden, link up with the U.S. 82d Airborne in the middle around the town of Nijmegen, and finally reach the British 1st Airborne and a Polish Airborne brigade near the town of Arnhem. Arnhem and the bridge across the Rhine River was the prize. With this gateway into Germany, the Allies could overrun the German defenses along the Siegfried Line and outflank Hitler's Legions. The daring plan was expected to end the war before Christmas 1944.

The linkup of the armored forces with all three airborne landings was planned to occur within forty-eight hours. It seemed a simple matter to drive the distance, especially since the Germans were so disorganized and demoralized after their traumatic retreat from France only a few weeks before.

Few things in war, however, go as planned.

Baker and Swanson struggled forward in the dark carrying their heavy packs. Movement in fog this thick was agonizingly slow as Baker had to stop to listen for sounds of the enemy as well as check his compass bearing to make sure they were on course. Sight was of little value in these conditions. The fog denied observation until it was too late. Sound became the vital means of locating the enemy. Using his compass and the process of dead reckoning, Baker led Swanson to the western bank of the canal.

This particular canal was a small, tributary-like canal that was a branch of a much larger channel eventually linking with the rivers and waterways in this area of the Netherlands. These canals that crisscrossed Holland made cross-country vehicle movement a nightmare. This was particularly true for the big British Sherman tanks and Firefly tank destroyers of British general Brian Horrocks's XXX Corps. The canals were even more of a headache for the bigger German Mark IV and Mark V Panther tanks and the German Sturmgeschutz (StuG) assault guns. As a result, any canal crossing site in Holland earned immediate military significance and became prime real estate.

Baker leaned over the side of the canal. He looked back at Swanson. "Ready?"

"As ready as I'll ever be," Swanson whispered.

Baker exhaled, hard and still, slowly lowering himself over the concrete wall of the canal and into the chilly water. The current was not strong, but the canal was deep and the water was cold. For a brief second, Baker felt a flash of panic shoot down his spine as he felt the weight of the satchel charge pull him down. Brief as a thought, his mind shot back to the time when he had first learned to swim. He remembered the icy fingers of fear he had felt as the water lapped around his neck. He might have let the water take him that day had it not been for the sternness of the man at the side of the pond who had challenged him to go on in spite of his fear, the same man who had given him the pistol he carried.

Baker held on to a crevice in the wall of the canal. The sides of the Willemsvaart canal were steep concrete and stone.

Swanson slid as quietly as he could into the water next to Baker.

"Now all we have to do is get to the other side without getting shot," Baker whispered. "I'll go first."

"Understood," Swanson said as he found a handhold in the wall and held on while Baker prepared to swim to the other side.

Baker couldn't see the other side of the canal. It wasn't that the distance was so great, it was simply that the impenetrable fog limited visibility. He stopped for a moment and listened carefully. He didn't want to think what would happen if the Germans were waiting for him on the other side of the canal.

Hearing only the sound of the water flowing in the canal, Baker unwound a length of rope that was tied to his web belt. He handed the rope to Swanson. "Take this so we don't get lost in the fog. I'll swim across and you wait here. When I tug on the line, follow the rope and swim across to me."

Swanson nodded.

Baker pushed off the western bank of the canal, glided for a moment in the chilly water, quietly swimming toward the other side. His heavy load of explosives tugged at him and pulled him down. He struggled to keep above water by moving forward. In a minute, he was across the canal, reaching the wall of the eastern side.

At the far wall he treaded water while desperately searching for something along the wall of the canal to hold on to. Stretching as far as he could reach, his right hand found a metal mooring ring. He held on to the ring and tugged on the rope. After a while Swanson appeared in the fog and came up beside Baker.

Baker listened carefully for sounds of the enemy. With the fog and the countryside as flat as an anvil's face, every sound seemed loud and close by.

Somewhere to the east a dog started barking.

"That damn dog is going to give us away," Swanson whispered.

"Nothing we can do about that now," Baker replied quietly. "The crossing must be right in front of us."

As he moved through the water along the eastern wall of the canal, he heard the sound of the Germans working on the crossing point.

Swanson heard the noise, too, and pointed up ahead.

"Yeah," Baker whispered. "We must be close."

Swanson took a deep breath as he looked toward the crossing point. "Damn, I can't see it."

Baker slithered through the murky water to a better vantage point to observe the crossing site. Quickly, he searched for a handhold in the concrete wall. His hand found another barge ring.

The dog was barking louder now.

"It's ten feet in front of us," Baker whispered. "Start placing the charges."

Swanson handed a spool of det cord to Baker. "Hang on to your pack charges. I'll be back after I place these two."

Surrounded by the fog, Swanson swam forward. Baker waited patiently, listening to the German voices on the bank above him. After a few minutes that seemed like hours, Swanson returned.

"Hand me your packs."

As Baker handed Swanson the explosive charges, he heard the grinding of tracks against steel road wheels.

"Kraut tanks," Swanson whispered, reinforcing Baker's observation. "They must be moving to the crossing point."

"We're running out of time."

Baker handed his two demolition packs to Swanson.

Swanson took the charges and swam forward once more, carefully searching the side of the canal for a place to tie down the charges.

The dog became more agitated and barked incessantly. Baker felt his heart beating hard in his chest.

The minutes ticked by in endless anticipation as the dog's barking seemed to be coming from just above him.

Baker's heart froze at hearing more German voices. In the thick fog he couldn't tell where the Germans were, or how many, but he could hear their footsteps up above.

"*Schieben Sie hoch. Lassen Sie uns gehen!*" a gruff voice shouted from above.

Baker held his breath for a moment. Holding on to the mooring ring, he held his pistol ready.

Tense seconds turned into anxious minutes as Swanson worked to place the last two charges.

Baker waited and clicked down on the thumb safety of his .45 caliber Colt automatic pistol.

"Okay, they're set," Swanson whispered.

Suddenly, Baker looked up and saw a German soldier pointing a rifle down toward the water.

"*Wer ist dort?*" the German screamed and then fired his rifle.

German 88mm Multipurpose Cannon

2: BY BRASS
AND BLUFF

Obviously, boldness is the thing. We will rush the bridge.
—Lieutenant Colonel J.O.E. Vandeleur,
Commander 3d Battalion, Irish Guards,
32d Guards Brigade, Guards Armored Division, XXX Corps

Fifeen Days Earlier, Sunday, September 10, 1944.

It was early morning and there was no sleep. Staff Sergeant Mathew Baker lay on an uncomfortable army cot in the damp air of his gloomy tent, thinking about the war, his eyes wide open. The camp was as quiet as an un-drawn sword. But the quiet, Baker knew, would not last long.

Baker closed his eyes, praying for sleep. He was weary, but not from lack of trying to rest. In spite of hitting the sack before midnight, he felt as if he had not slept at all. Still in his pants and T-shirt, he laid on the cot most of the night, his mind swirling with thoughts of men he had once known and friends who were recently killed, wounded, or missing. His thoughts pummeled his con-science like waves striking against a rocky shore. In the moments when he did sleep, he saw the vague faces of dying men, men he thought he knew but somehow couldn't make out.

In these moments, his heart felt like an empty glass. After the hell of the fighting in Normandy, he wondered if he was tough enough for what lay ahead. He also won-dered if he had the strength to keep his humanity.

A loudspeaker played reveille.

It was 0530 and dark. Sunrise would not occur for another two hours. During these summers of the war, ever since 1940, the British had set their clocks two hours ahead of GMT, on what they called British Double Summer Time (BDST). So at 0530 hours British Double Summer Time (0330 hours, or 3:30 a.m. GMT) on Sunday, September 10, it was pitch dark. This manipulation of the clocks made the days start early and, it seemed, the nights last longer.

He fumbled in his pocket for a match. Reliable as ever, the army match sparked, sputtered, and failed to light.

"Specially designed for damp environments," joked a cynical voice from a second cot a hand's reach away.

Baker didn't reply. He pulled out another match and tried again. This time the match stayed lit long enough for him to find a nearby candle that was situated on an empty ammunition box. He lit the candle, and the darkness fled.

And as it did, so did the faces in his visions. He blessed the candle.

The dim light inside the tent revealed Corporal Tom Zanovitch, already half dressed and putting on his boots. Next to the candle was Baker's steel helmet, with the R painted in white on its side. Baker was the leader of a squad of jeep-mounted reconnaissance scouts of the 101st Airborne Reconnaissance Platoon. They were a special unit, hand-picked from the best in the Division.

The two paratroopers executed the routine they had performed the past few weeks to prepare for another day. Outside the tent, the noise escalated—men cursing, metal equipment clanging against metal, all the sounds of an army camp coming to life. The camp was a city of tents, a canvas metropolis, complete with mess hall and field showers. The 101st Airborne camp was sited near the Royal Air Force's Ramsbury Airfield in the United Kingdom, four miles east of Marlborough in Wiltshire. It wasn't much to call home, but since the fighting at Normandy, it had been a haven for Baker and his men.

Baker and Zanovitch wore baggy paratrooper pants and olive drab T-shirts. Corporal Tom Zanovitch, the older of the two men but Baker's junior in rank, was in the middle of lacing up his brown jump boots when he asked, "So, Sarge, what's the plan today?"

"The usual," Baker replied. "We'll check the weapons, go over our jeeps one more time, and wait for 'the word.'"

"Baker, you are just too serious," Zanovitch replied. "What you need is a good joke."

"As if you have any to tell," Baker chided. "Good ones that is."

"I'll take that as a challenge," Zanovitch answered. "Have I told you the story of the four soldiers who reported to Saint Peter?"

Baker laughed. "No, and I bet you've been waiting to tell this one all night."

"Not at all," Zanovitch replied. "But since you asked, here it is.

"One day, four young doughboys turn up outside the Pearly Gates. Saint Peter explains that before they can pass they must answer one simple question. Up walks the first guy. Saint Peter asks, 'What's two plus two?'

"The first soldier answers: 'Three.'

"'No,' says Saint Peter.

"'Five.'

"'No,' says Saint Peter.

"'Four.'

"'Yes; in you go.'

"Up comes the second soldier. Saint Peter asks him, 'What's two plus two?' He answers, 'The square route of sixteen.'

"Very impressed, Saint Peter allows him to pass.

"Up comes the third soldier. Saint Peter asks him, 'What's two plus two?'

"'It's greater than two.'

"'Yes.'

"'But less than six.'

"'Yes.'

"'It's greater than three.'

"'Yes.'

"'But less than five.'

"'Yes.'

"'It's four.'

"'Well done, in you go,' Saint Peter commands.

"Up comes the fourth soldier. Saint Peter asks him, 'What's two plus two?'

"'Five. Geronimo!' and without a pause, the soldier charges past Saint Peter and pushes through the Pearly Gates.

"Observing the commotion, an angel hovers over to Saint Peter and asks, 'What was all that about?'

"Saint Peter answers, 'It's perfectly obvious. There must be a war on earth and those four men were all soldiers who have been killed.'

"'I follow you so far, Saint Peter, but how can you tell that they deserve to enter the Pearly Gates?' inquires the angel.

"'It's really very simple. The first guy was an engineer, as smart as seaweed and as crude as mud, but he kept hammering away until he got through.

"'The second guy was an army pilot, who gave me more information than I really required.

"'The third guy was an artilleryman, who was uncomfortable with any firm answer, so in true artillery fashion he bracketed in on the correct answer until he hit the target.'

"'But what about the fourth guy?' inquired the angel. 'He got the answer wrong and then, without so much as a thank you, tore through the gates anyway. Why didn't you stop him?'

"'Ahh,' said Saint Peter, 'that guy was a paratrooper, braver than Lancelot and dumber than dirt, but you've just gotta love 'em.'"

Baker shook his head just as the tent flap opened and a young, baby-faced private entered.

"Here's your mail, Sergeant," the youth said as he handed a letter to Baker. "First sergeant wanted me to get these out before mess call."

"Don't you know how to knock, *Private*?"

"Knock? On the side of a tent?" The soldier answered, incredulous.

"Yeah, knock, you knot-head. Well, anything for me?" Zanovitch barked.

"Sorry, nothing for you Zanovitch," the young paratrooper responded.

"That's Corporal Zanovitch, tadpole," the older man growled.

"Yes, Corporal," the soldier replied.

"I was soldiering when you were still in diapers, and if you ever call me anything but corporal again, you'll see so much KP duty you'll be praying for battle."

"Franky, did Top give you any news about our alert status?" Baker asked, using the soldier slang "Top" for the company's first sergeant.

"No, Sergeant. I doubt if anything is going to happen," the kid-soldier said. "I'll tell ya, Sarge, I am tired of false alerts and dry runs. They've canceled more than a dozen operations since I joined this outfit in July. Twice we have loaded up and waited on the airfield, only to be told to stand down. Hell, Patton's tanks are moving across France like banshees with their asses on fire. The way things are going, the war will be over by Christmas, and I'll never hear a shot fired in anger."

"Listen to this tadpole," Zanovitch said with a laugh. "Baker, look at our warrior who is raring to go. Franky is eager to take on the Nazis. Hell, he just wants to get out of KP duty."

"Well, why shouldn't I be raring to go? That's why I joined the paratroops. That's why I was selected for recon, isn't it?" Franky pleaded.

"You were selected for recon, Franky, because all the grown men are wounded or dead," Zanovitch chided. "Now we are recruiting babies to fight. What is this man's army coming to, I ask you?"

Franky stood stupefied, unable to answer the question posed to him.

"Don't worry, Franky, you'll get your chance soon enough," Baker said solemnly, as he looked at Franky and tried to turn the conversation away from the new soldier's inexperience and age. "Don't wish for things you don't want."

Baker turned to Zanovitch and gave the man a look that said: "Lay off the little guy." Zanovitch was the most experienced soldier in the squad, had served in the French Foreign legion before returning to the United States to join the U.S. Army, and was one of Baker's gruffest personalities when it came to handling newcomers in the unit. Baker worried that Zanovitch enjoyed tormenting the new guys a bit too much. Baker wanted to build a team and didn't need Franky feeling any more insecure than he already felt.

"But . . ." Private First Class Franky protested, "all this sitting around is starting to get to me."

"Corporal Zanovitch, the private has a point," Baker announced. "Don't we have something for this soldier to do?"

"Franky, you'll never learn," Zanovitch said with a grin. "I'll be by your tent in thirty minutes to inspect your M1 rifle and web gear, and it had all better be spotless and in good order. Tell the rest of the squad that you volunteered them as well. Inspection at 0800, laid out in proper order, right after breakfast."

"Yes, Corporal," Franky whined, but stood in the entrance to the tent as if waiting for something more.

"Well, don't just stand there. Dismissed," Zanovitch barked.

Private Franky ran from the tent like a quail spooked by a bird dog. Zanovitch chuckled.

"You're too hard on him," Baker offered. "He's as green as grass. He needs your experience, not your sarcasm."

"You're as moody as a dame on the rag," Zanovitch replied. "You're kidding, right?"

"No, damn it, I'm serious," Baker replied. "The guys used to make fun of Legget the same way."

"Baker, the problem with you is that you care too damn much," Zanovitch replied. "Legget got everything he deserved, except maybe getting shot near Carentan, but that is what happens in war. He had to learn to stand by himself. A man has to be tough in this business, or he'll not last long."

"Franky's a kid," Baker protested.

"No, he's a soldier. He may have lied about his age to enlist, but he is of legal age now and has been through basic training and jump school. He's a paratrooper, and your life, mine, and maybe a lot of others will depend on whether he acts as a man or acts like a kid," Zanovitch insisted.

"Zanovitch—" Baker replied, but before he could finish his sentence, Zanovitch cut him off.

"No, you know I'm right," Zanovitch insisted. "That's

what I call 'being stuck between a rock and a hard place.' To be a good combat leader, you have to love your men. But to win in combat, you have to risk the men you love."

There was a short silence between the two men. Baker's stare pierced through Zanovitch, but he didn't reply. There were times when Baker had an intense dislike of Zanovitch, but not when the bullets were flying. In combat, Zanovitch was the kind of man Baker wanted at his side.

Outside the tent, a bugle played over the loudspeaker, announcing mess call.

"Well, let's get some chow," Zanovitch replied. "I have a bunch of rookies to inspect, and I'm in a foul mood."

"By the way, check them out carefully. The scuttlebutt is that we're headed to Holland," Baker offered. "It's not confirmed yet, but I believe this time we will have a 'wet run.' I think we'll get 'the word' today or tomorrow."

"Fine with me," Zanovitch answered, as if he hadn't a care in the world. "I ain't ever been to Holland. I can kill Krauts in Holland, France, or Germany, I really don't care. But right now, I care to get some breakfast. Think the mess will have any real eggs—not that powdered shit they've been serving the past two weeks?"

Sunday, September 10, 0930 hours, in the woods northwest of the Belgian town of Hechtel:

A pair of Typhoon fighter-bombers roared across the sky at treetop level. The aircraft suddenly shot up toward the sun and then dived down to the east, stammering their deadly 20mm cannons at an unseen target.

"Ours or theirs?" A German *Feldwebel* with a bandaged left hand asked the man next to him. The two men sat in the black, Belgium mud in a hastily dug foxhole.

Feldwebel Weise, the man who asked the question, didn't even bother to look up at the aircraft. He was using a knife to pick fish out of a small can as he asked the question. He savored the pilchards as if they were a delicacy of the highest order and smiled. "God, I love the Luftwaffe."

The tall man next to the *Feldwebel* did not answer. There was no need to answer. The question was rhetorical and every German soldier on the Western Front knew it.

"If you see a silver plane, it's American, if you see a black plane it's RAF. If you see no planes at all it's the Luftwaffe," Weise continued.

The *Oberfeldwebel* grinned at his friend's gallows humor. The German air force, the vaunted Luftwaffe, had been chased from the skies of western Europe. If it was daylight, and there was an airplane in the sky, you could count on it being an Allied war bird, or *jabo,* in soldier's slang. The word *jabo* was derived from the German *Jäger*-Bomber, or "fighter-bomber" (literally, "hunter-bomber").

"If there is one thing I hate more than anything else on this earth," the tall, green-eyed *Oberfeldwebel* growled, "it's retreating."

The six-foot-one-inch *Oberfeldwebel* cast a commanding presence, even though he was sitting cross-legged in a muddy hole in a wood on the edge of a farmer's field. The *Oberfeldwebel* was only twenty-eight years old. His mottled green-and-brown camouflaged jump smock, or *Knochensack* ("bone-sack") as the paratroopers dourly called them, was soiled and torn. His M-38 Fallschirmjäger helmet was scratched and dented. A Russian-made PPSh-41 submachine gun, with its seventy-one-round drum magazine, gave the *Oberfeldwebel* the look of a Chicago gangster, and after one glimpse of his face there was no doubt as to who was in charge.

Since the *Oberfeldwebel* was one of the few "old hares" in the unit, he wore brown leather "Y" straps attached to his combat belt. Wearing brown, verses the newly issued black "Y"straps, was another sign that the *Oberfeldwebel* was a veteran and had fought in the first campaigns of this long war. The right side of the belt held a Walther P-38 pistol in a brown hard-shell holster and a standard bayonet for a K-98 rifle. Attached on the left side of the belt was a map case and a pouch containing three thirty-five-round box magazines for the PPSh-41 submachine gun. On the back of the belt was a *Feldflasche* (canteen) and *Brotbeutel* (bread bag) for personal items. Slung over his shoulder was a cloth bag containing a gas mask.

The *Oberfeldwebel*'s most distinguishing mark, however, was a decoration. Around his neck, tucked into his camouflage smock, such that it was barely visible, hung the Knight's Cross to the Iron Cross with Oak Leaves and Swords. The medal was attached around his neck with a striped black, white, and red ribbon.

This was no ordinary medal. The Knight's Cross to the Iron Cross with Oak Leaves and Swords meant that the man wearing the medal had already received the Iron Cross Second Class and First Class, and the Knight's Cross, before being considered for the prestigious Oak Leaves and Swords. The story behind each grade of the *Oberfeldwebel*'s awards was a saga of bloody heroism on distant battlefields that very few men had lived to tell about. Fewer than two hundred soldiers in the Wehrmacht and Luftwaffe had earned such a testament of honor, thus it was rare to see a man so young, and still a sergeant, so honored.

"We are not retreating, *Herr Oberfeldwebel* Graf,"

Feldwebel Karsten Weise mocked. "Haven't you heard the radio broadcasts from the Reich Minister for Popular Enlightenment and Propaganda in Berlin? Soon we will launch a powerful blitzkrieg that will roll the cowardly enemy back through France and drive them into the cold waters of the English Channel. Our V-1 and V-2 rockets will pulverize the enemy's airfields and ports. Soon the skies will be filled with the Stukas, Messerschmitts, and Focke-Wulfs of the Luftwaffe, the fields of Holland will tremble with the approach of our panzers, and the glorious infantry of the Wehrmacht will march forward en masse to break the enemy's line, etcetera, etcetera. There is no doubt that the war will be over by Christmas. Or some such shit."

Graf snorted. He had stopped listening to the speeches from Berlin long ago, but he still had an open mind when listening to Karsten's pessimistic assessment of the war. The problem with Karsten Weise was that he was right: The war was lost and Graf knew it, but he refused to say so openly. In 1940 he had dreamed of victory, but not now. He had long stopped thinking of victory and had set his sights on his men's survival. "How is your hand?"

"Fine," Weise answered, looking down at the dirty, bloodstained bandages on his left hand. "Merely a nuisance."

"Nuisance? Now you are playing the hero? Let me have a look at it," Graf replied as he crouched over to Weise, grabbed the sergeant's hand, and inspected the bandage. "This must be cleaned and a fresh bandage applied, or you may get gangrene. Professors should know better."

Karsten Weise, or "the professor" as some called him, was a cynic and a talker, but a solid soldier. He was younger than Graf, but older than the rest of the unit—the 6th Fallschirmjäger Regiment—that he had joined during the fighting in Normandy, a little more than three months ago.

During that short time, both men had lived one step ahead of death, and they had come to count on each other. They had fought in the battles near St. Come du Mont and Carentan—with Weise nearly crushed by an American tank in the deadly bocage fighting. Together they had lived to fight on through the difficult, one-sided battles in Normandy and escaped the bloodbath at Falaise, where the Americans and British nearly trapped all the German forces in France. Graf had saved him from death or capture more than once. Weise was thankful for the favor.

As they fought together, a bond of mutual respect grew. And when Graf needed someone to confide in, he turned to Weise, since the others in his unit were all new recruits. The German army had been decimated in the months since the Allies landed in Normandy in June 1944. The 6th Fallschirmjäger Regiment had been bled white, pulled out of the fire, reconstituted with youngsters, and was now back in the frying pan.

Graf pulled off the dirty bandage from Weise's hand and inspected the wound. As he shook his head, he pulled his canteen from its pouch and doused the gash across Weise's left hand. He put the canteen down, then tore open a packet of sulfur powder and poured it on the bloody line across Weise's hand. Next, he took a British compress from his gas mask bag, tore open the paper wrapper, and wrapped the clean bandage around Weise's wound. "That should do it. I want you to check this tonight as well. That's an order. Germany will need professors some day."

"*Jawohl, Herr Oberfeldwebel,*" Weise said with a grin. "But right now I think it has more need for antitank gunners."

The sound of distant tank and artillery fire resonated

across the field from the south. Graf understood that an unequal battle between a British Sherman Firefly tank and German infantry armed with antitank grenades called *panzerfausts,* or "tank fists," was raging somewhere to the east. The roar of a Firefly's seventeen-pounder cannon was answered by the detonation of two smaller *panzerfaust* explosions. The noise demonstrated that the Germans were still holding back the British.

Last night, in one of the blackest nights he could remember, his platoon fought a desperate skirmish near the Belgian village of Hechtel. The combat was quick and bloody, as the Tommies had fortified the buildings and were ready. Graf's men were repulsed and three of his men were killed.

Graf looked out from the foxhole he shared with Weise. A few hours ago they had dug the hole into the moist Belgian soil on a tree-covered rise northwest of Hechtel. Thirty-six bedraggled German paratroopers were with them, occupying similar fighting positions. Graf knew that his men were tired and hungry, because he shared their fate, ate what they ate, and led by example. The German paratroopers had been on the move since September 7, marching from one battle to another in an attempt to stop or slow the British advance.

Graf looked down at the puddle of water forming at his feet. The one thing they weren't short of in Belgium and Holland was water. Holland, just a few kilometers to the north, was a land that was mostly under sea level and crisscrossed by canals. The movement of military formations across the flat, wet terrain of the Netherlands was a nightmare. Bridges were vital. Tanks and troops could not move across Holland without control of the bridges.

The low rumble of tanks on the move, the clanking of heavy steel tracks on steel road wheels, filled the air to the east. Graf knew that the British Guards Armored Division, which they had been fighting the past two days, was on the prowl. In the distance, between the trees, Graf could see dark-colored British tanks moving in a column to the northeast.

"*Oberjäger* Küster!" Graf shouted, waving his arm. "Here. Now!"

A twenty-three-year old paratrooper corporal, an *Oberjäger,* carrying an FG-42 assault rife, looked up from his position and ran over to the *Oberfeldwebel.* Küster knelt down next to Graf's foxhole.

"The Tommies must have finished their tea and are on the move again—see them there . . . over there . . . a line of tanks and trucks," Graf explained, pointing to the east. He reached into the map case on his left side, pulled out a well-worn paper map of the area of operations, and studied the terrain. "The British are about a kilometer and a half away, heading northeast toward the town of . . . Overspelt. More than likely it's more of those Irish Guard bastards that we fought last night. Get to company headquarters and tell them we should pull out now while we still have time. Otherwise the Tommies will trap us on the south side of the Meuse-Escaut Canal. Understood?"

Küster scanned the east and took in the view.

"Have you noticed how many horses and wagons we need to move our supplies and artillery while the Tommies and Americans have trucks?" Weise interjected.

Oberjäger Küster shot Weise a look of disdain. "Yes, *Herr Oberfeldwebel*! I see them."

"Read back the message," Graf ordered.

"Tell *Leutnant* Hanzer that the Tommies are moving northeast with tanks, just one and a half kilometers from our position. The enemy is moving toward the town of

Overspelt. You recommend that we withdraw immediately, so that we are not cut off."

"Good lad. Now run over to company headquarters, deliver the message, and get back here as fast as you can," Graf ordered.

The young corporal offered a slight smile at the compliment, nodded, and took off running through the woods.

"I'm glad *Generaloberst* Student is now in charge of the defenses in Holland," Weise said with a grin. "Old Kurt's a good man. He will stop the Tommies. You need a *Fallschirmjäger* like him to make order from this chaos, not these panzer types. You know what the philosopher said: '*Ordnung ist das halbe Leben.* Order is half of life.'"

"Defense?" Graf answered. "What defense? The north bank of the canal has not been prepared for defense. No organization of the ground has been carried out. All the Wehrmacht units I have seen so far are in pitiful shape. They are out of fight, and the Tommies, well, they have so many damn tanks!"

"Well, maybe you can at least ask *Generaloberst* Student to provide us with some better rations?" Weise answered. "After my experience with you in Normandy, I am tired of eating horsemeat."

"Student has his own problems," Graf snorted. "Besides, consider yourself lucky that you can enjoy those excellent British rations we captured."

"But you are one of Student's star pupils," Weise complained with mock astonishment. "Surely you can pull some strings. If not for me, then for the youngsters?"

"Star pupil?" Graf said. "Yes, we served together in Russia. They sent me to die a dozen times, and yet I survived. I owe my life to *Oberstleutnant* von der Heydte and *Generaloberst* Student. Not that my life is worth much."

"You'll have to tell me about that sometime," Weise replied. "I've always wondered about the rumors."

"No, I think I'll keep those stories to myself," Graf answered.

"I have to admit, I admire von der Heydte," Weise replied, changing the focus of the conversation. "He is a soldier's soldier, and a philosopher to boot. Did you know he studied law and philosophy at the University of Cologne?"

"So that's why you like him; he's a professor like you," Graf joked.

"I'm hardly a professor, even if the youngsters call me that behind my back. Two years at the University of Munich does not give one a degree, let alone a professorship," Weise replied. "No, I admire von der Heydte because he cares about his soldiers—and because he is as anti-Nazi as you are."

"Feldwebel Weise, you are the only one who has survived from the original group of replacements in Normandy, which is surprising to me in ways I cannot begin to tell you," Graf said with a smile, "but mostly because you have never learned to shut up."

"Someone has to be your conscience. Who better than a professor?" Weise offered. "God knows that in battle, the only principle that drives you is victory."

"I do what is necessary," Graf answered solemnly. "Just don't mention my political views in front of the youngsters. I am a *Fallschirmjäger*, I have no politics."

"Of course, we are only instruments of the State," Weise announced cynically. He was quiet for a moment, then, looking to the west, offered: "What about the Tommies? It doesn't look like the boys from the 176th Division are even trying to stop them. Should we sneak up on them and pop them with a few *panzerfausts*?"

"No. There's too much power in this move. I didn't

want to alarm Küster or the company commander, but the enemy is also moving to our west."

"We have Tommies to the west as well?" Weise questioned.

"Yes," Graf replied calmly. "It seems that we are in an usual position for *Fallschirmjägers*. We are about to be surrounded and there is no one to offer us any support."

"How do you know that?" Weise said looking to the west.

"Look over at those trees. What do you see?" Graf said pointing to the east.

Weise strained his eyes to observe the tree line that was nearly two kilometers away to the west. After a moment he turned to Graf. "Smoke?"

"Exactly," Graf answered. "Exhaust smoke from British tanks and Bren Carriers. The enemy is moving north on both flanks."

"You are right," Weise answered.

"Get the men ready to move out," Graf ordered. "When Küster returns, I expect us to head north to the canal as fast as we can walk."

"Men?" Weiss countered. "More like children. Since we left France our ranks have been filled with youngsters. Oh, they are eager, like Küster there, who was Hitler youth like the rest, but they don't know one end of a *panzerfaust* from the other. Most of them hadn't fired their rifles until we disembarked the trains in Holland a few days ago. And some of our officers . . ."

Graf shot Weise a glance that looked as if it could melt through the armor of a British Sherman tank. "Enough. Look after the men and take special care of our MG42 machine gun. Tell Jäger Stöhr that we may need it soon, and if it doesn't chatter like a virgin on her wedding night, I will personally kick his ass—and yours."

"Okay, okay. What the lion cannot manage to do, the fox can," Weise replied with a grin as the sergeant grabbed his MP40 submachine gun. "*Oberfeldwebel* Wilhelm Graf, I'll check the children and make sure they are ready to go as ordered. Just make sure you mention my loyalty and commitment in your report."

Weise moved out of the foxhole and ran from position to position, issuing instructions to the men.

Küster came running back to Graf's foxhole, followed by Lieutenant Hanzer. Both men jumped into Graf's foxhole.

"Graf, what's the situation?" Hanzer demanded, looking distraught.

"*Herr Leutnant.* There is a column of British tanks, reinforced with infantry, moving to our east and another moving to our west," Graf replied calmly as he pointed out the enemy movements.

Hanzer looked to the east and saw British tanks, Bren Carriers, and trucks moving north. He looked to the west and saw the same thing. "No one told me. I have not received any word from battalion."

"*Ja,* well, in war, *Herr Leutnant,* things happen fast," Graf replied. "I am sure everyone is too busy pulling back to send us a message."

"My orders are to stay here and defend these woods," the lieutenant replied.

"*Generaloberst* Student's plan is to stop the Tommies from getting into Holland," Graf explained. "His only hope of doing so is to establish the main defense along the Escaut canal. We should move north and get there before it's too late."

The young lieutenant shook his head. "How can I do that without orders?"

"Sir, moving north is consistent with *Oberstleutnant*

von der Heydte's intent," Graf said, as he stood up in the foxhole. "The *Oberstleutnant* would be the first to tell you that when they made you an officer they expected you to know when to disobey orders."

The lieutenant nodded. "You are right. We'll move north, through the woods, and link up with the rest of the battalion."

"Good decision, *Herr Leutnant*," Graf said. "My squad will act as your rear guard."

Lieutenant Hanzer smiled. "You should be the officer, not me."

"They would never make me an officer," Graf replied with a smirk. "I'm too dangerous for them."

Hanzer grinned again. "Okay, I'll move the company north. You act as the rear guard and move north as soon as you can. Good luck!"

The lieutenant turned and ran back toward company headquarters.

Weise sprinted back to Graf and reported. "The men are ready."

"All right, *Fallschirmjägers*," Graf ordered, pointing north. "Grab your gear. The platoon will move north. Patrol formation, First Squad followed by Second. We're the rear guard, so if the Tommies come into the wood, we'll form on-line, First Squad to the left and Second to the right, then let them have it. Understood?"

The heads of the young German paratroopers nodded in acknowledgment.

"Move out!" Graf ordered.

"Well, we didn't stay here very long," Weise offered. "I was beginning to like these woods."

"If there is anything I hate more than anything else on this earth," the tall, green-eyed *Oberfeldwebel* grumbled, "it is retreating."

Sunday, September 10, around noon, in Eindhoven, Netherlands:

"Do you see that?" a seventeen-year-old Dutch youth exclaimed in glee to the girl standing next to him. "It is what we have been dreaming of."

Alexander Van Janssen and his sixteen-year-old cousin Mira Vogel stood on the second floor of their home in Eindhoven and watched as a disconsolate column of muddy and tired German soldiers marched north. Some in the column rode bicycles. The wounded were transported in horse-drawn carts.

"Yes," Mira answered with glee. "The day we have been waiting for!"

"Liberation!" Alexander replied, hugging his cousin and giving her a friendly kiss on the cheek. "The Germans are in full retreat. Look at them! They are no longer the conquerors. Now they look like scared rabbits running back to their holes."

Mira stared out the window. Standing five-foot-six, with a slim figure, shoulder-length brown hair, and deep blue eyes, Mira was a beauty. Due to the responsibilities of taking care of her ailing mother in a horrible time of war, Mira had gained a calm confidence beyond her years. She was smart, the best student in her class, and she had an uncanny ability to make people see things her way.

"Can you distinguish their unit markings?" Mira asked. "This would be important information."

"Yes, but I should be recording them as they go past," Alexander replied, distracted by the spectacle of the hated Germans in retreat. "There are so many different markings that they must be from parts of many units. I'd better get my notebook to write them down."

Mira remained at the window and looked out at the

scene below. Her heart was pounding, and she felt something that she had not felt in a long time—hope.

Hope. She had never really lost hope; there had always been that spark to keep her going, but she had fought so many battles against despair in the past four years that she often questioned if the final outcome would be the result of darkness rather than light. Now she was seeing the light fanning the flicker of hope as if adding kindling to a fire.

Five days ago, on Tuesday, September 5, panic had gripped the German forces as the Allied troops approached the Belgian-Dutch border. Approximately 65,000 Dutch Nazi collaborators packed suitcases and wheelbarrows and fled to Germany. The day was immediately called Mad Tuesday. For those citizens of the Netherlands who remained true to the spirit of freedom, Mad Tuesday was a day of jubilation.

As she gazed through the lace curtains at the long line of dejected German soldiers, the sound of their hobnail boots on the cobblestone streets sent her memories crashing back at her. In a flashing moment she was reminded of the hardships of the past four years. Before the Germans, she remembered only a life of bliss and happiness. Her father was alive, her mother was healthy, and life was good.

As the storm clouds of war gathered in 1939 and early 1940, most of the citizens of the Netherlands hoped that their country would remain neutral and the scourge of war would not visit their fair land. For nearly a century, the Netherlands had adhered to a strict policy of neutrality in European affairs; the Dutch had not engaged in war with other Europeans since 1830. During World War I, the Dutch were not involved and Germany had not invaded the Netherlands. Mira only worried about school and friends, not politics. For her, the thought of war was alien and strange. Holland was a land of peace and beauty. How could this ever change? Surely the red horse of the Apocalypse would journey elsewhere.

All such illusions came to an end on May 10, when the German 10th Army, spearheaded by airborne troops, invaded the Netherlands. The German attack was like a thunderclap—powerful and stunning. The Dutch people where shocked by the rapid and brutal attack. Mira was only twelve years old when the independence of the Netherlands came to an end with the screeching sound of Stuka dive-bombers and the clank of Nazi tanks in the streets of Dutch towns and villages. In spite of a declaration of neutrality, the German attack was massive and was not preceded by a declaration of war. The Germans respected Holland's neutrality no more than they did the national sovereignty of Czechoslovakia, Poland, Denmark, or Norway. Then it was to be Holland, Belgium, France, and Great Britain who would learn the deadly cut of the Wehrmacht's scythe.

Initially, the German forces faced sparse resistance from the unprepared and ill-equipped Dutch military. In 1940, the Dutch army had only one broken French Renault tank, five tankettes, and thirty-nine armored cars. The Dutch air force consisted of mostly biplanes. The Dutch infantry was armed with bolt-action rifles made before World War I.

With the power of a modern army equipped with tanks, dive-bombers, machine guns, and paratroopers, the Germans raced past the stunned Dutch border guards and charged into the Netherlands. German reconnaissance and airborne units seized the vital bridges over the many canals to secure them before the Dutch army could destroy these vital passageways. Additional German paratroopers landed on key communication sites, forts, and bridges to assist the rapid movement of the panzers.

Still, the Dutch are a proud people. Rather than surrender, they recovered from the shock of the preliminary stages of the German blitzkrieg and fought back valiantly with their World War I–era weapons. The Germans had expected to take Holland in a day, but the Dutch put up a stern fight. Mira's father, a member of the army reserve, was called up and was killed in the fighting near the town of Sint-Oedenrode on May 12. His death would not qualify as a footnote in the history books, but it had a devastating effect on Mira and her family.

Mira remembered that German paratroopers had landed at the seat of government at The Hague, hoping to capture the Dutch royal family. Their attempt failed and Queen Wilhelmina fled to Britain, eventually creating a government in exile.

The Netherlands is a small country, and the modern military might of Nazi Germany rapidly overwhelmed the antiquated Dutch army and air force, no matter how bravely they fought. The bravery of the Dutch soldiers, although in vain, slowed the German advance. After four days and the horrific bombing of the city of Rotterdam, the Dutch were forced to surrender.

In the weeks ahead, German tanks and infantry, supported by Stuka dive-bombers, executed a bold "go for broke" armored offensive through Belgium's Ardennes forest, followed by an audacious crossing of the Meuse River near the French border town of Sedan. The hopes of millions of free people were crushed when the German panzers and powerful Luftwaffe defeated the British and French armies on the continent of Europe. The British evacuated their forces from the port of Dunkirk. The French surrendered to the Germans on June 25, 1940. A darkness descended across Europe, from the

German border with Soviet Russia in Poland to the English Channel.

Free Europe was defeated; Nazi Germany triumphant. The people of the Netherlands now lived in a country occupied by a conquering army.

The German victory in Europe, the occupation of the Netherlands by a pro-Nazi Dutch government, and German troops changed life in Holland dramatically for Mira. Mira's mother, broken from the news of her husband's death in the initial invasion, became ill, never fully recovering as Mira did her best to care for her needs.

Still, Mira felt that her personal tragedy seemed small by comparison to what was happening across Holland. Weeks after the German victory, the Nazis began to arrest and deport Jews. All Dutch Jews were ordered to wear Star of David armbands to identify them to the Nazis. Later, the Germans arrested anyone who opposed their way of thinking. Labor leaders, Socialists, Roman Catholic priests, and many others were sent to concentration camps. Life in Holland took on an ominous quality that permeated daily life. In spite of this oppression, ordinary Dutch citizens risked their lives to hide and protect targets of Nazi oppression.

As the war progressed, the hardships multiplied. Shortages of every kind grew. No one in Holland, except collaborators and government officials, were allowed to have cars or purchase gasoline. Coffee and tobacco were hard to find. Sugar and chocolate were nonexistent. Rationing cards were used by the Germans to control the population.

Then came the terrible *Arbeitseinsatz*—the drafting of Dutch civilians for forced labor. Every male between the ages of eighteen and forty-five was obliged to work in German factories. Fathers left their homes and families to work in Germany. Many never returned. In 1942 and 1943, many of the factories in Germany that used these forced laborers were bombed day and night by Allied aircraft.

As a result, a substantial Dutch resistance movement grew against the German occupiers. Alexander and Mira were part of this resistance. They helped men and boys hide from the *Arbeitseinsatz* by passing messages. In May 1944, they helped pass messages to a resistance group in Eindhoven that assisted the escape of two British bomber crewmen.

Since those early days, Mira had organized a cell of six friends, all under seventeen years of age, to cause mischief among the Germans. They took down German military signs, painted slogans over German posters, and even poured sand into German truck engines, but mostly they passed information. Due to their work, they had become known as the Bicyclists, and earned the trust of the local resistance organization that had ties to British Special Operations.

Then, in June 1944, a wonderful flicker of light came to Europe to start forcing back the darkness. On June 6, 1944, the Allies conducted the largest amphibious operation in history and landed in Normandy, France. The landings took the Germans by surprise and had an electrifying effect on the occupied peoples of western Europe. After four long years of occupation, the people of France, Belgium, and the Netherlands began to believe that the liberation would come. By late August, after months of hard fighting, the Allies had crushed the German armies in France and sent the Germans reeling back to the Fatherland. Suddenly, the world Mira had lived in for the past four years was changing, and she wanted to hasten that change, becoming a part of it in any way she could.

"Could it all be coming to an end?" Mira said out loud, holding back her emotions. "Could the war be over by Christmas?"

"What?" Alexander said, returning to the window with his notebook and a pencil.

"Nothing. Never mind. We must alert the Bicyclists," Mira replied. The Bicyclists came from Eindhoven and a small village southeast of Eindhoven called Lieshout. Alexander and three other teenagers were from Eindhoven. Mira and a boy named Peter were from Lieshout. "I will ride to Anna's home here to tell her and then to Lieshout and tell our friend there."

"I don't recommend that," Alexander protested. "You should stay with me, count the troops, and write down their units. There are too many Germans on the street for you to go by yourself. It is safer if we go together, tomorrow."

"Don't be silly," Mira said with a laugh. "We must alert all the Bicyclists today. There is no time to lose."

"I'm not being silly, just careful," Alexander offered.

Mira took a long look at her cousin and gave him a hug. Alexander was a bit taller than Mira, but she was proud to say that he never looked down on her. As a cousin, he was special. Enthusiastic, intelligent, a bit awkward, but always a good person. Only a year apart, they had grown up together and, since the start of the occupation, had shared everything. For Mira, Alexander was her perfect confidant. She could tell him anything and know that he would never reveal a secret.

After her father's death and her mother's illness, Mira had depended upon Alexander and his parents to get through the difficult times. He was her rock in shifting sands, and she loved him for it. The last thing she wanted to do was to put his safety in jeopardy.

"Alexander, you know that you would just slow me

down. I can get through the German checkpoints much easier without you. They are always kinder to pretty girls than pimple-faced boys. You would only cause them to be suspicious."

Alexander shook his head. "You can insult me all you want, but I still think you should wait here, in my home, and return tomorrow. I can go with you in the morning."

"There isn't time," Mira pressed. "You see what is happening. The Allies could be here any day."

"We should not argue about this," Alexander insisted.

"Who is the leader of the Bicyclists?" Mira demanded.

"You are," Alexander said, reluctantly. "I can never say no to you. That is, perhaps, why you are our leader?"

"Exactly," Mira replied with a hug and a kiss to Alexander's cheek. "Besides, I cannot leave my mother at home alone with all this happening. I must go."

Mira took her schoolbooks from the table, tied them with a strap, and walked toward the door.

Just before she left, Alexander announced. "Please be safe. I will see you tomorrow, at noon?"

"Yes, of course. Don't worry. I will be fine."

She walked down the stairs and opened the front door. Her bicycle was parked near the wall that surrounded the small front yard that had been turned into a cabbage garden. She secured her books to the back of her bicycle and pedaled down the street.

The long line of German soldiers that faced her, going north, seemed to be trapped in a distant stare. Not one of them looked at her, which was unusual, as she had become quite adept at responding to the catcalls of German soldiers in the past year.

Mira turned left up the macadam road and headed northeast toward Lieshout. The route was relatively deserted and Mira breathed a sigh of relief, happy that the route was not filled with retreating German soldiers. For all her outward bravado, she was acutely aware of the danger of a girl her age milling about a mob of angry, defeated soldiers. During the occupation, most of the Wehrmacht soldiers, the men in the traditional German army, had shown restraint and discipline. There had been few cases of rape, robbery, or murder perpetrated on the Dutch people.

Mira, however, had experienced a frightening episode from a German SS soldier. In contrast to the German army, the Nazis regarded the SS as elite troops and the party's "Praetorian Guard." All SS personnel were selected on the basis of racial purity and unconditional loyalty to the Nazi Party. The SS soldier that Mira met in February 1944 was particularly bloody-minded and very drunk to boot.

Mira and her friend Anna had been walking to Eindhoven to meet Alexander. Her friend was a year older, nearly seventeen, and a beautiful girl. On their way, the drunken SS soldier accosted them. They showed him their papers, but he demanded much more. The man looked at them as if they were not human, as if they were merely things to be used. He pushed Mira away, lunged at Anna, pushed her to the ground, and started tearing off her clothes. In a fury of fear and hatred, Mira pummeled the drunk with her schoolbooks until he turned on her. This allowed Anna to break away. The drunken soldier chased Mira, screaming and cursing in German, but Mira was a fast runner and made her escape. Due to her quick thinking, the episode ended without either girl being seriously hurt. Nevertheless, she had nightmares about the way the man made her feel. From that moment on, whenever Mira came close to an SS man, it was as if she were standing next to a wolf, not a human being.

Suddenly, the small hairs on the back of her neck stood up; she had entered a wolf's lair. At a road junction up ahead she heard the noise of tanks. She pulled off to the side of the road as four big German assault guns lumbered down the route, heading toward the town of Eindhoven. The assault guns—she had learned that they were called StuGs—had SS men riding on the top. The soldiers on the armored vehicles smiled and waved to her, offering their love in broken Dutch if they could only stop for a moment, promising all kinds of food and delicacies if she would only offer them her charms. These soldiers did not have the look of the gloomy and dispirited lot of men she had seen moving north from her cousin's second-floor window in Eindhoven. These men seemed rested, disciplined, and ready.

In a few minutes they had passed and the dust settled. She breathed a sigh of relief, collected herself, and noted from the marking on the fenders of the assault guns that these soldiers belonged to the 9th SS Panzer Division. She wondered if this was important. She had never seen a unit of the 9th SS Panzer in Holland before. This was a new unit and, she knew from the markings, a part of an SS German tank division. Most important, they were advancing south, not retreating north.

"I wonder how long they have been here," Mira thought. "I must report this to Melanie."

She turned back to the road and pedaled on toward Lieshout and home.

Sunday evening, September 10, near the Escaut Canal that divides Belgium from the Netherlands:

"Colour Sergeant, I've got this feeling. I can't shake it. Ever since this morning, I've felt as if this is it. I'm not going to make it," Guardsman Kincaid announced.

A slim, five-foot-seven-inch Irish Guards colour sergeant who looked like a long-distance runner stared at the young soldier. Tenderly, he put a hand on Kincaid's shoulder and whispered, "I know, lad. Everyone feels that way when they go into battle for the first time. I feel that way. You just have to put it aside and consider yourself already dead. If you don't, you'll hesitate and that hesitation is what will kill you."

"You? You feel the same way?" Kincaid replied.

"Yes, every damned day," the colour sergeant answered, and then turned to face the man to his left. "Isn't that right Corporal Ackers?"

"Aye, as certain as a tail follows a comet," Ackers replied. "That's why, when the going gets rough, he sings so much. That same damned bloody tune, over and over again. Hell, if he didn't sing it, I'd be worried."

The three men inched up to the top of a pile of black slag to take a better look at the enemy. In the gathering dusk, the British Guards Armored Division spearheaded the British 2d Army's advance and raced for the Escaut Canal. Bypassing German resistance and rolling through any Germans that were crazy enough to try to stop them, the British force was led by the 3d Irish Guards (infantry) and 2d Irish Guards (tanks). These Irishmen's hope was to capture a bridge before the Germans could destroy it.

Crawling up to the lip of the slag heap, Colour Sergeant Cathal Gilchrist held his Sten submachine gun forward as he looked north up the N69 road that crossed the Escaut Canal from Belgium into the Netherlands. In front of him was the most beautiful sight he had ever seen: a bridge.

The bridge was a sturdy, German-built, wooden trestle bridge, capable of supporting tanks and heavy equipment. The Germans were defending the bridge in force, and Colour Sergeant Gilchrist could see the German positions on the northern edge of the bridge. Three deadly German 88mm multipurpose guns, capable of punching a hole in a Sherman tank or Bren infantry carrier like a hot poker through cardboard, were deployed on the far side of the bridge. German soldiers, oblivious to the fact that Gilchrist and his men were nearby, lounged around their sandbagged positions, smoking and talking as if the war was far away.

"This won't be an easy party," Gilchrist announced as he slid down from the slag heap to the group of well-armed Irish Guardsmen that formed his infantry section. "But we have a good chance of taking this bridge if we hit them hard and fast."

Corporal Donal Ackers shook his head. "I see that fire in your eye, Cat. The last time I saw that we were in a hell of a fight. Are you sure you still have all your nine lives left?"

Colour Sergeant Cathal (pronounced KOH-hal) Gilchrist was nicknamed "Cat" by his men for his uncanny ability to survive countless battles. From Dunkirk in 1940 and throughout the war to the current fighting in France and Belgium in 1944, he had survived without a major wound. His men believed that the bullet hadn't been made with his name on it, and his confidence was infectious, manifesting in everything they did. His one quirk was that he was fond of song and had been known to hum, whistle, or sing his favorite tune, "The Minstrel Boy." He even named his Bren Carrier, the ubiquitous fully tracked, lightly armored vehicle of the British army, in honor of this tune.

"No time for your superstitions, Ackers," Cat said with a grin. "We have a bridge to take. On my command, we rush forward. You, Avery, Friskin, Gaines, Kincaid, Sheffield, and McNevin are with me. Ross and Roy cover us from here with the Bren Guns. Logan, you support the Bren Guns with ammo. Keep the fire coming, but shoot to the right of the bridge, don't cross your fire over onto us. Assault team, no grenades, as we'll be running fast and I don't want us rushing into our own explosions. This will all be bullets and bayonets. All brass and bluff."

An officer quietly moved up to the group. Without any fuss, as if he were an ordinary soldier, the commander of the Irish Guards, Lieutenant Colonel J.O.E. Vandeleur, joined the assembly. "Cat, are you and your men ready?"

"As ready as we'll ever be, sir," Colour Sergeant Gilchrist replied.

"Remember, once you clear the far side of the enemy, check the bridge for explosives," Vandeleur warned. "Cut anything that has a wire and pull off any explosives you find and dump them in the canal. We must take this bridge before the Jerries can destroy it."

"Aye sir, it will be done," Gilchrist replied. "Men, get ready to move out."

"I have tanks near the factory to our right ready to fire in support of your move," Vandeleur added. "I'll send more infantry behind you, but you will be the tip of the spear. In addition, two Sherman tanks will move up to the south end of the bridge to provide covering fire for your assault."

Cat nodded. He looked as calm as ice, except for the fire in his eyes.

"Good luck, Colour Sergeant!" Vandeleur offered and then, without any ceremony, left the group to coordinate the attack.

Cat and his men moved out, crouching at first and then crawling on their bellies to move closer to the bridge, hugging the ground on the right side of the road to be sure they were not seen by the enemy. The movement took time and the light was fading. So far, the Germans seemed unaware that the British were preparing to attack.

"Cat! There's a bloody eighty-eight on this side of the

bridge," Corporal Ackers whispered as he pointed to the north.

Cat peeked up over a small mound and saw the enemy gun. Four Germans were standing next to the 88mm cannon. They seemed unconcerned. One was eating from a mess tin. Another was smoking a cigarette. None of them carried weapons. Two more Germans were standing in a halftrack positioned just off the road.

Cat viewed the enemy gun and whispered, "Wait for the supporting fire."

Cat's men moved on-line and waited. The seconds ticked by. Then, with a crash that broke the evening silence like a dozen hammers shattering plate glass, the British tanks opened up. A dozen tank cannons blasted and as many machine guns chattered. A huge explosion erupted in front of Cat's position at the same moment a British tank scored a direct hit on the German 88.

Cat and his men jumped up and charged. Two of the Germans who survived the destruction of their guns stood staring in shock at the attacking Irish Guardsmen. A quick burst from Cat's Sten sent them both to the ground.

Confusion reigned as the sound of explosions filled the evening air. The German crew in the halftrack quickly revved the engine and took off toward the bridge, followed by the charging Irishmen who were firing madly as they ran toward the bridge. The halftrack pulled ahead, and just as it reached the south side of the bridge it was hit by a high-explosive shell from a British Sherman tank. The halftrack pivoted violently forward from the force of the hit, screeched to a stop, and erupted in a ball of flames.

Cat moved close to the burning halftrack, took a flare pistol from a pouch on his web belt, and shot a green Verey light into the air.

At this signal two British tanks roared forward. The

Irishmen dashed onward as well, past the blazing German halftrack that was now lighting up the darkening sky. The two tanks followed Cat's men, firing to the left and right of the bridge. Tracers flew through the air in all directions, and Cat heard the familiar zip of bullets as they whizzed by his head. The German defenders rushed around like madmen, trying to man their guns and distinguish the locations of their attackers.

"The minstrel boy to the war is gone, in the ranks of death you will find him," Cat sang loudly as he raced for the far side of the bridge.

As Cat's men rushed across the bridge, firing and shouting, the Irish Guards' machine guns, manned by Guardsmen Ross and Roy kept up a high volume of fire. This covering fire cut down the crew of the German 88mm cannon on the far right side of the bridge.

"Move it lads! On the run!" Cat, leading the charge, shouted at the top of his lungs. Two German soldiers rushed toward Cat from the north side of the bridge. Without losing stride Cat leveled his Sten gun and killed them both.

A German machine gun opened up on the attackers. Luckily for Cat and his men, the German gunner aimed high and a line of tracers flew over their heads.

"Run, you bastards!" Corporal Ackers shouted. "Let's get them!"

"His father's sword he hath girded on, and his wild harp slung behind him!" Cat sang as he knelt on the north side of the bridge and pulled a red flare from his pocket. He quickly loaded the red flare into the Verey pistol and shot it skyward, signaling that they had made it to the north side of the bridge. The red flare cut through the evening sky like a meteor on a summer's night.

Behind Cat, the tanks of the Irish Guards 2d Battalion

rumbled forward. Crashing through the flaming wreckage of the shattered German halftrack, the two British tanks rolled across the bridge to the northern side. With machine guns blazing at point-blank range, the lead tank routed the German defenders before the German gun crews could put their 88mm cannons into operation.

The second tank passed Cat's position and blasted away at a German 88 about twenty yards ahead. The shock effect of the tanks was more than the German defenders could stand. At the same time, Ackers and his men had moved to firing positions among the German sandbags and fired at the remaining Germans. The defenders were so confused by the violent and sudden attack that they were running in all directions. Abandoning their guns, the Germans began to run or put up their hands to surrender.

As the battle was won, Guardsman Kincaid ran over to Cat's side. The young man was grinning from ear to ear. "We did it! We took the bridge. I knew we could do it!"

At that very second, a German popped up from behind a sandbagged position, aimed his rifle, and fired.

Cat heard the bullet whip by his ear. He automatically ducked, picked up his Sten gun and fired. Several shots hit the German in the head. The enemy soldier jerked backward, his face a bloody pulp, and he fell out of sight. Cat turned and saw Kincaid at his feet, a bleeding hole in his right shoulder. The boy grabbed Cat's ankle with a death grip. "Am I going to die?"

Cat knelt down by the boy and quickly surveyed the wound. "Don't worry, lad, you'll live to tell your grandchildren about this night. Stay put here and I'll get back to you."

"Aidman!" Cat shouted as he quickly pulled Kincaid

to the safety of a pile of sandbags. Cat then sized up the situation.

"The far side is secure!" Cat shouted. Realizing that the Germans had placed explosive charges on the bridge and that the bridge was still in danger of being set off by the Germans, Cat turned back to the bridge. "Ackers, stay here to defend the far side. The Jerries may launch a counterattack. Sheffield and McNevin, come with me to check the bridge for explosives."

"We are set here, you check the bloody bridge!" Ackers screamed.

Cat was aware that the bridge might explode any second. In the light of the burning halftrack, the three men rushed onto the bridge and found wires and fuses lining the sides of the roadbed. They started pulling at the wires with all their might. A group of British sappers ran onto the bridge and did the same. The British sappers, armed with wire cutters, began furiously cutting the tangled mass of wires. Other men frantically searched for wires and explosives, racing against time. Several sappers climbed over the side of the bridge, pulled off blocks of TNT and dropped them into the water.

It was all a matter of timing. Would they cut the wires or be blown to Kingdom Come?

In the dim light, the veteran colour sergeant saw a mass of wires running along the left roadbed of the bridge. In the light of the burning German halftrack he traced them back to a foxhole on the north end of the bridge and found a detonator. For a moment, his soul was shocked, like the vibration of a giant bell. A dead German and another seriously wounded German lay near the detonator. The wounded German, though mortally hit, was crawling toward the plunger, his hand outreached, ready to detonate the explosives. Cat quickly pushed the wounded German away and reached down and started yanking the wires from the detonator. Once the wires were removed, he hurled the detonator into the canal.

More Irish Guards tanks and infantrymen rolled across the bridge and set up a defensive perimeter on the northern side while other men continued to pull and cut wires. After a thorough search, a sapper officer declared the bridge safe.

Cat breathed a sigh of relief. The bridge was captured. The two thousand pounds of explosives attached to the bridge would not explode that night. The Irish Guards had secured a bridge across the canal and, in the process, had liberated the first few yards of territory in Holland.

Cat walked back to the sandbagged position where Private Kincaid lay. Kincaid was propped up on his pack and leaning against the sandbags and appeared in good spirits for a man who had just been shot. An aidman had plugged his wound and was fixing a bandage to his shoulder.

Other Irish Guardsmen started moving German prisoners to the rear. A line of disheveled Germans moved past Cat. One of the Germans, in broken English, looked at Cat and announced: "Well done, Tommy."

Cat smiled. Just as he was about to say something clever to the German, a hand touched him on the shoulder from behind. Cat turned and saw his commanding officer, Lieutenant Colonel Vandeleur.

"Cat, that was a bit of Irish dash if I ever saw it," Vandeleur offered. "Well done, Colour Sergeant!"

"Yes sir, the lads did a good job," Cat replied.

"I watched you from the southern bank and I dare say you probably surrendered one of your nine lives to fate today," Vandeleur said with a grin as he offered Colour Sergeant Gilchrist a smoke.

"All brass and bluff." Cat smiled and took the offered

cigarette. "I may have given up one life tonight, sir, but I still have plenty left."

"Yes, and I'm mighty glad for it!" Vandeleur said, slapping Cat on the shoulder. "And now we have a bridgehead into Holland and at the cost of only three men wounded. Who knows, maybe the war *will* be over by Christmas?"

The U.S. Waco CG-4A Glider

3: D-DAY, OPERATION MARKET GARDEN

"On the outside of our CG-4A Waco Glider someone had chalked the prayer: 'I hope to God the crew of this glider land safely,' to which I mentally added my name. . . ."
—CORPORAL H. SPENCE, I British Airborne Corps Signals, attached to the 101st Airborne for Operation Market Garden

Ramsbury Airfield, England, 1300 Sunday, September 17, 1944 (D-Day).

A squad of American paratroopers from the 101st Airborne Division Reconnaissance Platoon stood near the tarmac of the Ramsbury Royal Air Force Airfield looking up at the heavens.

In spite of the fog, the sky roared with airplanes. The hum of thousands of engines from a mighty wave of military aircraft consisting of bombers and fighters resounded overhead. Starting before dawn, thousands of bombers and fighters flew from bases in England to attack German targets in the Netherlands, preparing the way for the Allied airborne invasion.

"Man! That was the best breakfast I've had since I've been in England!" Private First Class Franky said to Private First Class Dawson as he looked up at the aerial armada flying overhead. Franky reached in his pocket, took out a packet of gum, and offered a stick to Dawson. "I wish they fed us like that every day. Hot cakes with syrup and real scrambled eggs!"

Dawson took the stick of gum from Franky, staring at him with amazement. "Franky, you're about to be a part of the largest airborne operation in history, an operation that will decide the fate of the war, and all you can talk about is how pleasant it is to eat the last meal of a condemned man?"

"What?" Franky asked.

The other men laughed.

Staff Sergeant Matt Baker listened to the banter but didn't join in. He had mixed thoughts about the impending operation but did not want his men to know his feelings. The plan was code-named Market Garden. A powerful British tank force would attack from Belgium into the Netherlands, moving rapidly through Eindhoven, Veghel, and Nijmegen to Arnhem. The road crossed several rivers and canals. So the bridges across these rivers and canals were vital to the attacking Allied force. To secure them, parachute infantry and gliderborne troops would drop alongside the route, capture the bridges, and make it possible for tanks and trucks to go to Arnhem unhindered. Once across the Rhine River at Arnhem it would be a short distance to take the industrialized German Ruhr area. If the plan worked, and the German war machine was eliminated, the war could be over by Christmas 1944.

In the pit of his stomach Baker felt uneasy, the same way he had felt before a big high school football game back home in St. Louis. In those days, he would talk with his lifelong friend George Risner about the "butterflies" he felt before the opening kickoff. Before the war, George and Matt had been inseparable. They had shared everything together and attended the same classes, played on the same football team, and even dated some of the same girls.

Those were good days, Baker remembered, but somehow they seemed odd, like a life he had dreamed about and could visualize but had not really lived. The war had changed everything.

The last time he had spent a happy moment with his friend George was in England, right before the D-Day jump. Later he met up with him in Normandy, during the drive on Carentan. Carentan was a key city as it was a road junction between the two Allied beachheads: Utah Beach in the west and Omaha Beach in the east. It had to be taken and the job fell to the 101st Airborne. The tanks of the 70th Tank Battalion, George's unit, were tasked to support the paratroopers.

Baker would never forget that horrible day at the village of St. Come du Mont. George was in the turret of his M5 Stuart tank, working with a group of paratroopers from the 101st Airborne to clear the Germans from the town. As he approached a vital road junction that led to the town of Carentan, German paratroopers from the 6th Fallschirmjäger Regiment were waiting in ambush.

Baker was walking along a hedgerow near the tank. He would never forget the sound of the German *panzerfaust* that was fired from a nearby hedgerow. The warhead hit Risner's M5 Stuart tank in the front. The tank rocked back when the warhead exploded. Smoke and fire seeped out of the driver and bow machine gunner hatches. Six *Fallschirmjägers* jumped out from the hedgerow with antitank grenades to finish off Risner and his crew. Risner, stunned but unhurt, brought his Thompson submachine gun up and fired a magazine of .45 slugs into the approaching Germans, killing one and wounding another.

Out of ammunition, Risner pulled a shiny, silver-colored .45 caliber pistol from his shoulder holster. The fire inside the tank was rising and poured out of the turret. Through the black smoke Risner fired off two rounds and killed the lead German. One of the remaining *Fallschirm-jägers,* a tall man in a camouflage battle smock, blasted off a fusillade of shots from a round-drummed submachine gun and riddled Risner with bullets.

Risner sunk forward, dropping the pistol. The weapon clanked off the side of the tank.

Baker rushed to Risner's aid, firing madly as he ran, but the Germans withdrew. The *Fallschirmjägers* had accomplished their task. They had stopped the American tank and had made their escape, dragging their wounded with them.

By the time Baker turned back to help his friend, the tank was fully ablaze and Risner was stuck upright in the turret, burning like the wick of a candle. The image was horrific.

Baker was not able to get the sight of Risner's death out of his mind.

Two days later, the burned-out tank sat abandoned at the intersection, with the charred body of Risner hanging out of the turret. The paratroopers that passed by saw this grisly sight and soon named the area Dead Man's Corner.

The fighting carried on. More of Baker's friends were killed, but the battle was won.

In July 1944, Baker and his men were shipped back to England to rest, train, and prepare for the next operation. Now, three months after George Risner's death, Baker was about to jump back into the war all over again and lead his men into another desperate battle.

Only now his list of friends seemed to be getting shorter.

The one man he had grown close to since D-Day was Staff Sergeant "Red" Hartsock. His relationship with Hartsock, however, was different from the one he had with Risner. It was a relationship of mutual respect but

also of competition. Somehow he would never be as
close to anyone as he had been with George Risner, and
maybe, after seeing Risner die in Normandy, this inabil-
ity to make close friends was intentional. As Corporal
Zanovitch was fond of saying, "The army is in the business of breaking things and killing people." Maybe
Baker just never wanted to see another close friend die.

There were seven men in Baker's reconnaissance
squad: Corporal Sam Corrion, Corporal Tom Zanovitch, Private First Class Jack Courtland, Private First
Class Dale McCreary, Private First Class Franky Laroche,
Private First Class Nathan Holden, and Private First
Class Mike Dawson. Corrion, Zanovitch, Courtland, Mc-
Creary, and Dawson were all veterans of the Normandy
operation. Frankly, Holden and Laroche were new replacements, straight from airborne training in the States.

It was Sunday morning and many of the paratroopers
had just returned from breakfast and church services.
The heavy ground fog heightened the drama as Baker ordered his men to fall in for a final inspection before they
entered their designated means of transport to the battlefield in Holland: the CG-4A Waco gliders.

He searched for a word that expressed "fear, terror,
dread, trepidation, apprehension, anxiety." His choice:
Waco.

Parachuting, combat, riding in a glider—an ascending
order of terror. Baker had jumped from airplanes and
mastered his fear. He had fought in combat and maintained his cool. He would never overcome the helpless
sense of dread he felt whenever he flew in a Waco glider.
He would rather parachute into a hot drop zone.

The CG-4A Waco glider had been widely used during
the D-day operation, but Baker and the veterans in his
squad had parachuted into Normandy. Since the 101st
Reconnaissance Platoon counted on the mobility of their

jeeps once they were on the ground, riding in a glider was not an option.

The Waco consisted of a steel tubing fuselage, a wooden wing, a plywood floor, and canvas covered. The aircraft they flew with such abandon and ease was a strut-braced high-wing monoplane that could carry more than its own weight in payload, and frequently did. The wing, constructed around a front box spar and a rear "I" spar, had wooden ribs and was plywood covered except for the trailing edge. The whole wing was covered with doped cotton fabric. The cockpit was made of welded steel tubing that was covered with fabric and plywood. In short, the glider was truly no more than a glorified kite.

Designed to be towed over the battlefield by a C-47 transport aircraft, the glider was released over the landing zone and then flown to the ground by a pilot and copilot. The Waco could carry thirteen troops or a jeep or cannon and four men. Intended to transport a lot of troops behind enemy lines fast, the gliders were built for a one-way mission. Needless to say, a large percentage of these ungainly craft crashed because of uneven landing surfaces and congestion in the landing zones.

More important, it took a special kind of pilot to fly a glider. The CG-4A Waco glider was not an attractive aircraft. The rest of the Army Air Corps pilots joked about its ugly looks, but few of them poked fun at the guys who flew them. The glider pilots were a special breed—tough, independent, and ready to fight. On their silver glider wings was a "G," which they said stood for "Guts."

Baker had trained in the gliders repeatedly since Normandy, learning emergency procedures and practicing the loading and unloading of a jeep. He and his squad, however, had only experienced one practice glider landing. And one experience was enough. He hardly considered the word *experience* the right expression for the sheer panic of crash-landing a canvas-covered Waco carrying a four-man recon team and a jeep into a field. As far as he was concerned, he would rather take his chances with a parachute anytime, but the Waco glider was what the 101st Airborne needed to land reconnaissance teams behind enemy lines, and that, as they say in the army, was the final word.

"Fall in!" Baker commanded.

The squad lined up. Each man was fully loaded for combat. With their helmets, weapons, grenades, canteens, and packs, each man carried sixty pounds of gear.

Baker inspected his men. As he approached each soldier, the man brought his weapon to inspection arms and opened the bolt in a precise, military routine. Baker would grab the weapon, inspect every inch of the weapon, and hand it back to the owner. Packs and canteens were checked and on-the-spot corrections made.

"Franky, your canteen is empty," Baker announced as he jiggled the canteen at Franky's side.

"Sorry, Sarge, I guess I forgot to fill it," Franky replied sheepishly.

"In combat, water is life," Baker replied. "We may be jumping into Holland, one of the wettest countries in Europe, but clean drinking water is vital to your survival on the battlefield. Fall out, fill your canteen, and don't forget again."

"Yes, Sergeant!" Franky replied as he fell out of formation to fill his canteen.

"Rookie," Corporal Zanovitch muttered.

Baker continued with the inspection. They were going to war. Baker knew that this was the calm before the storm. Were soldiers like Franky ready for what lay ahead? Could anyone ever truly be ready?

Franky returned to the squad, his canteen dripping wet with water.

"Okay, men, gather around," Baker ordered. "This may be the last time we have to talk before we're in Holland."

"Listen up," Zanovitch added, glancing at Franky.

"Our mission is simple," Baker continued. "We've gone over this countless times. As recon for Division headquarters, we find the enemy and report his size, activity, location, unit, time, and equipment. The more we report and the better information we provide Division Headquarters, the more lives we can save. Do as you have been trained, and we'll all get back home."

"And what about fighting?" Corporal Corrion asked. "From what they've told us, there's nothing but sick, lame, and lazy Krauts in Holland. They say this operation should be a cakewalk."

"You should know that score by now," Baker replied. "Anyone counting on this game being a shut-out had better think again. The Germans may be on the run, but they are a first-class team, and the war isn't over yet. My guess is that the closer we get to Germany, the tougher they will fight. Holland is right next to Germany. Just remember, we are recon. We find 'em first, shoot, scoot, and communicate. That's why we are mounted in jeeps."

"Beats walking, like we did in Normandy," Corporal Corrion offered. "I'd rather drive than walk any day."

"Just remember, once we are on the ground, get the jeeps out of the gliders fast," Baker ordered. "Don't hesitate. Seconds count in the drop zone, so I want to see everyone busting ass and moving fast."

"Yeah, if you have to, cut your way out through a canvas side," Corrion offered. "Just remember, your glider is *designed* to crash-land behind enemy lines."

"Okay, knock it off," Baker ordered. "Right face. Forward march."

Baker marched the men to a holding area to wait for the order to board the gliders. They arrived at their designated spot, fell out of formation, and waited. Rumors were rampant that the bad weather would cause a postponement in the operation and that the whole thing might be canceled like the past twelve operations; however, the commanding general, Major General Maxwell Taylor, came around to visit the troops and reported that the weather forecasts over Holland were for clear skies. He announced that the fog in England would lift before it was time to take off.

After a long, quiet wait a whistle blew and the order was passed down to load the gliders. "Board gliders!"

"Recon! Fall in. Route step, march," Baker ordered. He marched the squad out to their two gliders. The jeeps had been loaded the night before and carefully strapped down.

As they marched in full combat gear, laden down with their rifles, knives, grenades, ammunition, and K-rations, they walked past long lines of army air corps ground personnel. The air corps personnel stood in awe as the paratroopers marched to their planes and gliders.

"I bet they are mighty glad not to be in our boots," Zanovitch offered.

"I kind of wish I were in the air corps right about now," Corrion added.

A long line of C-47 Dakota transports filled the airfield tarmac. With twin engines running, the noise from the powerful Dakotas was impressive. Behind every C-47 transport aircraft were two silent Waco gliders with their nose cockpits bent open. The gliders were connected to the planes with long tow ropes.

Baker marched his squad to the gliders. Corrion took

charge of three men in the first glider, and Baker took Zanovitch, Courtland, and Franky in the other.

As Baker's men arrived at their designated glider, Baker halted the column. "Squad . . . halt. At ease."

"Hello, Sergeant," the pilot of the glider said as he greeted Baker and reached to shake his hand. "I'm Second Lieutenant William Fallow, and it's my job to get you to Holland. While we're in the air, I'm in charge. Do as I say, and we'll land safely. Once we're on the ground, it's all up to you."

Baker shook the lieutenant's hand and smiled. "I wouldn't have it any other way."

"Well, we're about to make history," Lieutenant Fallow offered. "Ready?"

Baker gave the lieutenant a nod and entered the glider. Together, Baker and the glider pilot checked the glider and the jeep inside, making sure everything was locked in place.

On command, the squad entered the Waco glider. Baker sat in the glider's copilot seat and waited for a long time while the engines of the C-47 roared nearby. The waiting was torture. Plane after plane passed by, filled with paratroopers on their way to the drop zone near Son, in the Netherlands.

Sitting in the copilot's seat, Baker had an excellent view of the airfield operations. As one C-47 passed by, Baker saw a paratrooper standing in the plane's open door. The man looked at Baker and waved. It was First Sergeant "Mac" Hassay, an old friend from Baker's time in the 502d Parachute Infantry Regiment in Normandy. Mac was now the first sergeant, the senior noncommissioned officer, for the 502d's Headquarters Company.

In the 502d, every soldier had a silver dollar–sized white heart painted on the left and right side of his helmet—a symbol used to identify the soldiers as members of the 502d. White hearts? Baker pondered the irony of this symbol.

Should we call them white hearts or steel hearts? Is that the kind of heart you have to have to survive this madness, a heart of steel?

Baker forced a smile and waved to his old friend, and watched Mac's Dakota take off and rise into the air.

After a seemingly endless line of C-47s took to the air, it was time for the gliders to take off. A C-47 in front of him rolled forward, twin propellers twirling at high rpms to pull two gliders behind it. Slowly the gliders moved down the tarmac, gradually picking up speed, and then as the C-47 became airborne, the gliders were jerked into the air.

At last, it was his turn. Baker's glider jerked with the pull of the tow rope and then rumbled noisily down the tarmac on its three rubber wheels. Lieutenant Fallow did a superb job steering the ungainly craft and making sure that their Waco kept the proper distance from the Waco to their right. As the speed increased, Lieutenant Fallow pulled up on his controls and the glider shuddered as it became airborne.

The wings buffeted and Baker thought the glider might fall apart as it gained altitude, but the sturdy wood-and-steel-tubing construction held firm and the glider was soon high above the ground. Baker assisted the pilot as best he could, keeping a lookout for other aircraft and helping Fallow gauge separation distance between their Waco and every other craft in the sky, but basically Baker was along for the ride. Fallow did all the flying.

Baker had been briefed that the journey to Holland would take three hours. Lieutenant Fallow kept his hands on the controls, keeping the glider at the proper altitude and at the proper distance from the glider to their right and the C-47 tow aircraft.

From Baker's vantage point, looking out through the Plexiglas cockpit, the air movement to Holland was an extremely impressive sight. Hundreds of planes and gliders filled the air in well-disciplined "V" formations. As he looked left and right, he saw an endless chain of planes in perfect formation as far as the eye could see. The entire spectacle was a mighty demonstration of airpower. Baker suddenly felt he understood the magnitude of the undertaking.

This was also Baker's first chance to really get a good look at England from the air. The green fields and busy villages were a beautiful sight in the bright sunlight.

They had been flying for half an hour when the pilot pointed to a group of fighters heading toward them. "That's our fighter escort. P-51 Mustangs. Right on time."

Baker nodded. The sleek, silver-colored P-51s flew escort above, below, and to either side of the glider formation. Baker was reassured by the sight of the fighter escort. He did not relish the thought of meeting up with the Luftwaffe while flying in an engineless, unarmed glider. Without a parachute—glidermen did not have parachutes—they wouldn't stand a chance if German planes hit them in the air.

As they progressed toward the Continent and then crossed into Belgium, the blue-green water of the Channel gave way to land. Passing over what had recently been occupied Europe, Baker had for the first time a bird's-eye view of the effects of Allied bombing that he had heard so much about. They flew over dozens of destroyed factory buildings, damaged bridges, and destroyed railway lines.

Over Belgium the landscape was as pretty as the English countryside, with large green fields cut by small canals. Now and then, they passed one of the large canals, such as the Albert Canal, which was rimmed with tall Lombardy poplar trees. As Baker looked down he could see people below pedaling along on their bicycles and waving.

The Germans had just been kicked out of Belgium, and the front was rapidly approaching as the glider neared the Dutch border.

"There. See the orange panels?" Fallow asked. "Our lines were separated by air-recognition panels to show strafing pilots which troops were friend and which were foe. North of that line is the enemy. We will be at the LZ in fifteen minutes. Better warn your men."

Baker looked back at his three companions sitting in the back of the glider next to their jeep. "We're crossing into Holland now. Fifteen minutes till landing."

Less than a minute after the glider flew over the line of air-recognition panels and into Holland, the shooting started. German 88mm flak peppered the sky. Tracers flew wildly into the air and a burst of small-arms fire passed through the glider's wing, right next to Baker. The noise sounded like corn popping.

Baker gave Fallow a glance that was a mixture of surprise and wonder.

Fallow smiled, presenting a brave face. "All in a day's work. Don't sweat it."

Baker grew tense as he watched the troop carrier formations hold firm despite the fire. It was like walking into a water hose and not flinching, only this was lead being shot from the hose, not water.

Baker was in awe of the bravery of the pilots. He watched a blazing C-47 keep formation long enough to reach the drop zone, disgorge eighteen paratroopers, and then plummet to the earth. The burning aircraft hit the ground in a ball of fire and black smoke. The pilot and aircrew never made it out.

Baker sat transfixed as he watched the drama unfold before him, the largest daylight airborne operation in history, as if he had a ring-side seat at a championship boxing match. What was being asked of these pilots was unbelievable. What they were doing was exceptional. The result was a sky full of paratroopers who landed exactly on target at the drop zone at Son.

Suddenly the operation became personal as Baker heard more snapping sounds and realized that the enemy's small-arms fire was zeroing in on his slow-moving glider. A couple of rounds cut through the canvas wing.

Baker shot a nervous look to Lieutenant Fallow, who was too busy with the glider controls to respond.

A few more bursts of flak dotted the sky as they closed in on the landing zone. An explosion erupted nearby, above them, and Baker heard a zing as shell fragments pierced the left wing. A large hole was ripped in the canvas, but the sturdy wing of the Waco held.

They started their final approach to the landing zone.

"Prepare to land!" Lieutenant Fallow shouted.

Baker looked back at his men and scanned the landing zone. Hundreds of parachutes from the rifle parachute units that had already landed covered the ground of the drop zone. Above this area, the sky was filled with C-47s releasing their gliders, which circled to the ground in wide spiral arcs.

Baker's glider bounced in the air as another shell burst close by. Off to his left another C-47 was hit by German antiaircraft fire and burst into flames. Unable to release its tow ropes in time, the C-47 plunged toward the ground dragging two helpless gliders with it. The C-47 flew away from the drop zone and crashed. Just before impact, one glider broke free and raced to the ground. The other glider wasn't as lucky and plunged into the burning wreckage of the exploding C-47.

Baker looked down and saw the C-47 burning on the ground and thought about its crew and the men in the glider.

"This is it!" Lieutenant Fallow shouted as he reached for the tow rope release lever. "Brace yourselves!"

The glider suddenly shuddered and turned steeply, and Baker realized that his Waco had cast off from the C-47 tow plane. The scene changed violently as Baker's glider headed toward the ground. Fallow pulled hard to the right to avoid hitting the other glider. He circled over the DZ and then dropped the nose downward.

Time moved in slow motion as Baker watched the ground approach. The speed of the Waco glider seemed to increase as the ground drew ever nearer, until suddenly the glider touched down. The glider held firm under the tremendous strain of the impact, then broke a wheel as it hit and screeched across the flat Dutch field. It tore up about a hundred yards of real estate before finally coming to a halt.

In seconds, it was over. The glider stopped; there was silence.

Baker caught his breath, glad to be alive. He glanced at Lieutenant Fallow.

Fallow was grinning from ear to ear. "We made it."

A touch of euphoria overcame Baker. He and his men had survived the glider flight to Holland, and the landing couldn't have been better. His adrenaline was pumping as he patted Lieutenant Fallow on the shoulder. "Okay, now it's my turn."

Baker and Fallow struggled with the cockpit latches. After a mighty push the cockpit released and folded up on hinges in the ceiling. At the same time the men inside the glider worked furiously to disconnect the chains that held down the jeep.

"Move it. Out! Everybody out!" Baker ordered.

In minutes they were moving the jeep out of the glider and onto the landing zone at Son.

"Good luck, Baker!" Fallow shouted with a grin as Baker and his men began to move out.

"Thanks, sir! Good luck to you," Baker shouted as he snapped the pilot a proud salute. Baker made a quick check to see that his men and gear were secure in the jeep, then gave the signal to move forward. "Let's go!"

Baker's war had begun.

On the Dutch side of the Meuse-Escaut Canal north of the Belgium town of Neerspelt, inside the defensive line of the 2d Battalion, 21st SS Panzer Grenadier Regiment, part of SS Kampfgruppe Heinke, 1410 hours:

"I want this to be perfectly clear," SS *Obersturmführer* Carl Kodritz snarled as he looked down at Graf. Graf stood in a trench and the tall SS officer, on the ground, towered above him. The SS officer didn't try to hide his contempt for Graf or his *Fallschirmjägers*. An SS *Hauptscharführer* named Gunter, carrying an MP-40 submachine gun, stood at Kodritz's side, like a bouncer at a bar waiting for orders to throw a rowdy customer out of a tavern. Graf guessed that before the war, that was just what the master sergeant did for a living.

"While you are here, *Oberfeldwebel,* you are under SS command," Kodritz emphasized. "*My* command. If your men attempt to withdraw from this position, they will be shot and I will hold you personally responsible. *Generalfeldmarschall* Model has issued strict orders.

This line will be held. I will not have cowards in my command."

Graf didn't balk or show any emotion to the SS officer's insult. He had dealt with this kind of arrogant bastard before and knew the rules and regulations of the German military. Graf chose his words carefully. From the look of this SS lieutenant, he was not a man to be trifled with, even if he was too young to have seen much combat. "My *Fallschirmjägers* are not in the habit of running away, *Herr Obersturmführer.*"

"From what I have heard, the Sixth Fallschirmjäger Regiment does as it pleases," the SS officer growled. "Just like your commander—von der Heydte is his name?—did at Carentan."

As before, Graf did not reply to this second insult. Kodritz was referring to a battle in Normandy where the 6th Fallschirmjäger Regiment under the command of Major von der Heydte withdrew from the town of Carentan when the situation had become hopeless. The town was surrounded by American paratroopers of the 101st Airborne, the Screaming Eagles, as they were called. The *Fallschirmjägers* had been in constant battle for days and were outnumbered, outgunned, out of supplies, and exhausted. As a result, von der Heydte disobeyed orders, withdrew his men, and saved much of the regiment from death or capture. The regiment lived to fight another day in Normandy and was essential in gaining time and holding back the Allied tide.

The day after von der Heydte withdrew from Carentan, an SS Division attacked to retake Carentan from the Americans. The attack failed and the SS Division commander wanted von der Heydte court-martialed for his unauthorized withdrawl. Instead, General Student, the commander of all German *Fallschirmjägers,* personally intervened and promoted von der Heydte to lieutenant colonel instead.

"If I had been in charge of your beloved von der Heydte, I would have had him shot for disobeying orders," Kodritz growled. "In any case, do your duty here or suffer the consequences."

Graf brought his right hand to his helmet and saluted, in the military fashion. Kodritz turned, without returning the salute, and marched to the rear, followed by the SS sergeant.

"A pleasant fellow if I ever saw one. We are lucky to have such brave leaders," *Feldwebel* Karsten Weise replied cynically to Graf.

The field telephone next to Graf rang. Graf picked up the transmitter-receiver:

"*Jawohl, Oberstleutnant,* all is in order here. We are ready. Yes. I will call for mortar fire through you as soon as I see the Tommies on the highway. I will do my best. Good luck to you, too, sir."

Oberfeldwebel Graf placed the field telephone transmitter down on the field telephone set. The day was bright and sunny, but Graf had an ominous feeling, the same way he used to feel in Russia before a major attack by the Red Army. Maybe it was his run-in with SS *Obersturmführer* Kodritz, or maybe it was just that he didn't like the SS, or more likely, it was because the past two days had been ominously quiet.

"What did the *Oberstleutnant* say? Do we stay here with the SS or come back to the Regiment?" Weise asked. "I don't think we are welcome here."

"We stay," Graf replied unhappily. "We are to coordinate the joint defense of the Hechtel-to-Eindhoven highway and call for regimental mortar support to aid the SS in their mission to block the road from the east. Von der Heydte is upset that the road is the boundary between the Sixth Fallschirmjäger Regiment in the west and the SS in the east. The road as the boundary! What idiot staff officer made this decision? Either the Fallschirmjäger Regiment or the SS Kampfgruppe should have been given the ground on both sides of the road and the sole responsibility to block the road to Eindhoven."

"Well, maybe nothing will happen today?" Weise offered. "It's past noon. The Tommies normally attack at dawn."

Graf shook his head. "Check the positions again and make sure the men continue to dig the trench line deep. I want this trench shoulder high—as deep as they can make it. Make sure that the *panzerfausts* are protected and placed at the very bottom of the trench until they are needed. More spade work will save lives if Tommy attacks us in force."

"Your shoulders or mine?" Weise asked with a grin.

"Professor, not now," Graf snapped. "I am not in the mood."

Weise nodded and moved off to inspect the men.

Graf surveyed his platoon. Since September 11, an uneasy quiet had settled over the battlefield. His men occupied trenches and bunker positions that were dug into the wet ground to the east of the Hechtel-to-Eindhoven road. The positions were created only in the past thirty-six hours. The trenches were not deep enough, and only a few were covered with timber to provide overhead cover.

What worried him most was that his platoon was getting smaller with each passing day. No reinforcements had arrived from Regiment. He had started with forty-two men when he arrived in the Netherlands on September 7 and had lost eight killed—three only last night—and four wounded in the fighting in Belgium. The survivors of the past few days of fighting totaled only thirty men. He swore a silent oath that he would do his best to keep the rest of his youngsters alive, but he knew that the task would become more difficult in the days ahead.

Armed with one Maschinengewehr 42—MG42 machine gun—and dozens of *panzerfausts*, Graf realized that their main defense against any attacking British tanks would be the short-ranged *panzerfausts*, an ingenious percussion-ignited grenade that was shot from a hollow tube. It worked much like a rifle grenade, but the warhead was bigger and consisted of a shaped charge designed to burn through the thickest British tank armor. The *panzerfaust* was an easy to use weapon with the firing instructions printed on the warhead, but Graf worried that only a few of his men had actually trained to fire them.

To fire the *panzerfaust*, the gunner cocked a small arming rod located on top of the barrel, turned the safety switch to the left, aimed it at the target, and squeezed down on the arming trigger. The warhead, which was mounted to the launching shaft, was armed in flight, after leaving the tube.

The *panzerfaust* was a desperate, close-in weapon, but for infantry in the defense, it was highly effective. The range of the *panzerfaust* was between ten and thirty meters, but only a skilled gunner or a lucky shot would hit a moving target.

Graf wished he had more time to train his men on how to use their weapons and rudimentary tactics. In the old days, he would train his squad for days. Now, with the Allies held back by the German defenses along the Meuse-Escaut Canal, he had no time to train them at all. Moreover, Graf knew that this small strip of water would not hold the British back for long. On the tenth, the Tommies had surprised and seized the bridge across the canal before the dunderheads of the Herman Goering flak units guarding the crossing site could destroy the bridge. Graf feared this mistake would cost the German defenders dearly.

To confirm his fears, the past few days had been filled with the sound of Allied tanks and vehicles moving up toward the canal. The British were too far away to see, but the sound of their movement traveled a long way at night, and Graf knew they were preparing an attack. From the sound of their movement, he knew the British were planning a big push, one that would have considerable weight to it, but when?

Yesterday, he was dispatched by the regimental commander, *Oberstleutnant* Friedrich von der Heydte, to co-locate with the SS mechanized infantry and act as liaison for the Regiment to the SS, who were occupying defensive positions on the eastern side of the road. The SS infantry battalion was reinforced with three 88mm cannons, two 57mm antitank guns, and dozens of *panzerfausts*.

Van der Heydte, however, was concerned that the defense was not coordinated between his paratroopers and the SS. He feared that in the thick of battle, with each separate German force looking out for itself, the enemy might split the boundary and race down the road. To make sure the defense between the two units was coordinated and that the SS would have the benefit of the *Fallschirmjägers* mortar platoon, von der Heydte had placed Graf and thirty-man platoon with the SS.

Graf was expected to communicate with 6th Fallschirmjäger Regimental Headquarters by field telephone wire. If all else failed, he was to fight with the SS and do his best to stop any British advance north.

"Graf, do you hear that?" Weise asked.

Graf took off his helmet, holding it in his left hand. A

strange humming sound emanated from the south. Initially it sounded like the buzzing of tiny insects, but then it grew louder. Soon the buzzing turned into a steady rhythm, the rhythm of engines—lots of engines. From his position in the forest east of the road, Graf looked up at the southern skyline. The sky was filled with small, dark dots. Graf stared at the horizon, unsure of what he was seeing.

Suddenly, with a roar of turbo-supercharged Pratt & Whitney engines, Graf witnessed a line of low-flying aircraft heading right for the SS defensive line. A pair of big, American P-47 Thunderbolts raced directly at his position at treetop level, followed by waves of other fighter-bombers. The wings of the fast-flying P-47s sparkled as four fifty-caliber machine guns in each wing blazed away at Graf.

"Jabos!" Graf shouted as he jumped for his foxhole, dropping his helmet to the ground. He fell on top of Sergeant Weise, then rolled and tried to get as small as his large frame would allow.

The mud kicked up all around as Graf hugged the wet dirt. Men screamed up above his trench, but he dared not raise his head.

A dozen aircraft now noisily darted past, just above the woods, like angry vultures looking for prey. Their heavy machine guns rattled while the bullets shattered the trees. Bullets and wood splinters fell like a deadly rain from the sky.

Graf looked up and in a quick glimpse saw a British Typhoon pass overhead. Right over Graf's trench the aircraft launched a dozen high-explosive rockets at an unseen target to the north. The rockets made a horrific screaming sound as they launched from the wide wings of the Typhoon.

"My God!" Weise screamed. "This must be the main attack!"

Graf didn't answer. There was nothing to say or do. Living through the ordeal was all that one could hope for.

Then, unexpectedly, the aircraft flew farther north, hunting other prey. More aircraft flew high overhead, fighters, fighter-bombers, and big four-engined B-17 bombers, hundreds of them, but these seemed to be heading to other targets farther north.

Graf waited for a moment and listened to someone screaming, then shouted: "*Fallschirmjägers.* Sound off!"

"Küster, present!"

"*Jäger* Stöhr, here!"

Becker, Berna, Dörnefeld, Eckolt, Emmerrich, Henning, Hensel, Horst, Merckel, Miller, Vibbard, and Wigand responded in turn. The rest of his men replied in turn.

"Good, all the little rabbits are safe," Weise offered with a grin. "So who is screaming?"

Graf lifted his head above the trench and saw the smoldering wreck of a Pak 41 antitank cannon. He reached for his helmet and put it on his head. Nearby, he saw the twisted metal gun shield of the antitank cannon and a wounded SS man. The SS soldier lay in the mud, grabbing his abdomen and kicking his feet wildly. Blood was gushing from the man's belly, and Graf, a veteran of many scenes like this one, knew he would not live. Three SS men gathered near him and pulled him away from the destroyed gun and into their foxhole. After a few moments, the man stopped screaming.

Graf sat back in the trench cradling his PPSh-41 submachine gun. The SS men were as young as his "little rabbits" and probably had even less training than some of his men. Training or not, they would quickly be put to the test. From the number of *Jabos* in the initial wave of the attack, Graf knew that Weise was right and that the British were about to launch a major attack.

Weise pointed to the sky. "Graf, I can't believe it. Look!"

Graf scanned the sky and saw long V-shaped formations of transport aircraft. In perfect formation, line upon line of C-47 Dakota paratroop planes flew overhead. Graf lost count, there were so many. The Reich had never had so many paratroop transport aircraft, even during the heyday invasion of Crete in 1942!

"Amazing!" Graf exclaimed. "If only we had such power."

Puffs of flak burst overhead as the German antiaircraft guns greeted the Allied aircraft and tried to take down some of the planes in the swarm passing overhead. A few of the slow-flying aircraft were hit, caught fire, and plummeted to the ground. The rest bravely kept their formation and flew north.

A sinking feeling engulfed Graf's soul as he looked up at the armada flying high in the sky. In Russia, he had fought against staggering odds, but the enemy was mostly on the ground and the Red Army's attacks usually consisted of heavy artillery fire, followed by massed infantry and tanks. Now, in the west, the Allies were flaunting their military-industrial muscle and were employing air and ground warfare in a massive way. Their airplanes filled the sky. The display of Allied military might was staggering and at the same time demoralizing.

With so many parachute transport planes in the air, it was obvious that the Allies were launching several parachute divisions behind German lines. The ominous meaning behind this revelation, even for a veteran like Graf, sent a chill down his spine.

He reached for the field telephone transmitter, cranked the ringer, and waited for the voice at the other end.

"Graf, prepare for a major assault!" the voice of a *Fallschirmjäger* lieutenant on the other end ordered. "Call us as soon as you have a target for the mortars."

"Of course, *Herr Leutnant*," Graf answered, trying to sound calm. "We will do our duty."

Before he could say anything more, an artillery shell exploded fifty meters in front of his position. He threw down the phone and ducked instinctively. As soon as he had ducked down and was kneeling in the trench, it was as if a dam had abruptly burst. A tidal wave of twenty or thirty heavy-caliber, twenty-five-pounder shells burst in a jagged line in front of his position, each explosion about ten meters apart, sending searing metal screaming through the air. The next wave detonated ten meters closer to the German trenches.

Graf realized that the British were opening up their offensive with a barrage of artillery on a grand scale. They were walking the artillery onto the German position, meter by meter.

"Everyone down!" Graf screamed as he lunged to the bottom of the trench and hugged the dirt again. With one hand on his *Fallschirmjäger* helmet and the other clutching his Tommy gun, Graf pressed his body into the bottom of the trench. Weise was on the ground next to him, quivering from the power of the onslaught.

The ground shook as if a giant was pounding a table with a sledgehammer. Treetops disintegrated as the shells exploded in the air over the defensive line. Cannons were tossed into the air, flipping like toys as they were struck by high-explosive shells. Somehow, above the tremendous ear-splitting noise and the intense concussion of the blasts, Graf heard the shrill voices of men screaming.

The shelling continued. Explosion after explosion rocked the earth. Hot metal zinged inches over the trench line while shattering anyone or anything the fragments came into contact with. Dirt, smoke, and the smell of burning powder filled the air as shell after shell detonated all around the hastily dug foxholes and trenches of Graf's paratroopers and the men of the 2d Battalion, 21st SS Panzergrenadier Regiment.

The world seemed to spin beneath him. Graf bounced in his trench as the concussion of the shells pulled him up, then smashed him back against the dirt. Blast upon blast pummeled the position.

Each time he thought he could not be more afraid, but with each passing moment the fear rose in his chest. He had been under artillery fire before and had endured massive Russian artillery barrages, but nothing had been like this. He felt a sense of insanity rising in his throat. His experience kicked in and he kept control, as he always had in these situations, when most men could not. He was sure they would all die.

Then suddenly, with each passing second, the explosions moved farther away, heading north. Graf took a deep breath of air and felt the euphoria of being alive. At the same time, he was consumed with a white hot anger toward his foe, an enemy who had wreaked such havoc on his men and against whom he could not strike back; but that was about to change.

The ground was covered in a thin blanket of gray smoke. His ears were ringing, his rage burning, but he channeled the fire, as he always had, focusing on the situation at hand. He groped for his PPSh-41 submachine gun, ran his hand over the bolt to clear away the dirt, and prepared the weapon for action.

"*Fallschirmjägers* report!" Graf shouted at the top of his lungs.

At first, no one answered. He heard the sound of a boy crying and the last murmurs of men dying.

"*Fallschirmjägers* report!" Graf repeated.

"Küster!"

"Stöhr, here!"

"Berna here!"

"Dörnefeld, alive."

Eckolt, Emmerrich, Henning, Hensel, Merckel, Miller, Vibbard, Wigand, and the rest responded.

Two men were missing. Graf looked over the lip of the trench and saw a foxhole ten meters away where Becker and Horst had been. There was nothing there now but a smoking hole, a *Fallschirmjäger* helmet, and pieces of clothing.

He scanned the defensive line. Dead soldiers and wrecked equipment from the 2d SS Panzergrenadier Battalion littered the ground. Wrecked antitank cannons, now smoldering piles of scrap metal, dotted the defensive line. A bloody leg lay a few feet behind Graf's trench.

Medics moved to the trenches to remove the wounded. Men cried out in pain as they were manhandled to the rear. The SS battalion had taken heavy casualties. Most important, all of their antitank cannons had been knocked out.

Sergeants shouted orders. The survivors of the multiple air and artillery attacks stood up in their trenches, checked their weapons, and prepared to fight.

"Get ready for ground attack," Graf ordered. "Bring up the *panzerfausts*."

Graf's *Fallschirmjägers* obeyed. Slowly, the men shook off the shock of the artillery barrage and prepared to fight.

Graf reached down for the field telephone and picked up the transmitter. He cranked the ringer and listened, but there was no response. Graf threw the transmitter down. The British artillery fire had obviously cut the line.

"*Jäger* Stöhr, is the MG42 ready?" Graf shouted as he

looked to his left at the thin soldier manning their only machine gun.

Stöhr, a boy of eighteen, nodded confidently. "*Ja, Herr Oberfeldwebel.*"

Graf grabbed Weise by the shoulder. "Stay next to Stöhr and direct the fire of the machine gun."

Weise grunted and moved down the trench to stand next to the machine gunner. He checked the weapon, examined the ammunition, and patted Stöhr on the back. "MG42 is ready for action, *Oberfeldwebel.*"

"Küster, Miller, Emmerrich. Bring *panzerfausts* and stand near me," Graf growled, like a wolf ready to go on the prowl.

The three young *Fallschirmjägers* rushed over from the right side of the trench line. Each soldier carried two *panzerfausts* in addition to their rifles.

"I see them coming!" Weise shouted. "Eleven o'clock. The Tommies are launching tanks right down the road."

A big, green-colored British Sherman tank clanked down the Hechtel-to-Eindhoven road at fifteen miles an hour, spraying the area to the right of the highway with machine-gun fire. On the far left of the 2d SS Battalion's line, a group of young soldiers were quickly gunned down by the advancing British tank.

The SS men ducked for cover. The entire defensive line seemed stunned. With their antitank guns destroyed and their officers nowhere to be seen, the young SS soldiers hid in their trenches and waited for someone to issue orders.

Graf saw the lead British tank advancing straight down the road. A line of other British Sherman tanks followed in close order. If something wasn't done soon, the enemy tanks would pass the German defenses and advance, unchecked, toward Eindhoven.

Suddenly, in a burst of smoke and flame, the lead

British tank jerked to a halt as it was hit by a *Fallschirm-jäger panzerfaust* from the west side of the road. Ober-stleutnant von der Heydte's men, on the other side of the road, were on the attack!

"Covering fire! Force the British tank commanders to button up!" Graf ordered to Weise.

Weise obeyed instantly and directed Stöhr to fire the MG42 machine gun at the turret of the second tank in the column. As the fire splashed against the side of the second tank, the British tank commander ducked down inside the turret and closed his hatch. Weise then directed the fire of the machine gun to the third tank. As the bullets from the MG42 smashed against the armor of the third Sherman tank, the tank commander also buttoned up his hatches to protect himself from the searing machine-gun bullets.

"Let's go, boys!" Graf shouted as he slung his PPSh Tommy gun over his neck, grabbed a *panzerfaust,* and ran like a greyhound toward the second tank in the column.

Emmerrich, Küster, and Miller followed on the run. A dozen SS boys, seeing Graf and the other paratroopers running toward the British tanks, took heart and leapt from the trench line and joined the attack.

The British tanks, now blocked on the road as the lead tank exploded in a shower of sparks and flame, turned their turrets on the advancing German infantrymen and plastered the trees with machine-gun fire. Half of the SS men were cut down like wheat by a scythe. Miller was also hit and spun backward, mortally wounded as a volley of tank machine-gun fire struck him in the chest.

The ground erupted in geysers of dirt in front of Graf as the British tankers frantically fired at the advancing German *Fallschirmjägers*. While the British tanks chopped up the remaining SS *Panzergrenadiers,* Graf, Emmerrich, and Küster charged the stalled tanks from the right-front. The British tankers, buttoned up and looking through narrow vision blocks, could not see Graf and his men approaching them through the trees and smoke to their right.

As Graf closed the distance with the tanks and moved into *panzerfaust* range, he knelt next to a tree and took up a firing position. He cocked the *panzerfaust*, took aim at the second tank in the column, and fired. The grenade lobbed forward through the air and hit the right side of the tank's turret.

There was a dull, crumping sound as the *panzerfaust* warhead ignited against the turret in a splatter of sparks and fire. The tank immediately burst into flames. The hatch opened and thick black smoke belched from the turret. A figure tried to bail out of the front hatches of the hull, but Graf grabbed his PPSh and plastered the tank with submachine-gun fire. The British tanker was hit and, with his feet still in the hatch, his body dangled over the side of the hull.

Spires of black smoke rose from the two burning tanks. The oily black smoke rose high into the sky like a funeral pyre.

Küster and Emmerrich fired at the third tank. Küster's *panzerfaust* flew true but low and hit the British tank on the lower-left side, disabling the track. Emmerrich, a new soldier who was not experienced with the *panzerfaust*, fired, but in his excitement he failed to pay attention to the end of the tube. Screaming as the hot gases burned into his right leg, he dropped the *panzerfaust*, and the warhead missed the target, hitting the road and exploding behind the third tank.

Another tank in the column turned its turret on the three German paratroopers and fired. Küster ducked for cover behind a dirt mound and Graf took cover behind a tree. Emmerrich, wounded and in agony from the *panzerfaust* accident, turned, but was caught out in the open and was torn apart by machine-gun bullets.

At that moment, from the west side of the road, a *panzerfaust* hit the third tank in the turret and the British vehicle burst into flames.

The road was now effectively blocked. It would take some time for the British to push three burning tanks to the side of the road.

As if on cue, British Bren Carriers moved forward and stopped short of the third burning hulk. Riflemen piled out of the infantry carriers with their rifles and submachine guns at the ready. A whistle blew, orders were shouted in English, and the British infantry rushed forward on the right side of the road.

Soon the enemy infantry was fixing the German defenses with fire on the left and moving to flank the trench line on the right.

Grenades landed nearby. Ear-splitting explosions kicked up geysers of dirt as the advancing Tommies closed in on the defenders.

Many of the SS troops were in full retreat. There was no one to hold the line. Graf saw the inevitable conclusion to the fight and made a decision.

"Withdraw!" Graf shouted to Küster as he withdrew and fired his PPSh Tommy gun from the hip at the British.

The two *Fallschirmjägers* ran back to the trench line just as British infantry began moving through the woods. As Graf was running for the trench line, he swore that he heard the sound of someone singing.

"At them men!" Colour Sergeant Cat Gilchrist bellowed as the Irish Guards leapt from the armored protection of the Bren Carriers to the muddy ground of

Holland. Gilchrist held his Sten submachine gun in his left hand and signaled his men forward with his right. "As my grandfather used to say, death never comes too late. On line. Forward, half right! Let's give it to them!"

Two platoons of Irish Guards Infantry led the charge, with one platoon in reserve following. First Platoon was on the right. Cat's platoon took the left flank.

The Germans fired at the advancing British from the trench line, but their fire was ragged and uncoordinated. Only one German machine gun at the far left of the line put up effective fire against the British attack.

"Corporal Ackers, move your section to the left," Cat ordered. "Clear this open ground fast!"

Corporal Ackers blew a whistle and the veteran soldiers of his section spread out to the left and moved on line, firing as they rushed. Then they deployed his section on-line with the Bren light machine gun to the right. Cat was on the right along with Guardsmen Barclay, Gaines, Logan, Roy, and Weller. The well-trained infantrymen moved forward in quick rushes, one section at a time, as the other section fired at the enemy.

Ackers's section took up prone positions and fired. The Bren Gun in Ackers's section chattered away as Cat's section rushed forward to a small rise that was perpendicular to the German line. Cat ordered his men to go to ground and pour a deadly enfilade onto the enemy line.

German soldiers started to run from the trench line. The moment of truth had been reached and the SS infantry could take no more.

"Everyone, to the trench line!" Cat ordered and started to sing. "In the ranks of death you'll find him!"

Ackers's men ran forward. The Irish Guardsmen fired and screamed like banshees as they attacked, routing the German defenders. A wounded SS soldier rolled from behind a tree and fired a pistol at Cat as the Irish colour sergeant raced forward. Guardsman Barclay was hit in the chest, staggered, and fell. Cat leveled his Sten gun at the German and fired off his remaining magazine of 9mm shells. The Sten is a devastating close-range weapon. One long burst and the German was dead.

Dead Germans lay all about the trench line as Cat's men rushed them from the right side. A few wounded Germans were bayoneted as they tried to crawl away. The Irish Guard attack was fast and hard. There was no time for a sporting approach to battle, this was close combat and split seconds decided who lived or died.

Off to Cat's left-front, an SS trooper jumped up from the trench and threw up his arms to surrender. The German soldier was young, probably no more than nineteen years old, but he moved too quickly and Ackers, unsure of the situation, fired a burst from his submachine gun first. The German was hit in the face and fell backward.

"Guardsman Roy! Your Bren Gun to fire in that direction," Cat ordered as he pointed at the German machine gun up ahead. "PIAT, on that Spandau!"

Guardsman Roy removed the curved magazine at the top of his Bren Gun, replaced it with a fresh magazine, and plastered the enemy machine-gun position with fire.

Cat could see the short, distinctive helmet of a German *Fallschirmjäger* behind the trench. He fired, but the figured ducked in time. Suddenly the barrel of a submachine gun rose above the lip of the trench and a fusillade of bullets forced Cat to the ground.

"Mother Mary!" Cat cursed. "Gaines, fire a PIAT on that bastard!"

Gaines was the best PIAT gunner in the platoon. The PIAT (Projector, Infantry, Anti Tank) was a spring-loaded grenade launcher. It was heavy, difficult to cock, and cumbersome, but in the hands of a good gunner it could launch a three-pound grenade sixty to seventy meters.

Gaines aimed his PIAT and let loose. The bomb traveled through the air and hit the *Fallschirmjägers* trench. The explosion sent up a shower of rocks and mud.

The firing tapered off as Cat held his men in position. Whatever Germans were left alive had fled east. Several wounded SS soldiers lay on the ground moaning.

Cat's men took up positions in the German trench line and faced to the east. The reserve platoon moved through Cat's line and pushed farther east, taking an odd shot every now and then.

Cat sat down in the trench where the PIAT bomb had exploded and saw the dismembered leg of a German soldier just a few feet from the position.

Corporal Ackers walked over to Cat staring at the bloody leg. "Whoever had been in this hole must have been blown to kingdom come."

"Yeah," Cat replied. He opened up his left breast pocket, took out a package of cigarettes, and handed one to Ackers. Ackers took the cigarette and lit up. "What's our status?"

"We lost two men, Barclay and Weller, both killed," Ackers said. "But we fared better than the lead tanks. I saw at least three brewing on the road, and we've just begun this fight. If we have to battle like this for every yard of the forest that lines this bloody highway, there'll be hell to pay."

"Yeah," Cat replied. "There will be hell to pay before we own Hell's Highway."

Eindhoven, Netherlands:

It was a beautiful sunny day in German-occupied Holland. Like every Sunday, Alexander Van Janssen and

Mira Vogel had attended church services at Saint Catherine's Church.

Rumors were rampant. Everyone in the Netherlands knew that the Allies weren't far away. During the homily, the priest declared from his pulpit that "something" was about to happen. Alexander and Mira knew what he was alluding to. As Alexander and Mira left the Gothic-style church, the organ softly played the first notes of the national hymn of the Netherlands.

Expectation filled the air.

As they left the church, the two youngsters saw that the streets of Eindhoven were busy with German traffic, but unlike the previous week, now there was organization in the German effort. The time of panic had ended. There was no more of the frantic disorganization of Mad Tuesday. It was clear that the Germans were getting ready to fight.

As they walked down the cobblestone streets of the city of Eindhoven, pushing their bicycles with them, a commotion started at the far end of the street. Alexander and Mira stopped at a corner just as a squad of German soldiers ran past them. As they observed from the street corner, they saw a group of German soldiers arresting railroad workers and herding them into a truck. One old man protested his arrest and a German soldier hit him with the butt of his rifle.

The old man fell to the ground, blood spewing from his mouth. Two other detainees shielded the old man and helped him up into the truck.

"Look how they treat us, and so near the church," Alexander announced, his voice ringed with anger at what he was watching. "Sometimes I wonder whose side God is on."

"God is not on anyone's side," Mira answered dispassionately. "We are called to be on God's side."

Alexander smiled. "How many railway workers went on strike today?"

"From what Melanie told me, all of them. Every single one," Mira answered proudly.

Melanie was Mira's contact with the Partisan Action Netherlands, or PAN, resistance group. It was a group in Eindhoven that was established in 1943 and had grown to nearly a hundred members. Consisting of mostly young, idealistic men and women like Alexander and Mira, PAN members were eager to help push the Germans out of the Netherlands. Mira's Bicyclists did not belong to PAN, but cooperated with PAN on several occasions to help people hide from the Germans. It was through her PAN contact Melanie that Mira passed information on the German army that the Bicyclists collected so carefully.

"Will I ever get to meet Melanie?" Alexander asked.

"In due time," Mira replied with a smile. "You know how important it is to maintain secrecy."

Mira felt she could trust Melanie, which was a code name and not the person's actual name, but she also knew that PAN had its limitations. After D-day, in June 1944, hopes for liberation grew high. Many PAN members became impatient and increased their anti-German activities. When Mad Tuesday occurred, one PAN group took up arms and attacked the twenty-five-man German garrison at the Eindhoven airport. A short firefight ensued at the airport and then the PAN members dispersed. The Germans maintained control of the airport and made several arrests over the next few days.

PAN members also approached German soldiers they knew to try to persuade them of the hopelessness of Germany's situation, and invited them to surrender. Few German soldiers took the offer. Instead, the German soldiers reported the PAN members, who were then arrested and executed—the punishment for belonging to a resistance organization.

In short, Mira knew that their actions, though heroic, could not overcome the might of the German military. If liberation was to come, the Allies would have to drive the Germans out of Holland. She was convinced that the best use of the Dutch resistance, and particularly the Bicyclists, was not to fight but to provide the invading Allies with intelligence on German units, troop movements, and headquarters.

"Look—something is happening," Alexander announced.

Unexpectedly, people started to come out onto the street. The German soldiers also seemed to gather in the open streets. The guards who, moments before, were busily beating old men and forcing them into the back of a truck, stopped worrying about the railway workers and pointed to the sky.

A whistle blew. A German officer screamed orders. Excited German soldiers scurried away as the truck moved out. It was as if an anthill had been kicked over and the ants were scurrying everywhere.

Alexander and Mira looked up at the heavens. What they saw was incredible, unbelievable, and absolutely wonderful. From the southern horizon, the sky was filling with aircraft flying north. The aircraft flew in disciplined V formations with each aircraft nearly evenly spaced from the other. Most of the aircraft had white and black stripes on their wings. They were Allied aircraft.

Alexander and Mira watched in stunned silence. To their ears, the hum of hundreds of Allied aircraft flying overhead sounded like the music of angels.

A siren blared in the distance. More German soldiers ran around the streets, pointed skyward, and started to set up machine guns.

"Those are not bombers," Alexander shouted in glee,

above the noise of the engines. He hugged Mira and they both smiled.

Sporadic German machine-gun fire sounded throughout the city. Tracers arced up into the sky. In the distance, a German 88mm cannon blasted away at the approaching Allied aircraft.

The aircraft armada now stretched across the entire sky, from south to north a great carpet of aircraft filled the heavens. Some of the younger residents of Eindhoven climbed out on their roofs, oblivious to the danger of the German machine-gun fire, to watch the spectacle.

Mira turned north and saw what looked like snowflakes falling from the sky. She stared in wonder at the magnitude of what was happening. Soon, it dawned on her that the snowflakes were parachutes. "Paratroopers! Those are transport aircraft. It must be a parachute drop. Liberation is coming!"

"So what do we do now?" Alexander asked.

"We must gather the Bicyclists," Mira answered. "Go and pass the word. The Allies will be here soon. This is our country. We must play our part in the liberation."

Oberfeldwebel Wilhelm Graf

4: D+2

Heavy rain fell during the night, and in the morning of D+1, Monday, September 18, there were thick clouds over the Continent and fog over the Allied airfields in England, delaying the second day's lift of glider infantry and supplies. By noon the 101st's paratroopers had liberated Eindhoven, but not until seven that evening did the Guards Armored link up with them. British engineers went to work building a prefabricated Bailey bridge to replace the blown canal bridge at Son. By dawn on D+2, September 19, 1944, the British Engineers completed their work. The way to Nijmegen and Arnhem was now open....

Dawn, Tuesday, September 19, 1944, 0600 hours, along the Pastoor van Ravensteinstraat road, Son, Netherlands:

"'Land of Song!' cried the warrior bard, 'Tho' all the world betrays thee, One sword, at least, thy rights shall guard, One faithful harp shall praise thee!'"

"I swear the man never gets tired of that tune!" Corporal Donal Ackers exclaimed as he saw Colour Sergeant Cat Gilchrist amble back from the bridge at Son. Ackers stood up in the back of his Bren Carrier. "Well, Cat, why are you in such a good mood? Is the damn Bailey contraption ready? We've been ready to go since zero three hundred!"

"Calm down, Ackers, we'll be on the roll shortly," Cat replied with an air of triumph. Cat was wearing his British P-1944 Turtle MK IV steel helmet, full battle gear, and carrying his trusty Sten submachine gun in his left hand. "I just talked with the engineer colour sergeant of the Fourteenth Field Company. They have the Bailey bridge completed, all one hundred and ten feet of it, and are testing the bitch now to see if she will hold together."

"Let me run my Bren Carrier across it," Ackers answered. "That'll test it for sure."

"Well, you won't get your turn until the tanks of the Household Cavalry and Grenadier Guards cross first. Once they cross, we'll move over to the other side and follow them as the lead of the Irish Guards."

Ackers shot Cat a grin. "What's that you say? The Grenadier Guards will lead the attack, now that we've fought as the vanguard and pushed Jerry all the way from the Belgium border to Son? No wonder you're in a good mood. That's the best news I've heard since we started this bloody operation."

"Aye, and the Grenadier Guards are welcome to the honor," Cat announced.

"Too bad the Yank paratroopers couldn't take this bridge intact," Ackers added. "If they had, we'd surely be having breakfast in Nijmegen by now."

Cat nodded. "They tried. On the seventeenth, when they landed in the fields northwest of here, they ran for the bridge. No matter, the Jerries blew it up in their faces."

"Maybe they should have run faster or landed right on the bloody bridge instead of in the fields," Ackers countered. "Wasn't it in the plan for the Yanks to take these bridges *before* we arrived?"

Cat smiled. "And when have you seen plans—*any* plan—go as written?"

"Corporal Ackers, tea's ready," Guardsman Avery interrupted.

"Care for some tea, Cat?" Ackers offered.

Cat reached back to grab his water bottle and removed the attached metal cup. He offered the cup to Guardsman Avery. "Don't mind if I do."

Wearing a brown leather glove to protect his hand from the heat, Avery filled Cat's cup with tea from a large tin can. The cavalry armored cars and tanks of the Grenadier Guards revved their engines. The armored cars of B Squadron, 2d Household Cavalry, which were already lined up on the road, drove forward.

Cat watched as a dozen armored cars rolled toward the bridge and then noticed that a jeep trailed the last armored car. The jeep was driven by a man in an officer's visored cap. There was no one else in the vehicle, just the officer. The jeep stopped in front of Colour Sergeant Gilchrist's Bren Carrier and pulled off the road.

A man jumped out and sauntered confidently toward Cat and his men. The man's cap had a brown leather visor and red piping, which designated him as a senior officer. The rank on his shoulder, a crown with crossed swords and sheath, designated him as a lieutenant general and the commander of the British XXX Corps.

The officer, Lieutenant General Brian Horrocks, stopped in front of Colour Sergeant Cat Gilchrist with a wide grin on his face. "Cat, is that you. Still alive?"

"*Section,* atten*shun*!" Cat shouted as he placed the cup of tea on the fender of the Bren Carrier and brought his Sten gun up to a rifle salute. Corporal Ackers, Guardsman Roy, and Guardsman Avery, who were standing next to Cat, snapped to attention.

"None of that now, stand easy men," the general announced. "I should be standing at attention for you lads after the thrashing you have given the Hun these past days."

The general wore an open battle jacket with a fleece-lined collar; he carried no combat gear besides the binoculars that hung around his neck. His only weapon was a thin riding crop.

Cat relaxed and smiled. "It's good to see you, too, sir! Are you looking for Lieutenant Colonel Vandeleur?"

"No, Colour Sergeant, I just talked with Joe down the road, and he is mighty proud of you and your boys," Horrocks offered with a wide grin. "I'm headed to see General Taylor, the American Hundred and First Commander, but thought I would stop by and chat with you and your lads first."

"Is that the Thirty Corps commander?" Guardsman Roy whispered to Corporal Ackers. Roy's eyes were wide and the expression of awe on his face was as if he was standing in audience to the king.

"Aye, you bet it is," Ackers answered softly, "and a hell of a fighter he is."

A Sherman Firefly pulled out onto the road and clanked north to the Son Bridge. In succession, one tank after the other pulled out onto the road and followed the lead Sherman. The general stood next to Cat as the British tanks of the Grenadier Guards passed by.

Every soldier who saw their commander seemed to swell with pride. Cat knew that the men of XXX Corps would do anything for their much beloved commander, and, in turn, they knew he felt the same.

"Cat, I'm glad to see that you are well," Horrocks said. "I was afraid that, by now, you would have run out of those 'nine lives' you're reported to have stored up. Someone must be watching out for you."

"Care for some tea, sir?" Cat offered, attempting to shift the conversation from himself to anything else.

"Yes, thank you, I would like that," Horrocks answered and then looked to Corporal Ackers and Guardsman Roy. "Does Cat still sing 'The Minstrel Boy' and usually a bit out of key?"

Ackers and Avery chuckled.

"Aye, sir, he sings, whistles, or hums that damn melody

all the time. We wouldn't know him if he didn't," Ackers replied.

"I have to admit, I was moved when I first heard him sing it," Horrocks replied, putting his hand on Cat's shoulder. "It was during the evacuation from Dunkirk in 1940. We had to leave all our heavy equipment, but we were able to rescue the men."

Cat's men gathered around their commander as he told his story.

"I was on a fishing ship with about sixty tired, wet, and demoralized men when Cat sang the tune, 'The Minstrel Boy,'" the general reminisced. "By the time we saw the white cliffs of Dover and landed in England, we weren't demoralized anymore but eager to get back at Jerry. One man's courage and a song played a big part in turning all that around."

Cat remained silent, but his eyes beamed with pride.

"That was a tough time, sir," Cat replied.

"Yes, but we're on the attack now," Horrocks said with a gleam in his eye, "and Jerry is on the run. If we hurry, we may be able to give him a good bashing."

A second column of tanks rumbled by, crushing loose rocks into the macadam road. The rocks crackled as the big, thirty-ton steel monsters surged by the men. As the armored vehicles passed, the commanders standing in the turret of each tank recognized the man standing with Cat and his men near the bridge. The tank commanders snapped salutes and offered comments to General Horrocks as they passed by.

Horrocks, in his element and looking the model of optimism and confidence, waved back at the tank commanders with his riding crop and shouted: "All the way to Nijmegen boys. Don't stop for anything!"

Guardsman Avery handed General Horrocks a cup of tea.

"Thank you, Guardsman," Horrocks said and then sipped the lukewarm tea from his cup as another big, green-colored, thirty-ton Sherman tank rolled by. "What's your name?"

"Guardsman Avery, sir!"

Horrocks took a sip of tea. "Avery, this is the best tea I've had since this bloody operation commenced. Secret blend?"

"Field tea, sir!" Avery grinned. "We do our best."

"And your best is mighty good," Horrocks added with a toothy smile.

Cat looked at Horrocks and nodded at the passing tanks. "It's good to see the Grenadier Guards finally earning their pay, sir."

"Yes, but you and your lads certainly deserve a bounty for your fighting the past two days," Horrocks said with affection. "You have done a splendid job. Simply splendid! I could not be more proud of the Irish Guards."

"Thank you, sir," Cat replied. "It's been a bit touch and go, especially with the narrow width of our attack and Jerry's unexpected stubbornness. But tell me, sir, if you don't mind my asking, how is the battle going?"

"Cat, this is something you and your men have to be discreet about," Horrocks replied solemnly. "I wouldn't want any of the other units to get the wrong idea."

Cat's men nodded.

"You can count on us," Guardsman Avery offered.

Horrocks smiled. "Well, then, here it is, we can win this fight, but every minute counts. The entire corps is attacking down one single, narrow road, and we are already thirty-six hours behind schedule—thirty-six hours! Our First Airborne boys up at Arnhem are catching hell. We have to make it to them in time."

Cat's men listened carefully, hanging on the general's

every word and honored that he trusted them enough to tell them such high-level information.

"And Cat, you're right: We're not up against third-class Jerry units like the intel boys told us we would be," Horrocks explained. "We're fighting determined *Fallschirmjägers* and elite units of the Ninth and Tenth SS Panzer divisions. These are some of the best soldiers in the German army."

"Yes, and Jerry has been fighting hard to stop us," Cat said. "Will we make it in time, sir?"

"That is the big question," Horrocks said, and then took a final sip of tea. He finished the cup and handed it back to Guardsman Avery. A wide grin broke out across the general's face. "But with troops like Guardsman Avery here, how can they stop us?"

The men laughed. Ackers pushed Avery's helmet forward on the young soldier's head.

"So, remember, we must drive on," Horrocks added. "Speed is the vital thing. We can't let Jerry delay us along Hell's Highway—that's what the Yanks are calling the route now. We have to keep moving and reach the American Eighty-second Airborne at Nijmegen and then join our First Para boys at Arnhem at their bridgehead across the Rhine. That's the prize and that's the prize we will take!"

"We'll do our part, sir," Cat replied.

"I know you will," Horrocks replied. "Before this fight is over, I'm sure I'll be calling on the Irish Guards to save the day."

The men grinned, proud to have shared a moment with their general.

The last tank in the lead serial passed and this break provided Horrocks a brief moment to get back on the road.

"All right, lads, I've got to run off and discuss plans

with General Taylor," Horrocks announced. "Good luck to you!"

Cat and his men snapped to attention as General Horrocks moved back to his jeep, slid into the driver's seat, and quickly chased after the last Sherman tank.

"Well, that was a fine meeting," Avery announced.

"Aye, with officers like that leading us, how can we fail?" Corporal Ackers replied.

Cat looked south down the road to see another column of Sherman tanks heading to the bridge. "Mount up and get ready to move. We'll follow the end of the next tank column all the way to Nijmegen."

Sunset, Tuesday, September 19, 1944, Eindhoven, Netherlands:

"It's fantastic. A dream come true," Mira Vogel announced as they stood on the sidewalk and watched a close column of British tanks, armored cars, Bren Carriers, and trucks drive down the cobblestone street.

Mira and Alexander Van Janssen were joyous. Yesterday the Americans had liberated their beloved city of Eindhoven. In the afternoon the lead tanks of the British XXX Corps were in Eindhoven and pushing north to Son. The Germans put up a token fight and were either killed, captured, or fled.

Alexander took his red notebook from his haversack, making sketches of scenes he observed. He quickly sketched Mira, depicting her as she smiled and waved to the Allied troops, then he proudly displayed the image to her.

"You will be a great artist someday," Mira announced with glee.

"Someday?" Alexander replied in mock protest.

Mira and Alexander laughed. Their world had just turned from night into day.

People of every age lined the streets. It was a massive celebration of freedom and joy. Dutch girls hugged and kissed every American and British soldier in sight. The Americans and British soldiers were happy to oblige, and it took all the authority their sergeants and officers could muster to keep their men focused on fighting the war and not joining the party.

"The town was awash in orange! Everyone wants to see the Americans and British," Alexander offered with glee. Orange-colored sheets and streamers made from every kind of cloth hung from the windows. Orange was the color of Free Holland and had been banned by the Germans. Now it was everywhere. "The young and old have all come out to celebrate."

As they walked by a small square, a British truck was parked and three big British soldiers were handing out food to a mob of Dutch children. Mira and Alexander walked over to watch the soldiers distribute chocolates and bread.

A soldier threw a half-loaf of bread to Mira. She smiled. "Thank you!"

The two walked away and munched on the bread as they walked.

"Look at this bread," Alexander exclaimed. "I can't believe that bread could be so pure white!"

They came to the main road and watched a line of British trucks, halftracks, and Bren Carriers roll slowly through Eindhoven. The big trucks and Bren Carriers were filled with jovial British soldiers standing in the back and waving to the crowd. The crowd waved back and passed to their liberators all types of gifts, from flowers to apples and bottles of beer.

Alexander carried some green apples in his haversack and tossed the fruit to the British soldiers who were riding in the big, open-topped army trucks. The soldiers caught the apples and threw back chocolate bars to the crowd. The children scurried to pick up these delicacies. Alexander and Mira laughed at the sight of so many exuberant people celebrating, and then they walked off together toward the church square.

"What an amazing difference a couple of days has made," Alexander said as he looked at Saint Catherine's Cathedral and saw a group of American paratroopers sharing their rations and chocolate with a throng of Dutch children.

"We should celebrate and not forget this moment," Mira said as she observed the kindness of the American paratroopers. "Let's go meet our liberators."

Alexander reached in his bag and offered apples to the three paratroopers sitting on the steps of the church. "*Dank u wel*—Thank you!"

The nearest American soldier took the apples, passed them to his friends, and smiled. "Sure, kid."

Mira bent over and gave the grimy paratrooper a kiss on the cheek. The man looked to be in his mid-twenties, but he had intense blue eyes that seemed to pierce Mira's soul. She glanced into the soldier's eyes and realized that the eyes carried an age much older than the man. "My name . . . Mira. *Feestelijk inhalen*. Welcome to Eindhoven. Thank you for liberating us!"

"My name is Baker. Staff Sergeant Matt Baker. Thanks for the apples," Baker said to Alexander and then looked at Mira. "And for the kiss."

Mira looked at her liberator for another long moment. "Baker. I will remember you."

Mira and Alexander smiled and walked away, back into the cheering crowds.

British vehicles continued to roll through the streets as

the sun set and the sky darkened. Since there was still a war on and the town was in blackout, the people of Eindhoven began to filter back to their homes.

As they walked to Alexander's home, Mira put her arm around her cousin and smiled. They walked for ten minutes as vehicles passed by. Throngs of smiling people filled the streets as dusk arrived.

"Today was a great day," Mira said. "A day for all time. But tomorrow, we have a rendezvous. Not all of the Netherlands is free. Tomorrow, Melanie will be in Eindhoven and we must meet her."

"Finally, this Melanie that you have told me about for the past few weeks will be here," Alexander replied. "She must be quite a woman to help organize all the resistance groups in the Netherlands. What time will we meet her?"

"You and I will meet Melanie at noon on Thursday," Mira answered with a grin.

"What is so funny?" Alexander questioned. "What aren't you telling me?"

"You'll see on Thursday," Mira said as she looked at her watch. "But now it's getting late. We should—"

Suddenly a bright light popped in the air above the city. Mira and Alexander looked up, naturally drawn to the super-bright light of a burning flare. The flare was soon followed by another, then six more.

The air filled with a whistling sound, then the rumble of explosions.

Mira scanned the sky. In the light of the flares, Mira could see a dozen large aircraft flying in a V formation high over the city.

"Oh my God," Alexander exclaimed. "It's the Luft-waffe! The Germans are bombing the city."

Mira looked up dumbfounded. Machine-gun fire rattled into the air. Strings of tracer bullets leapt up from several points around Eindhoven, and the boom of anti-aircraft cannon echoed in the dark night sky.

Two blocks away, bombs detonated in a deafening roar. The explosions moved toward them like a wave, growing louder with each passing moment. The flashes from the explosions and the concussion from the bombs rocked the ground.

The city was on fire as more bombs fell from the heavens. A column of British trucks caught on fire. Soldiers ran from their vehicles as the ammunition loads the trucks were carrying ignited. Flames rose from the burning trucks and lit up the sky.

Mira had no way of knowing how many German planes were in the sky above Eindhoven, but it seemed as if they filled the horizon. British cannons shot shells into the sky and bright orange-red bursts buffeted the Luftwaffe's tight V formations. The Germans took evasive action, flying higher in the air to avoid the antiaircraft fire. In spite of a determined effort, the British antiaircraft guns were unable to stop the high-altitude German attack.

The city was in pandemonium, bathed in fire and fear. People screamed in panic and ran for the cover of nearby buildings. A dead man lay in the street, unattended. Mira saw bloodstains on the pavement.

Mira and Alexander ran to a brick apartment building as a house exploded across the street from them. Broken glass and fragments of bricks sailed through the air from the explosion. Dust engulfed the street. The broken remains of the house across the street burned like a bonfire, and on the street Mira saw burning vehicles and carts. The air was hot, and it became difficult for her to breathe.

Alexander frantically tried to open the door, but it was locked. He then pounded on the door, and a tall, silver-haired woman in her forties answered.

Mira and Alexander were covered in white dust. Mira was shaking like a leaf but was unhurt.

"Quickly, follow me," the woman ordered and ushered them downstairs into her basement.

They gladly entered the home and followed the woman through a hallway and down creaky wooden steps into a cool, dark basement. The ground trembled. Bombs blasted nearby and dust fell from the ceiling rafters. Inside the cellar was a small window at street level. A horrifying flicker of light cast spectral shadows through the windows from the fires burning outside.

The entire world seemed to be on fire. Explosion after explosion. It was beyond belief and worse than her blackest nightmare! Mira's beloved Eindhoven, a picture-book city, was being destroyed and her people assaulted!

Inside the basement, Mira could see a married couple with four young children, all girls, in one corner. The oldest girl was no more than ten and the others younger by a few years in succession. An older couple, probably the grandparents of the family, sat against the wall next to the family of six.

The girls were crying and the father and mother huddled them in their arms for protection. The silver-haired lady sat on the floor with the grandparents. Mira and Alexander took a place to the right of their silver-haired benefactor.

The bombs whistled, shrieked, and exploded with ever-increasing rage. The house shook as the stair handrail crashed to the floor. The dust that filled the room glowed eerily from the flames outside the house.

"We are all going to die!" the grandmother moaned.

"Be strong, Mother," the silver-haired lady replied. "Be strong and of good courage; do not be afraid, nor be dismayed . . ."

Mira could not hear the rest of the prayer. A bomb detonated outside and threw everyone to the floor. Mira lost consciousness for a second, then opened her eyes. She tasted a copperish flavor in her mouth and realized that her nose was bleeding. She held her nose with her right hand—she felt as if they were going to die.

The bombing seemed to last forever. Then, just when she thought she might go mad, it stopped. Mira heard the children crying. She looked across at the silver-haired lady who now lay on her side with her face toward Mira. The woman wasn't moaning. A red gash had been seared across the lady's face.

"Mira, are you all right?" Alexander asked, gasping for air.

"Yes, but we have to help her," Mira replied as she looked at the silver-haired lady who had saved their lives. A piece of the concrete wall blasted off by the bomb had hit the woman in the face. The lady's eyes met Mira's, and somehow, through the blood, the woman managed a brave smile before she died.

Mira sobbed. Alexander held her gently in his arms and rocked her back and forth.

"If I live to be a thousand, I will never understand," Mira sobbed. "What did I call this day earlier? A day for all time? This day will certainly live in my soul forever and this evening in my worst nightmares."

"Don't talk," Alexander murmured as he swayed with her in his arms, "just cry."

Graf clenched his PPSh in his arms as if it were the sword of the Archangel Michael. The weapon was heavy, with a fully loaded seventy-one-round drum magazine, but Graf carried it as if it were weightless.

Graf remembered his mother, a kind and very religious woman, telling him about Saint Michael and the great battle that had occurred in heaven at the beginning of time. The Archangel Michael was the leader of God's army during the Lucifer uprising. It was Michael who cast Satan out of Paradise. Later, Graf learned that Michael was also considered by many soldiers as the patron saint of all paratroopers.

Graf wondered how, or even if, Germany would cast out its Lucifer.

Men like Kodritz confirmed his disgust for the Nazis. The human animal goes quickly from the sublime to the brute, he thought.

Right now, however, he had to focus on the matter at hand—survival. He walked quietly through the sparse woods, leading a five-man patrol behind enemy lines.

It was two hours after dusk. Eindhoven was burning and the fires lit up the sky to the south. His mission was to lead a patrol behind enemy lines and capture a prisoner. Kodritz's superiors wanted information on the Americans. Graf had been ordered to take his *Fallschirmjägers* and get the job done. It was just another dangerous foray behind enemy lines for Graf, but for his footsore and exhausted men, it was an ordeal of fear and stamina.

This made Graf more determined than ever to accomplish the mission and bring his men back to friendly lines before daylight.

Friendly lines? The thought made Graf smirk. SS *Obersturmführer* Kodritz's *kampfgruppe* seemed less friendly every day. He yearned to take his men back to their own 6th Regiment, but the needs of the current crisis made that impossible.

After the battles to slow the British advance along Hell's Highway, Kodritz's *kampfgruppe* had withdrawn to the northeast. The 6th Fallschirmjäger Regiment was forced to withdraw to the northwest. Separated by kilometers of ground and split by a lethal enemy in the middle, Graf realized that the standing orders "that all attached units were to stay with the units they were assigned on September 17" made tactical sense.

Graf halted the patrol, listening carefully. He heard explosions to the south in Eindhoven.

The bombing of the city didn't bother him. He knew that the decision to launch Luftwaffe bombers on a night raid against Eindhoven was not out of blind revenge but was a sound, tactical decision. The German air force, no match for Allied fighters, could only operate at night.

Reports from informers inside the city told the Germans that the British trucks were traveling nearly bumper to bumper in the serpentine streets. The bombing would hit parts of these vital British convoys, and the ruins of the city would cause delays to the British advance, giving the Germans the one resource they needed the most—time.

Eindhoven, therefore, was a tempting target and an opportunity that could not be passed up. Civilians would be killed, but such is war. The Allies had shown no reluctance to bomb German cities these past four years, killing thousands of civilians in the process. Graf saw no reason why the citizens of Eindhoven should be any different.

Sergeant Weise moved up to Graf, whispering, "Do you hear something?"

"No, just listening," Graf said.

"Tell me, why didn't any of the SS men go out on patrol tonight?" Weise asked. "Why are we always getting the shithole jobs?"

"It's normal. I did the same in Russia," Graf replied. "You save your own men. You send the strangers on patrol."

"That Kodritz will be the death of me yet," Weise replied.

"Enough chatter about our 'esteemed' commander," Graf said in a cold voice.

"Esteemed indeed," Weise replied. "I suspect that, under your hard shell, you're at heart a sentimentalist. In all the time I have been with you, I really don't know you."

"And you won't get to know me if we don't survive this patrol," Graf growled. "Send the rabbits forward and take up the rear."

"As you order," Weise replied, and sauntered off to bring up the rest of the patrol.

Graf sat quietly as he waited for Weise to return with the rest of the patrol. He looked down at his Russian-made PPSh Tommy gun and his mind wandered back to the day when he took the weapon.

He was on a patrol, much like this one, in July 1942, deep behind Soviet lines. He led a section of elite Brandenburg Commandos in the mountainous Caucasus region of Russia. They moved for several days through rough, wooded terrain to raid a Russian mountain outpost. About five kilometers from their objective, Graf heard something, ordered the rest of his men to wait, and walked ahead of the patrol.

As he moved through the bushes, he came face-to-face with three Soviet soldiers. There was no time to call for help. Graf reacted immediately and killed one Russian with a burst from his German-made MP40 submachine gun. The leader of the Russian patrol responded with a hail of bullets from a Russian-made PPSh41 submachine gun. Graf dove for cover behind a large log as the other Russian thrust at him with the bayonet.

Graf dropped his submachine gun, grabbed the Russian soldier's rifle, and pulled him down. Reaching for his fighting knife, he stabbed the Russian in the chest. As the Russian died, Graf looked for his submachine gun, but it had slipped down the slope, out of reach.

The Soviet soldier with the PPSh pummeled the log with bullets as Graf hugged the ground with only a knife in his hand. Splinters from the log flew all around as the Russian tried to blast through Graf's cover. The firepower was impressive, and Graf was sure that this would be his last day.

There was no way out. No escape. No options.

Then, the shooting stopped and Graf knew that his foe was reloading. Jumping over the log he rushed the Russian with a mighty cry as the man was fumbling with a new drum of ammunition. Before the Soviet could click the drum in place, Graf plunged the ten-inch-long blade under the man's chin with a powerful uppercut.

The Russian died quickly, seeming to drop the PPSh into Graf's hands. For Graf, this was an omen. From that day on, Graf had carried the Russian weapon.

Weise returned with the patrol. Graf waved his hand forward, signaling for the squad to move out and follow his actions. He stepped forward, picking his feet up high and placing each step deliberately, to make the least noise possible. In a night patrol like this, stealth was life. Graf might move only a few hundred meters in an hour, but by moving slowly he would not be heard by the enemy. In this darkness, he knew that stealth would bring his men home safely.

The patrol moved west in single file with Graf leading, then *Oberjäger* Küster, *Jäger* Wigand, and *Jäger* Merckel, followed by *Feldwebel* Weise.

The sounds of explosions to the south and east rumbled in the thick, night air. Graf came to the edge of the woods and gazed across an open field.

The field was about two hundred meters square, with

woods on all sides and a trail leading in and out that traveled from north to south. At the west edge of the open field, just where the woods began again, Graf saw the glow of a cigarette.

He signaled for his men to come forward. Quietly, deliberately, they crouched near their leader.

"The *Amis* are on the other side of this open area," Graf announced softly. "Weise: You, Wigand, and Merckel will stay here and provide covering fire, but only fire if you hear me start shooting. Do not shoot unless I fire. Is that clear?"

Weise nodded.

"Küster will come with me," Graf continued. "We will grab a prisoner and bring him back here. Once we are all together again, we'll head back to the *kampfgruppe.*"

Graf waited a moment and scanned the open field a second time and studied the intermittent glow of the cigarette.

"Küster, you will gag the prisoner and tie his hands behind his back," Graf ordered. "I will bring him to you. He will be conscious, unwounded, and probably scared to hell. The last thing I want to do is carry a prisoner back through this forest, but you must silence him and tie his hands."

"Understood, *Herr Oberfeldwebel,*" Küster answered. "I have the gag and rope to tie him with."

Graf nodded.

With his bandaged hand Weise signaled Wigand and Merckel to lie down in positions to either side of him.

Once Graf saw that Weise's men were set, he moved with Küster to the right, inside the concealment of the fir trees. As they came to the northeast corner of the open area, Graf heard voices in English.

"George, do you have any food left?" a voice said in English.

"Naw, I ate my last ration for lunch today," a second voice answered. "I hope we get supplied soon. I don't like fighting on an empty stomach."

Graf signaled for Küster to get down. Quietly, Graf then took off his helmet and placed his PPSh submachine gun next to Küster.

Graf signaled for Küster to watch and remain silent. The tall *Oberfeldwebel* crouched motionless, watched and listened for several minutes. Finally, he realized that the nearby enemy outpost consisted of only two Americans. They were close together and only about twenty-five meters away from Graf. He concluded that the Americans were a listening post that had been placed forward of the Allies' main line of defense.

Graf stood up and slowly strode toward the Americans. As he walked forward, he pulled out the six-inch steel fighting knife from its scabbard and held it out of sight, behind his back.

"George, did you hear something?" A voice whispered in English.

"Yeah," the other man whispered in return. The American put out his cigarette. "Halt! Carrier!"

"Carrier!" Graf sounded back in perfect English.

"Maybe he didn't hear us say the challenge?" a young voice said. "Pigeon!"

"Pigeon!" Graf answered. "I'm an American. Man am I glad to find you guys. Don't shoot, I'm coming in."

"What the hell are you doing out there by yourself?" a voice replied. "We nearly shot you."

Graf drew closer. In the dark, the American who challenged him couldn't tell whether Graf was friend or foe.

Graf moved swiftly toward the Americans from their flank and was within arm's reach of the nearest sentry before the man recognized the danger. The American saw Graf in the weak light and, for a moment, hesitated. That moment was all it took. The soldier had his weapon forward, but Graf deftly pushed it aside. With a quick upper slash of his knife he plunged the sharp fighting blade into the man's throat. The pointy edge of the knife exited the back of the man's skull. The American fell to his knees, grabbing his throat with both hands, gurgling blood.

With lightning speed, the tall German sergeant fell upon the second American. Like an eagle striking from the clouds, Graf hit his second opponent in the face with the wooden handle of the knife. The powerful blow knocked the soldier down, sending his helmet flying and causing the man to drop his M1 rifle. The American fell to the ground on his back, stunned. Graf then pounced on him, placing the knife along the soldier's throat.

"If you wish to live," Graf said in perfect American-English, only inches from the man's face, "remain silent and do not resist. If you make a noise or resist, I will kill you instantly."

The sentry's eyes expanded in wide circles as he stared into his assailant's icy glare.

Graf saw that the American was probably nineteen or twenty years old, not much older than many of his men. He looked back at his first victim, to make sure the man was dead, and saw the man's legs twitch for a few seconds and then stop.

Graf looked back into the eyes of the second American. "Next time you challenge someone, you idiot, don't let them reply with the challenge code word. Your friend is dead because of your incompetence."

Graf moved up to one knee and, still holding the knife at the man's throat, carefully pulled the boy up. Quickly, Graf checked the dazed soldier for weapons, removing a bayonet and several grenades. Confident that his enemy was unarmed, Graf pushed him forward. With the

American in front, and Graf's knife at the prisoner's neck, Graf herded him back to Küster.

In short order Küster unhooked the American's web gear and searched him for knives and other weapons. Küster took the man's watch and cigarettes and dumped out the remaining contents of the prisoner's pockets. Küster then took out a long cloth from the pocket of his camouflage smock. He placed this rag in the American's mouth and tied it tight at the back of the prisoner's head. He then took the rope from his belt and tied the American's hands.

Graf wiped the blood from his knife on the heel of his boot and then sheathed the blade. Placing his helmet back on his head, he picked up his treasured PPSh. "Let's move."

Küster grabbed the prisoner by the neck and directed him through the woods. Moving rapidly, the three men stepped back to Weise, Wigand, and Merckel.

"I see you succeeded again, Graf," Weise said in a hushed voice. "The usual trick?"

Graf nodded. "I was lucky to run into amateurs."

"Ah, this surviving one skirmish after another, however fortunate and exhilarating, is terrifying business, but it surely beats the alternative, heh?" Weise grinned. His grin was so wide that his white teeth gleamed in the dark. "Someday, my friend, you may meet your opposite number—a veteran who is as crafty as you—and balls alone won't save you."

"Save your advice," Graf replied as he signaled for everyone to stand and move out. "Everyone up. Weise, follow us as the rear guard. I want to get back before sunrise."

German Sturmgeschütz IV or StuG. Waffen SS and elite Wehr-macht divisions had StuG brigades as a permanent part of their divisions.

5: D+5, BLACK FRIDAY

*Our situation reminded me of the early American west, where
small garrisons had to contend with sudden Indian attacks at
any point along great stretches of vital railroad.*
— MAJOR GENERAL MAXWELL TAYLOR, Commanding Officer,
101st Airborne Division

*The Germans attacked the Corridor between Uden and Veghel
from the east on 22 Sep and blocked all traffic for 24 hours.
German forces launched several attacks on Veghel. All were
stopped but the corridor is still cut. It is vital that Hell's Highway be cleared and the advance towards Nijmegen and Arnhem continue.*
— Situation report September 23, 1944, from G2 Section,
101st Airborne Division Headquarters

**Sunset, Friday, September 22, 1944, near the village
of Veghel, Netherlands:**

"Mac, it's good to see you," Baker replied with a grin
as he left his jeep and walked over to meet First Sergeant
"Mac" Hassay. The two men embraced as brothers in
arms.

Six days had passed since the landings on September
17, 1944, that initiated Operation Market Garden. It had
been a long, bloody road from the landing zone near Son
to the town of Veghel.

The 101st secured the village of Son, but the Germans
destroyed the vital bridge that crossed the Wilhelmina
Canal there before the Americans could stop them. The
city of Eindhoven fell to the 101st Airborne on September 18. Reacting quickly to the destroyed crossing site
at Son, the British Engineers erected a Bailey Bridge in
record time. By then, however, the advance of XXX

Corps toward Nijmegen was already off schedule. To compound this delay, the German Luftwaffe, in a bloody night raid, bombed Eindhoven the night of September 19, burned a portion of the town, ignited a convoy of ammunitions trucks, blocked traffic moving north, and killed hundreds of civilians.

Bad weather had delayed the operation as well. The fog was so thick on September 19 that Allied aircraft couldn't fly. The weather on September 20 and 21 was almost as bad, grounding aircraft for portions of each day. Hindered Allied supply drops delayed the arrival of reinforcements.

All the while the Germans frantically counterattacked. Their goal was to reduce the isolated lodgments of American and British paratroopers, recapture vital bridges and road junctions, then stop the British XXX Corps from moving north along Hell's Highway.

The terrain in the 101st area was ideally suited to defense. The land was marshy and heavily wooded, cut by numerous waterways. The XXX Corps attack axis was reduced in some areas to only a forty-foot-wide route— the width of two tanks. Blocking this route and stopping the British from reaching the British airborne troops at Arnhem was the German's top priority.

From September 17 through September 22, on a dozen battlefields from the towns of Best, Eindhoven, and Veghel, the footsore 101st Airborne was hard-pressed to keep Hell's Highway open. With little rest and sparse supplies the American paratroopers fought a battle that the 101st's commander, General Max Taylor, characterized as "Indian fighting," the constant scurrying from one threatened sector to another. During those six days, Baker's jeep-mounted reconnaissance squad had become the division commander's fire brigade, rushing from crisis to crisis along Hell's Highway to report the situation and, when possible, help drive off the Germans.

"Matt, you're still tougher than a fifty-cent steak! I'm glad you're still alive," Mac replied and returned the smile. Mac was wearing the same dirty paratrooper pants and combat jacket that he had worn since the first day. He carried an M1 rifle. His steel helmet boasted a white square painted on the side to designate that he belonged to the 502d Parachute Infantry Regiment. The rank on his sleeve, three stripes on top, three rockers on the bottom, and a diamond in the center, designated Mac as the "Top" sergeant of the company, the first sergeant. "With all you and your recon teams have been through since we landed last Sunday, I thought for sure I would see you on the casualty list."

"Top! Believe me, the Krauts have tried their best, but I've been lucky so far. What's the situation?"

Mac shook his head. "It's a bloody mess. Kraut Panther tanks appeared out of nowhere and had a field day destroying trucks, jeeps, and armored cars along Hell's Highway. General Taylor ordered the 506th to counterattack and retake the town. They did, but we lost a lot of good men in the process. Later, the 327th Glider infantry and some six-pounder antitank guns arrived to reinforce the 506th. One six-pounder knocked out a Panther by hitting its track, but that didn't stop the Krauts. They really want that town.

"Hell's Highway is particularly narrow, near Veghel," Mac continued. "The Krauts know that if they can block the Highway here, and stop our supplies and equipment from traveling beyond Veghel, Operation Market Garden is doomed. As a result, the Germans could win a great victory."

"So where does that leave us?" Baker asked.

Mac pulled out a map from the cargo pocket on his trouser leg, studied it carefully, then pointed to his left at the town of Veghel. "We have an observation post in the church in Veghel, and he spotted Kraut infantry and tanks moving toward the woods to the southeast of the town. All the rifle companies are committed to the fight, so I scraped up all the headquarters personnel I could find, and here we are."

"So we have to stop the Krauts from flanking the town," Baker replied.

"Yep, and if you can get division headquarters on your radio, maybe they can provide us with artillery support."

"Artillery will help, but do you really plan to stop them with this group?" Baker scrutinized the headquarters troops that Mac had scrounged up. The men looked relatively clean, shaven, and rested—in short, untried. Most were tech-sergeants: signals men, staff personnel, and cooks. One soldier lugged a .30 caliber machine gun, but looking at him, Baker wasn't sure the man knew how to use it. Half carried the standard M1 rifle, but the rest were equipped with only M1 carbines. Baker guessed from the look of their gear that most had not fired a shot in anger during the past six days.

Baker and his men, on the other hand, looked like trained, professional killers. Baker and his recon squad had been in combat for only six days, but it might as well have been six years compared to what these headquarters personnel had experienced.

"They're soldiers. They're paratroopers. And they're all that stand between us and a German breakthrough," Mac replied. "Besides, you brought Zanovitch and a bazooka. And McCreary, too! How can we lose?"

Zanovitch smiled. "Mac, I never miss, you know that."

"Good to see you, Top," McCreary offered with a grin.

Only veterans of the Normandy operation could call First Sergeant Hassay "Mac." The rest, out of respect, called him First Sergeant or "Top." Few ever argued with Mac, and those who tried never won the argument. Baker knew that Mac was a professional soldier of the old breed, a man who had been in the infantry for over fifteen years and a rarity in this citizen-soldier army. If Mac said it could be done, it would be.

"Yeah, unfortunately I only have these three knuckle-heads with me and only one bazooka," Baker offered as he looked at Corporal Zanovitch, who cradled the M9 Antitank Rocket Launcher like a baby in his arms, Mc-Creary sporting an M1 rifle, and Holden with a radio over his shoulder and carrying an M1 carbine. "The rest of my squad is off on a separate recon mission. So, Mac, what do you want us to do?"

Mac pointed at a raised road to the east about a football field away. "We need to get to that road. That berm will be hard for tanks to cross. We can defend from there. Division has promised that the Irish Guards are sending tanks and infantry to support us. Let's hope they arrive in time."

Baker scanned the tree-lined road to the east. In Holland, with the land so flat and wet, many of the roads were built on earthen berms. These raised banks keep the roadway dry, and evenly spaced poplar trees provide a picturesque view, but the berm also makes an effective, hasty fighting position.

"Zanovitch, park that jeep in the woods and grab the bazooka," Baker said. "And take good care of her."

"Don't worry. I'll put her next to a couple of big trees; I don't want to be walking all over Holland."

"You can say that again. Riding beats walking any day."

Private Holden nodded in agreement.

Zanovitch put the jeep in gear and drove off.

Mac turned back to his map and continued discussing the situation with Baker.

After a few minutes Zanovitch returned carrying a bazooka and a full pack of bazooka rounds. Before Baker could question them about his precious jeep, a shell shrieked overhead as one of the headquarters soldiers screamed, *"Incoming!"*

In an instant, Baker, Mac, and the other twenty-five soldiers dove for the ground. German artillery shells exploded three hundred yards to their right, and then half a dozen detonated a few hundred meters behind them. The ground shook. Searing hot metal flew though the air.

Baker heard the sound of whizzing shrapnel as more shells exploded nearby. A volley of explosions erupted in the woods behind him. He hugged the ground and pushed into the dirt, trying to make his body small.

The twenty-seven American soldiers lay on their bellies, spread out at the edge of the woods waiting for the storm to pass. The barrage of high-angle mortar fire—the kind of mortar shells that make a whistling sound as they fall on you—dropped in groups of three followed by quiet moments of dreadful anticipation. The shelling lasted for nearly two minutes and then, just as suddenly, stopped.

Baker picked up his head and looked around. "Zano, McCreary, Holden. Everyone okay?"

"Roger. We're all in one piece," Zanovitch answered.

McCreary looked to Zanovitch. "Whatever happened to all that talk in England about shoot, scoot, and communicate? Seems like we've been doing more shooting than scooting lately—not to mention getting shelled by Kraut mortars."

"Welcome to the Airborne," Zanovitch chided.

First Sergeant "Mac" Hassay lifted his head from the dirt. "Everybody up! Up and to the road. Follow me!"

Baker and the other men jumped up and ran forward, following the first sergeant toward the road.

The Americans ducked a little lower as another volley of German shells flew overhead, detonating near the town to the north. The sky was darkening. The rain had stopped, but the temperature was remarkably cool for September. The ground was muddy, and running through muddy fields was difficult.

"Man, I hope our jeep is all right," Zanovitch muttered as he jogged behind Baker.

Mac picked up the pace and led Baker's squad and the group of "green" headquarters personnel to the road. When they arrived, Mac raised his hand and signaled the group to halt. "This is our position—on this side of the berm. Spread out, two yards between men."

Obediently they plopped down on the western side of the berm and formed a firing line.

"Here? By ourselves?" a young soldier asked. "If the Krauts have tanks, how can we stop them? How will we stop a German tank attack?"

"We will hold this position," Mac answered as he walked behind the line of American soldiers. "Lock and load your weapons. Be quick. We can expect the bastards to attack any minute now. Baker, set the bazooka up over there."

Baker positioned his men on the right side of Mac's line, along the berm, facing east.

The headquarters troops dutifully prepared for combat, and Mac made sure they didn't waste any time. Under his close scrutiny, the soldiers dropped their field packs and unloaded bandoliers of ammunition. A few of the veterans scraped holes at the top edge of the berm with their entrenching tools, checked their rifles, and placed M1 Garand rifle clips within easy reach of their weapons. Mac directed the soldier with the .30 caliber machine to set up the weapon on the left wing of the line.

The men waited. They were nervous. Baker lay quietly, observing the tree line for targets, and listening.

"Did you hear about that guy in H Company, Five-oh-deuce, who saved his squad by falling on a grenade?" a soldier down the line to the left asked a buddy.

"Yeah, Private Joe Mann. Mac told me about him." His friend answered.

"What makes a fellow do that?" the soldier asked

"Guts . . . pure guts," his buddy replied. "From what Mac told me, Mann single-handedly destroyed a Kraut Eighty-eight and an ammo dump with a bazooka. He then killed a mess of Krauts with his M1 and was wounded four times in the process. When they bandaged him up he had both arms in slings. During a counterattack a potato masher landed in his trench. There were six other wounded guys in the same trench. Mann must have realized that they would all die, so he covered the grenade with his body."

"Damn, where the hell do we get guys like that?"

"Okay, cut the chatter," Mac ordered. "Simon! Over here."

A thin, young private first class carrying an M1 rifle ran over to Mac.

"Yes, First Sergeant!" Private First Class Simon answered.

"You used to be in H Company, right?" Mac asked.

"Yes, First Sergeant!" Simon replied. "I was in a rifle squad. They moved me up to Headquarters after we returned from Normandy."

"Son, I need a veteran infantry soldier for this job," Mac said, calmly. "You are going to be our observation post. Run forward to those woods. When you hear the enemy coming, hightail it back here. Don't fire unless you have to. I want to surprise the bastards."

Simon glanced at the woods to his front and then back at Mac. He gave Mac a brave look, then took a deep breath. "Okay, Top."

"Good man," Mac answered and patted Simon on the shoulder. "But don't be a hero. Just listen and when you hear them coming, run back here."

Simon nodded.

"Weapons on safe," Mac ordered. "I'm sending a man forward."

Mac patted Simon on the shoulder and Simon got up and ran toward the woods.

Baker watched the paratrooper make it to the tree line and enter the dark woods, then lost sight of him.

"My guess is that the Krauts will hit before dark," Mac said to Baker. "Before they do, we'd better make radio contact with our artillery."

Baker nodded. "Holden, you heard the man. You're the radio operator. Start operating."

Mac looked at Baker, smiled, and then walked down the line, checking his soldiers' weapons and giving them encouragement.

There is no better man to be with in a fight, Baker mused.

Mac reminded Baker of his father, Colonel Joseph Baker. Baker's father was a professional soldier. Matt never understood his father, but lately he had grudgingly learned to admire what his dad had stood for. Mac, also a professional soldier, had served with Baker's father before the war. Because of this, Baker always felt that Mac treated him differently than the other paratroopers in their outfit. It was Mac who insisted Baker be promoted to sergeant after the 3d Squad's original squad leader, Sergeant Saunderson, was badly injured in a practice parachute jump several weeks before the Normandy, D-Day operation. Baker never asked for the promotion, or the responsibility of leading a squad, but Mac wouldn't listen to Baker's objections. It was as if Mac knew that Baker was made of sterner stuff. Now, Baker was a combat veteran and a staff sergeant in charge of a squad in the Division's reconnaissance platoon.

Baker trusted Mac. In combat, Baker knew, trust was everything.

The paratroopers aimed their weapons to the east and crouched low against thick dark Dutch dirt.

Another volley of mortar shells exploded in the trees behind them. The blasts were far enough away to be safe, but close enough to make everyone nervous.

Baker turned to watch the mortar explosions. The Germans were firing blind, hoping to hit something. He then looked to his right, to check on his men. McCreary was flat against the side of the berm, aiming his rifle at the woods and ready to fight. Holden sat below the top of the berm working his radio. Zanovitch sat next to Holden, checking the rockets for his bazooka and laying them out within easy reach in preparation for battle.

While all this was happening, the sound of heavy combat erupted to the north, in the town of Veghel.

"It looks like the Krauts are hitting our guys in the town hard. My guess is they will send a flanking force around to the south, through the woods to our east," Mac explained. "Hold 'em by the nose and kick them in the ass—that's tactics."

Baker realized Mac was right. If the Germans did come out of those woods, they could roll up the entire American defense of Veghel from south to north. "You're right, Mac, we have to stop 'em from flanking the town."

A German mortar shell whistled overhead.

"Jesus Christ!" a soldier lying somewhere to Baker's

left muttered. "This is it, then. I sure don't want to die here."

"Calm down," Mac countered. "Things aren't so bad here. If the man upstairs calls you, this is as good a place to die as any other. At least here we have a purpose. We stand our ground, protect the flank. We hold the bastards off until the Brit tanks arrive."

Baker couldn't help but crack a slight smile, even as more German shells detonated to the rear. Mac's leadership was holding them together. If anyone could get this "pickup team" to fight, it was Mac.

Baker scanned the ground. In front of their firing line the field was open for two hundred and fifty yards and then ended in the woods. If the Germans came out of the woods, Mac's idea to surprise them just might work. If they could ambush the Germans, and even the odds a bit before the Germans knew how few men they really had, they might have a chance.

That was the theory, but if Mac was wrong, the situation could rapidly deteriorate into a "last stand" rather than a successful defense.

Baker took a deep breath. The fighting the past six days has been costly, but he realized that this fight could be the most critical battle yet.

In the past six days he had come to know Zanovitch, McCreary, and Holden better than ever before. War does that. He had shared everything with them, yet now he had to risk their lives. What had Zanovitch said back in England about being stuck between a rock and a hard place?

The weight of his responsibilities as squad leader pressed down on him. He realized that Zanovitch was right: to be a good combat leader, he had to love his men. He also knew that to win in combat, he had to risk the men he loved.

That was another part of the great dilemma, Baker

thought. In combat, decisions always seemed to be a choice between bad outcomes. You never had enough information and hesitation was deadly. You had to size up the situation, decide rapidly, and ignore your fears.

Baker realized that Mac was good at this. Mac could decide and make even a bad decision work.

"We are the right of the line!" Mac shouted as he walked behind the headquarters clerks and cooks lining the berm. Confident and calm, Mac spoke as if he was a paragon of authority. "Don't forget. You are the Screaming Eagles. The 506th is on our left, in Veghel, but there is no one to our right. Nothing but road and open field. If the Germans break through here, they'll be able to turn into Veghel or run all the way to Eindhoven. We can't let that happen. *You* won't let that happen."

No one replied. No one needed to say anything. It wasn't fair that a ragtag group of headquarters clerks and cooks, reinforced by one jeep section of Division's Reconnaissance Platoon, were ordered to stop a major German attack, but there was no one else. These soldiers, even though most of them were not frontline infantrymen, understood what was at stake.

"Mac!" McCreary announced. "It looks like Simon's coming back."

"Hold your fire," Mac ordered.

Like a deer fleeing from a pack of wolves, the paratrooper Mac had sent forward ran back from the woods toward the American line. Private First Class Simon sprinted as if he were trying out for the Olympic two-hundred-yard dash. Only in this case no one was racing against him, there was just the fluttering wings of death beating above him as the paratrooper raced for his life.

From the woods, Baker thought he heard the faint sounds of armored vehicles.

Simon finished his sprint from the woods and dived to the ground next to Mac. "The Krauts are coming," Simon reported, pausing to gulp in air and catch his breath. "Lots of them. And the bastards have tanks. I could hear them."

"How many tanks?" Mac quizzed the panting soldier.

Simon caught his breath. "I don't know. Two, maybe three. I didn't want to stay and ask them how many more were coming."

Mac grinned. "Well done, son. Now find a place in the line and get ready to fight."

Baker gritted his teeth, and then looked at Corporal Zanovitch. "Zanovitch, stay low until I call for you. Unless the Kraut tanks show us a flank, that damn bazooka is more likely to piss off the Panzers than destroy them."

"Don't worry, Sarge," Zanovitch answered. "Front or flank, I never miss."

"Holden, any contact with the artillery?" Baker asked.

"I relayed a message through Division G3 to the artillery. They can support us with mortars. They've promised us 105's as soon as they're available."

"Good job, Holden," Baker pulled out his map to check the grid coordinates. "Tell them we need artillery at grid CS 382847. Got that?"

"Wilco."

The thud of explosions in Veghel rose to an ominous level. The flare-up in the town signified a major German attack. If the Germans broke through the town, Mac's paltry group of fighters would be flanked and wouldn't stand a chance. Infantrymen cannot outrun a tank.

Baker could feel the fear crawling up and down the line of American paratroopers. He recognized it, like a doctor recognizes the symptoms of a fever. Baker knew fear, had lived with it ever since Normandy, and was familiar with its icy grip. He knew that the only antidote for fear was leadership.

Soldier, leader, human being—that was the challenge in three words. To be the first and second without losing the third.

He wasn't sure it was possible.

Baker knew from experience that the strength of the sum of the three was the key. The problem was to sense how to blend the three into one, to do this in time, and derive a unique answer for every distinct situation.

An intimidating challenge with no clear path to success.

He knew from experience that the calculus of the battlefield was stern. The arithmetic of combat was severe and unforgiving. The cost of a wrong decision, or of hesitation, was measured in the lives of friends and comrades. It was an expensive price to pay—expensive as each loss chipped away at his confidence.

His mind searched for a rallying point. In infantry tactics a rallying point is the place you return to when everything has gone to shit.

Mac stepped back from the berm and announced, "Steady lads. You are the fighting 101st!"

The gunner of the .30 caliber machine gun looked at Mac, ashen-faced, then looked toward the rear.

It was as if Mac could read his thoughts. "Soldier. Machine gunner—*look at me!*"

The startled machine gunner turned his head to Mac.

"Martino, right?" Mac asked.

"Yes, First Sergeant," the machine gunner answered. The fact that the first sergeant knew his name had a visible affect on Martino.

"You need some help with that gun, son. Simon! Get over here and load for Martino."

"On the way, First Sergeant,"

Mac moved over to Martino and put his hand on the soldier's shoulder. "Martino, your machine gun is the heart of our defense. I'm counting on you. As soon as I give you the word I want you to fire hot and accurate. Fire short bursts at the base of the tree line, then work your way back as the enemy moves on us. You got that?"

The gunner bravely gave First Sergeant Hassay a thumbs-up gesture signifying that he understood.

Simon plopped down by Martino's side. "We'll be okay, Top."

"That's the pitch,"

"Nervous in the service, huh," Baker offered in a hushed tone as Mac passed behind him. "Will they stand their ground?"

"Yeah," Mac answered. "They'll hold. They have to."

Baker nodded, hoping that Mac was right. "Zano, how many rockets do you have for that stovepipe?"

"Five, Sarge, only five," Corporal Zanovitch answered. "I could use someone to help me load."

Baker turned to Mac. "McCreary is a good shot. I hate to take him from the line to assist Zano with the bazooka. Do you have a loader to spare?"

Mac looked over to his left. "Rodriguez, get over there and help those recon guys load that bazooka!"

Baker watched as a confident but very young Mexican-American soldier ran over from the far left of the line to help Zanovitch load the bazooka. The kid looked like he was no more than eighteen years old, but then again, they were all young, Baker thought. The comrades he had lost these past six days were all under twenty-five. War is a young man's business, and by its nature always generates a youthful harvest.

Zanovitch gave Rodriguez a crash course on loading the bazooka and emphasized that he must be well away from the back-blast when the weapon was fired.

"Otherwise the flame from the back of this stovepipe will melt you like last year's Christmas candle."

Then, like a bad storm, that monstrous sound . . . that deadly beat . . . that monstrous cacophony of battle grew louder inside the town.

The cool wind rustled through the trees. The noise of battle raged from the north, emanating from the town of Veghel.

The camouflage-clad, heavily armed *Fallschirmjägers* moved like skilled hunters through the forest, deliberately and quietly. The veteran German soldiers pointed their rifles and submachine guns forward, safety off and ready to fire at a moment's notice.

Oberfeldwebel Wilhelm Graf held his PPSh submachine gun in his left hand and raised his right hand to signal "halt."

Fifteen *Fallschirmjägers* immediately stopped and took cover behind trees and mounds of dirt, waiting for the command to move forward.

Graf and his fifteen *Fallschirmjägers* were at the right flank of the German line that was part of a company-sized *kampfgruppe* advancing though the trees. After two weeks of heavy combat, his platoon was reduced from forty-two to fifteen men.

The defense near Valkenswaard and the near-continuous fighting since September 17 had cost Graf dearly. He had lost more than half his men since the day of the great Allied airborne invasion.

Graf inched forward and peered through the trees at the open ground in front of him. His sixth sense warned him about this open area. He couldn't see any *Amis*—as they called the Americans—but he had learned, as only a veteran of countless battles knows, to trust his battlefield intuition.

A few German mortar shells exploded in the woods about four hundred meters to the west.

"Is that all the SS can provide as artillery support?" Feldwebel Weise asked. "A puny mortar barrage?"

Graf shrugged. "We're lucky we have that. How much longer until the assault guns catch up?"

"Who knows?" Weise replied. "The *kampfgruppe* is strung out for almost a kilometer. One StuG broke down on the road before we entered this forest. One moves like it is sick, belching black smoke from its ass like a chimney. The other is on the left flank. If the Panzer Corps is the elite of the German war machine, as the newsreels say it is, we're doomed."

Graf gave Weise a stern look and then glanced west to study the terrain. A north-south road bisected the open area. The road was built up on a berm. Graf recognized that the berm would provide valuable cover for his men.

Their objective, however, was to attack Veghel from the south, not to seize the road. To do this, Graf knew that the correct tactical move was for the *kampfgruppe* to attack as a combined arms team of assault guns and infantry support. Once the *kampfgruppe* was together at the west end of the woods, it should move rapidly across the open ground and then quickly seize a southern chunk of the town of Veghel.

Graf turned back to face Weise and saw the sergeant peering under the dirty bandages that covered the wound on his left hand. "How is it?"

"Better since I doused it with that packet of sulfur powder," Weise replied. Weise had taken the sulfur powder from a dead American paratrooper. "Amazing that the *Amis* can provide their soldiers with such wonders. How many soldiers could we save if we had such things?"

"They have sulfur powder, but we have Tiger tanks," Graf answered.

"Maybe so, but when is the last time you saw a Tiger tank?" Weise countered, pulling the bandage back to cover his wound. "I haven't see any Tigers lately. I'd rather have the sulfur powder."

Graf look behind Weise and saw someone barreling through the woods toward them. It was SS *Hauptscharführer* Gunter. The man looked out of breath, and he breathed heavily as he cradled an MP40 submachine gun in his arms. "What are you stopping for?"

"Look ahead, Gunter, you fool," Graf growled as he pointed to the field to the west. "We must send someone across to scout the far side of this open area before we move into it."

Gunter hesitated and looked at the open field. "There is no one there. You're afraid of shadows. Our orders are to attack with speed. The assault on Veghel is under way. There have been too many delays already."

"Do you obey every order you are given, no matter how stupid?" Graf questioned.

"No . . . , I mean yes."

Graf shook his head. "Our force is stretched out in this forest. We should wait for the assault guns to arrive before we push forward. If we don't, we'll likely hit the *Amis* piecemeal."

Before Gunter could reply, *Obersturmführer* Carl Kodritz moved up to Graf with six SS soldiers. The SS man nearest Kodritz had a long scar across the left side of his face.

"Gunter, what is holding us up?" Kodritz demanded.

"*Oberfeldwebel* Graf refuses to advance," Gunter announced. "He questions your orders."

Graf turned to Gunter. If looks could kill, Gunter

would be dead, buried, and letters of condolence sent to his family.

Kodritz looked as if he would explode. His jaw tightened; his face turned red with anger. He shot a fiery glance at Graf. "I have had it with your insubordination! The movement to Veghel and the attack on the town will continue immediately."

"Herr Leutnant," Graf protested calmly, but before he could say another word Kodritz moved forward within an inch of Graf's face.

"You will address me as *Obersturmführer,* not *Leutnant,"* Kodritz snarled. "If I cared for your opinion, I would order you to give it to me. I do not."

Graf bristled at the officer's comments but didn't bat an eye.

"Get this," Kodritz continued. "I don't like you or your kind. You say you fight for Germany, but deep inside you do not fight for the Reich. Germany is the Reich. I heard rumors that you criticize the Nazi Party. In the new Germany we will do away with people like you. Do you think you can hide behind your Knight's Cross forever?"

Graf didn't flinch. He stared in silence at the ranting SS officer.

"I will not accept excuses," Kodritz ordered. "Continue the attack, take the town, and cut the British from moving along the road to Nijmegen. Those are our orders."

Graf gazed back at the officer and held firmly to his PPSh submachine gun. A thought crossed Graf's mind that he could end the argument here and now, but he realized that this was not the time or place.

Kodritz saw something in Graf's eyes that made the enraged SS officer blink. The *Obersturmführer* turned and moved off to the left of the advancing line of infantry with his six SS soldiers trailing. Gunter, like a faithful hound, followed his officer.

When Kodritz and his group were out of earshot, Weise walked up to Graf and said: "How are we ever going to win this war with assholes like that?"

"With courage, my friend, with courage," Graf said with a determined grin.

"Kodritz is big on enthusiasm for the party, but not so big on tactical sense," Weise added. "He'll be the death of all of us yet."

Graf put his hand on Weise's shoulder. "Never forget, we don't fight for him. We fight for Germany."

Weise nodded. "Ah yes, the Fatherland. I almost forgot."

"I serve for duty and honor, not for them and their crooked cross."

"Can one be separated from the other? Nazis, butchers, mass murderers—this is the rising sequence. We have sold our souls for your duty . . . and this time she is deranged."

"You talk too much," Graf replied. "In this world talk is dangerous. If our SS friends hear you . . ."

"That is why I only talk of this with you, for I know you."

"Then you know that we must have a fixed opinion to survive this. One driving goal. To fight and win. Once we win, we can change them."

"Win? Once they win, everything will change."

"Winning has many forms. In 1940 it was Europe. Now, it is to save Germany. If we can fight the Allies to a standstill, they will offer terms."

"We cannot and they will not," Weise answered. "They will continue until we are beaten into the mud."

"Then we will do our duty and leave the rest to God."

"God left us in 1936, or hadn't you noticed?"

Graf shook his head at his friend's sarcasm and then focused on the issue at hand. "Up *Fallschirmjägers*! Skirmish-line formation. Move out!"

The sun sank below the horizon. The sky turned gray while the Americans waited. The noise of the battle in Veghel ebbed and flowed. Several of the houses were on fire, flames lighting up the dusky sky. The Germans were hitting Veghel hard, but it sounded like the 506th was giving as much as they took.

Baker looked at the woods to the east. Once the Germans rush out of the woods, he wondered, how long will this thin green line hold? The berm will help, but only if all of us keep up an accurate and heavy volume of fire. If we don't do that, we won't hold this berm, and we'll be smashed like coconuts hit by a hammer. Men cannot outrun tanks.

Baker waited, checked his Thompson submachine gun, and made sure the safety was switched to fire. His mouth was chalky dry and his palms were moist. A quiet voice inside his head thought about running, but he knew he wouldn't listen to that voice. Ashamed at his thoughts, he squeezed the pistol grip of his Thompson submachine gun. His thoughts swirled as he reflected on his days in high school back in St. Louis, Missouri, remembering the time when he was a boy. He remembered the day his father left him after his father and mother were divorced. He reminisced about his best friend, George Risner, and remembered when they played baseball for their high school team—Matt was the pitcher and George the catcher. They had made a great team. In the same vision he saw the image of George in a burning Stuart tank, number D-12, 70th Tank Battalion, near St. Come du Mont in Normandy. He recalled all these things in an instant, and then a shell exploded fifty yards behind him. Immediately, his soldier's instincts and training kicked in, and he was suddenly focused—totally focused—on the tree line to the east.

Mac moved back to the berm and crawled next to Baker. "Baker, can you have your man radio Division and ask them to tell the Brits we are here? If the British tanks do arrive, I don't want them shooting us up. I want the Brits to know they have friendlies on this side of the road."

Baker nodded and relayed the order to Holden.

Then Mac saw something in the woods and grabbed Baker by the shoulder. As Baker looked to the east, he spied a couple of dark shapes coming out of the trees.

"Hold your fire," Mac ordered. "Pass the word."

Quietly, the soldiers passed the order not to fire until ordered.

"Zanovitch, stand-by," Baker echoed. "We have to let them get close and make every shot count."

Zanovitch nodded. "Just tell me when and I'll give 'em hell."

More Germans exited the woods. At least twenty heavily armed Germans in camouflaged battle smocks moved into the open field in front of them. The German infantry formed a skirmish line and headed northwest. Baker saw German sergeants issuing orders and two men carrying MG42 machine guns over their shoulders. It appeared that the Germans did not know the Americans were close by, waiting in ambush along the road.

"Hold," Mac sounded.

"There sure are a lot of them," McCreary whispered as he aimed his M1 rifle at an enemy soldier.

The line of German infantry moved perpendicular to the road, unaware of the Americans and offering Mac an opportunity to enfilade the German line.

More Germans came out of the woods. At least thirty were now in the open field.

"Now!" Mac shouted. *"Fire!"*

The entire American line exploded in fire. Twenty rifles blasted away. Baker emptied a magazine of .45 caliber slugs watching two Germans fall. Martino's .30 caliber Browning machine gun rattled like a sewing machine with every fifth round a red tracer. In the waning light, Baker saw tracer bullets skipping across the field and into the ranks of German soldiers.

The German infantry faced left and charged, straight for the American line. Figures in *feldgrau* and camouflaged uniforms fell, others knelt and returned fire, some ran back to the woods.

Baker reloaded and realized that this was a large attack, at least company strength.

"Kraut bastards!" McCreary yelled, shooting and cussing at the same time. "Come and get it."

Explosions rumbled closer to the American line as the Germans corrected their mortar fire onto the road. Several shells crashed into the dirt behind the Americans, not hitting anyone but landing close enough to scare the hell out of the headquarters troops as hot metal screamed overhead and nipped the trees that lined the road.

"Holden, we need that artillery," Baker screamed. *"Now!"*

Holden was on the radio, shouting into the transmitter. "Fox Six, if you can hear me, the Krauts are hitting us now. They have tanks coming our way. At least two, possibly three, enemy tanks. Grid CS382847. Request armor and artillery support, over."

"Keep firing! Keep up the fire!" Mac ordered, in total charge of the action.

"Our artillery is on the way!" Holden yelled. "Fox Six

this is Romeo! Enemy infantry is two hundred yards in front of our position. Grid CS382847. I say again, 382847. Request artillery and tank support. Over!"

A bunch of dark-uniformed men rushed down from the crest at the American lines.

"Here comes their main assault! Keep up the fire!" Mac screamed. Dozens of Germans ran toward the berm shouting as they fired their machine pistols and rifles. The noise from the firing was overwhelming. The branches of the trees were falling from the intense fire like leaves on a fall day.

Holden continued to shout into his radio. McCreary was nearby, firing his M1 rifle and screaming at the top of his lungs.

The .30 caliber machine gun sent a fusillade of hot .30-06 lead at the attackers. The American machine-gun fire cut down the Germans as they charged forward, but the Germans kept coming. Baker fired a burst from his Thompson submachine gun at a group of attackers that were nearly at the berm.

American artillery began falling in the woods to the east. Shells burst inside the trees in bright red-orange flashes.

"That's the ticket, boys," Mac shouted. "Pour it on 'em."

"Zanovitch, I haven't forgotten you," Baker shouted. "Stay down until I order you up! The rest of you, keep up the fire! Holden, keep that artillery coming."

Holden nodded to Baker. "Fire for effect is on the way."

Baker rose back up to the lip of the berm with his Thompson submachine gun ready as mortar shells arced overhead and crashed into the German tree line. Flushed by the mortars, five Germans jumped up from the field and rushed toward the road to Baker's right-front. Baker saw them, and immediately pulled the trigger of his Thompson and dropped one of the attackers. McCreary popped up as well and opened up with his M1 rifle. Baker and McCreary hit two more attacking Germans while the other two made it safely behind the other side of the berm.

Baker slipped back behind the berm and pulled McCreary down with him. Quickly, Baker unhooked a grenade from his load-bearing harness and signaled for McCreary to do the same.

McCreary unhooked a grenade and made ready to throw.

"Together, on three!" Baker shouted.

McCreary nodded.

"One, two, three!"

Baker and McCreary threw their grenades over the road to the right-front of the American line where the two Germans were last seen. The spoons from the grenade fell off and Baker watched as the grenades sailed through the air. Three seconds later there were two explosions and Baker heard someone on the other side of the berm screaming in German.

Then, above the sound of the shooting and shelling, Baker heard the distinctive sound that all infantrymen fear more than anything else on the battlefield: the rumble of tank tracks. Two German StuGs, armored assault guns, broke through the trees and moved into the open field.

The Germans took cover around the assault guns and advanced as the StuGs churned forward.

Baker ducked down behind the berm. "Zanovitch, stand by. Any minute now."

Zanovitch nodded.

Rodriguez knelt next to Zanovitch with a bazooka round in his hand.

Baker nodded. "Holden! Get 'em on the radio. Where are the damn Brits? We need tank support."

Holden placed his M1 carbine down and reached for the shoe box–sized SCR 536 radio slung around his shoulder. "Wild Boar Six, this is Romeo over."

Holden reported triumphantly. "They're almost here. At least four Brit tanks."

"Mac, did you hear that," Baker shouted. "The tanks are on their way."

"Good! Hold on, boys. The cavalry's on the way!"

McCreary slid down behind the berm and turned to Baker. "StuG, right-front, one hundred yards!'

A StuG blasted away with its big, 75mm cannon. The shell hit the berm in front of McCreary and showered them with dirt and rocks.

Baker peaked over the road again and saw the StuGs closing the distance to the American line. One assault gun on the right was moving fast toward the road. The other, farther to the left, was approaching more slowly and was coughing up black smoke from its rear exhaust manifold.

Encouraged by the presence of their advancing armor, more Germans charged out of the woods. Martino's machine gun kept up a constant fire and crumpled the German line. The German attack staggered as Martino squeezed off short bursts, just like the instructors taught at Fort Benning. All the while, Simon lay to Martino's side and fed the machine gun with white cloth belts of .30-06 ammunition.

"Zano! Tank. Right-front!" Baker screamed.

At that moment, the lead StuG turned on its tracks and fired again, but this time it zeroed in on the American machine gun.

Baker felt the concussion of the explosion as the high-explosive 75mm shell hit in front of the American machine gun. The shockwave threw Baker to the ground. Baker rose and turned to see Martino and Simon. Both men were blown back off the berm and were lying on their backs in the mud. Their lifeless bodies were a bloody pulp of torn flesh and broken bones.

Baker stared at the bodies of Martino and Simon and burned with anger.

The battle swirled around him, consuming his senses, heightening his fear. Keeping his wits, he knew, was the key. Maintaining his focus on leading, trapping, and outthinking the enemy was central. Doing it amid all this, ah, yes, that was the problem . . . that was the dilemma . . . and that was his job.

More bullets thudded into the dirt near Baker. An explosion ripped the trees just to the far left of the American line. One soldier clutched his neck and clawed at the ground with his feet. The man suddenly reached up with both arms, as if to grab some unseen person, and then his arms fell, and he was still.

Baker saw Mac knocked down by the blast, but the tough first sergeant rolled to his feet firing his M1 rifle over the berm.

Peering over the berm, Baker saw a StuG moving to his left. The big armored assault gun was looking for a way to cross over the berm and, in doing so, offered a perfect flank shot for the bazooka. "Now, Zano! Bazooka team, *up*! Target the right tank. *Fire!*"

Zanovitch ran up to the center of the road and kneeled. The bazooka loader tapped Zanovitch on the helmet, indicating that the bazooka was loaded and ready to fire. Zanovitch took a couple of tense seconds to sight his weapon as bullets flew all around, and then he fired.

The rocket left the tube with a *swoosh* as a ball of fire jetted from the front and back of the bazooka. Baker could feel the heat from the back-blast. Zanovitch's aim was true, and the rocket hit the German assault gun on the right side.

The stricken StuG tried to back up, but stopped after a few yards as its track rolled off the support rollers.

Zanovitch and Rodriguez rushed back behind the safety of the berm.

"I got the bastard!" Zanovitch said with a wide grin. "I told you I never miss."

At nearly the same moment a series of explosions sounded on the east side of the berm. Baker heard the hollow-thud sound of a high-velocity round penetrating armor, followed by a loud secondary explosion. The sound of the explosions was coupled with the sound of heavy machine-gun fire.

Baker rose up to the lip of the berm and saw both StuGs billowing thick black smoke. The German infantry was in full retreat. He looked to the north and saw four British tanks, followed by Bren Carriers, churning through the muddy field.

"The Brits are here," Baker shouted. "Thank God!"

The Bren Carriers jerked to a stop, ten yards behind the tanks. In an instant, five Irish Guardsmen in the back of each carrier jumped out with their weapons, ready to fight.

"I thought we already cleared the Jerries from this area," Corporal Donal Ackers shouted.

"What's wrong?" Colour Sergeant Cat Gilchrist yelled back. "You don't like helping out the Yanks?"

"Don't worry, Corporal Ackers," Guardsman Logan replied. "I'm ready for a fight today. You can stay behind if you're squeamish."

"Listen to the man," Ackers replied. "You've got to do your own growing, no matter how tall your grandfather was. I don't need you to do my fighting for me."

The British tanks in front of the Irish infantry fired a volley of high-velocity 75mm shells. Four rounds, fired in volley, lit up the darkening sky.

"All right, lads, on line, Bren Guns on the flanks!" Cat ordered. "The Yanks are to our right. Don't shoot at them; they don't take kindly to that. The Jerries are to the left. Give 'em lead when you see them."

The British Sherman tanks advanced on-line as the Irish Guards followed behind. Two German assault guns burned in the field. In one StuG, the one farthest from the British tanks, the ammunition had ignited and the vehicle exploded in a shower of sparks and fragments.

In the dim light, Cat saw German soldiers running for the woods to the east.

"Section, action left! Bren Guns ready!" Cat ordered.

The Irish Guardsmen swiftly deployed in precise battle drill and faced southeast. In the distance, figures in *feldgrau* scampered toward the wood.

"Bren Gun One up!" Guardsmen Friskin shouted.

"Bren Gun Two ready!" Guardsman Logan sounded off.

"Fire!" Cat ordered.

The British line opened up on the fleeing Germans. The Bren Guns chugged away with their slow rate of fire, cutting down the enemy like tall, green grass to a scythe. At the same time the British tanks wheeled left and blasted away with machine guns and cannon fire.

"His father's sword he hath girded on!" Cat shouted.

"Aye, it's that song again!" Donal commented. "I only get worried when he isn't singing!"

The German attack was broken, but a dozen Germans were still running and returning fire at the Irish infantry. Cat rose to a crouch to move to the right of the line. Suddenly, Cat saw a tall German jump up from behind a mound of dirt not ten yards in front of him.

For Cat the action played out in slow motion. His foe was a tall, thin German paratrooper. The man carried a submachine gun with a large, round magazine and he aimed the weapon directly at Cat.

Cat instinctively swiveled to meet the threat and brought up his Sten gun. Before Cat could fire, Guardsman Kelly, directly in front of Cat, rose up to a kneeling position and fired.

The German fired off a stream of bullets as Cat fell flat on the ground. The German hit Guardsman Kelly.

Cat aimed at the enemy soldier and blasted away with his Sten gun. At the same time a grenade exploded in front of Cat in a spire of dirt and smoke. Through the smoke and dim light Cat fired off a second burst from his Sten gun. When the smoke cleared, he suddenly lost sight of the target. Like an apparition, the German paratrooper was gone.

Cat knelt down next to the man who was hit and watched as Kelly's eyes turned from horror to calm to nothing. Gently he passed his hand over Kelly's face to close his eyes.

"Damn!" Cat cursed. He wanted to do something for Kelly, but there was nothing to do. Realizing that his men were still in danger, Cat quickly recovered. "Casualties?" Cat yelled.

Ackers crawled over to another soldier who was hit. The wounded Guardsman had dropped his Enfield rifle and was curled up in a fetal position. "It's Guardsman Heaton. He's taken one in the arm. He'll live."

One man killed and one wounded, Cat thought in anger. He scanned for more targets, eager to even the score.

The tanks moved closer to the wood line and blasted the trees with machine-gun fire. The Germans melted away.

After a few more minutes of this, the tanks ran out of enemy to shoot at and ceased their fire.

Cat surveyed the battlefield. Twenty or more Germans lay dead in the field with half a dozen or so wounded. "Check for wounded! Bring any prisoners to the west side of the berm where the Yanks are."

His men quickly fanned out. A shot was fired as one wounded German would not surrender to Corporal Ackers. The German tried to grab his pistol as Ackers approached. One blast from Ackers's Sten gun and it was over. After a thorough search, one wounded SS soldier and two wounded German paratroopers were carried behind the berm.

Cat walked over the road and saw a group of fifteen American paratroopers from the 101st Airborne Division manning a firing line along the road. At least seven Americans lay dead from the fighting, and their comrades were lining the bodies up near the wreckage of a mangled machine gun.

Cat waited in silence as three Bren Carriers climbed up the berm, crossed over the road, rolled down the west side and stopped near the Americans. A British medic jumped out of one Bren Carrier and walked up to a tough-looking American first sergeant.

"Can I help you with your wounded?" the medic asked.

"First Sergeant Hassay," the man said as he extended his arm to shake hands with the medic. "We have three wounded, and I'd appreciate it if you could check them out."

The medic shook hands with the American and then stepped past the dead bodies to treat the three wounded paratroopers.

Cat walked over to an American staff sergeant, who was sitting on the side of the berm with a Thompson submachine gun cradled in his arms. The staff sergeant stood as Cat neared.

"Thanks," the American offered. "You guys arrived just in time."

Cat nodded. "My name is Colour Sergeant Cathal Gilchrist. Irish Guards and I lost a good man tonight saving your sorry asses."

"Yeah, well, we lost a few good men ourselves," the American replied. Baker reached. "I'm Staff Sergeant Matt Baker, 101st Airborne Reconnaissance Platoon."

"I don't really care who you are, Yank. I just want to gather my men and get the hell out of here."

Baker's face hardened. Before he could reply to the British sergeant's rude comment, three British soldiers came over the roadway carrying a wounded SS sergeant.

"Doc, as soon as you're free, come check out this bloke," a British corporal announced.

The medic, who had finished tending the American wounded, moved over to treat the German.

"Did you check this man for weapons?" the medic asked.

"Blimey, Doc, do I look like a rookie recruit?" the corporal answered. "Of course I checked him."

"Hmmph, I suppose you checked that Hitler Youth lad the other day as well?"

"Doc, I told you, that was Avery's fault. I've since educated the lad on the proper procedures. Now, can you have a look at this wounded bastard, or should I just shoot him and put him out of his misery?"

The medic strode over to the German. The man was an SS sergeant lying face up and holding his stomach with both hands. He had obviously been shot in the stomach. The man had a long scar across the left side of his face from a past wound that had healed. The medic drew a bandage from his aid bag, ripped open the brown wrapper, and knelt next to the wounded enemy soldier.

"I don't know if you can understand me, but I'm going to pull your hands away and place this bandage over your wound."

The German didn't respond.

The British aide man moved the German's hands. At first the German didn't want to move his hands from the wound, but relented when the medic insisted. As he moved his hands away a spurt of blood gushed from the wound. The British medic immediately placed his own hands over the area and applied direct pressure to stop the bleeding.

Baker, Cat, and the Irish Guardsmen stood and watched as the medic removed one hand, keeping the other on the wound, and deftly placed a compress on the hole in the German's stomach.

"Corporal Ackers, could you fetch my bag with blood plasma from the Bren Carrier?" the medic asked.

"Aye, Doc, be right back."

The SS sergeant's eyes opened wide. "You give me blood?"

The medic looked shocked when the enemy soldier, who was silent while being bandaged, suddenly spoke in English.

"Yes," the medic replied. He took a knife and cut the German's shirtsleeve, exposing the wounded man's arm. The medic then checked the man's arm for a vein to stick in the plasma needle. "You've lost a lot of blood. If I don't give you this plasma, you'll probably go into shock and die."

"British blood?" the German asked in English.

"Yes," the medic answered.

"I refuse," the SS sergeant announced. "It could be Jewish blood."

The medic looked at the German in disbelief. "Refuse? You can't refuse. Jewish blood, Christian blood, British blood, it doesn't matter! If you don't take this plasma, you'll die."

"No blood," the German insisted.

The medic looked at Cat. "Colour Sergeant Gilchrist, I need your help here. This German refuses treatment."

"I heard him," Cat announced. "Leave him be. If our blood is not good enough for him, then he can die and go to Hell."

"That's a mean thing to do," the medic replied. "I tell you, this man will die without the plasma. We should force him to take it, at gunpoint if needed."

"We'll do no such thing," Cat replied. "Being mean is part of the job. In this racket it's the tough guys who lead the survivors. Screw him."

The medic looked on dumbfounded as First Sergeant Hassay and Private Holden walked up to Baker.

"Holden just received word that you are to report to division headquarters as soon as possible," Hassay said to Baker. "And they want me to put the ranking Brit here on the radio."

"That'd be me, Colour Sergeant Gilchrist, Irish Guards," Cat announced. "What's their radio identification number?"

"Identification number?" Holden asked as he handed the radio to the British colour sergeant. "You mean their call sign, Sarge? It's Kangaroo Three One," Holden said as he handed the radio to Cat.

"Don't call me 'sarge.' You Yanks may not care for proper discipline, but in the British army you call me 'colour sergeant,'" Cat took the radio, walked a few steps away, made the call, and then walked back to Staff Sergeant Baker. "It seems, Staff Sergeant Baker of the 101st Airborne Division Reconnaissance Platoon, that you and I both have been ordered to report to your division headquarters's intelligence section."

Baker looked at Mac. "I wonder what the G-two has in mind for us now?"

Mac shrugged. "It's usually not good."

Baker turned to the British sergeant "My jeep is back there in the woods. You can ride with me—that is, if you want to ride with a Yank."

"Fine, it's probably the fastest means of getting there," Cat snapped. "Let's get moving and get this over with."

Baker turned to Mac and put out his hand. "Well, Mac, I guess I'll be seeing you."

"Thanks for your help tonight." Mac shook Baker's hand and then pulled in close to whisper. "And don't kill that Brit asshole on the way to division headquarters, no matter how much you may think you want to. Don't forget, he *did* save our butts."

Baker nodded. The two men then looked at each other for a moment and wondered if they would ever see each other again.

"Come on, damn it, let's get a move on," Cat snarled. "I haven't got all bloody night."

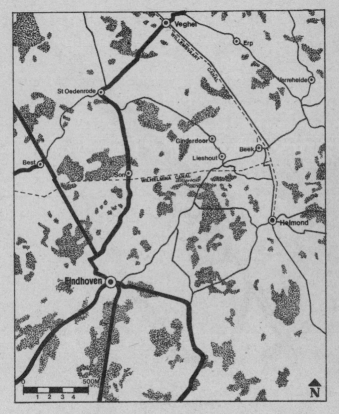

The Netherlands: Hell's Highway Area of Operations

British Sten Gun

6: D+6

Hell's Highway was strewn with wreckage from a British convoy, which the Germans had smashed the day before. The trucks were still burning.
—SERGEANT SCHWENK, 101st Airborne Division

Sunrise, Saturday, September 23, 1944:

The sun was breaking through the trees and *Oberfeldwebel* Wilhelm Graf was frowning.

It looked as if today would be the first good weather since the British and American attack. Graf didn't like it. Good weather meant Allied airplanes. The last thing he needed was a sky full of P-51 and P-47 *jabos*.

High overhead to the west, the sky filled with distant formations of Allied transport aircraft towing gliders. This was another bad sign. The formations flew north, out of view, but their length and depth meant that the British and Americans had more combat power to pour into the fight.

Closer to earth, the situation with his men was dire. Supplies were sparse and they had not been issued food and medical supplies in the past three days. Yesterday, before the big attack on Veghel, they had been resupplied with a meager allocation of ammunition, but it was not sufficient to turn the tide of battle. To acerbate the problems between his men and the SS even further, when supplies did arrive, Kodritz made sure they were issued to the SS first. Graf's men received the leftovers. As a result, his men were forced to scrounge food, water, and bandages off the enemy or the Dutch civilians.

Graf and his men occupied fighting positions in a forest near the Dutch village of Erp. His men rested, cleaned weapons, and shared their meager rations. After the past week of fighting, they were exhausted.

Luckily, the Americans and British were just as tired, content to stay in Veghel. Graf was happy with their decision.

"A hell of a way to fight a war," *Feldwebel* Karsten Weise complained.

Graf, Weise, and nine other *Fallschirmjägers* were all that was left of Graf's forty-two-man platoon after more than a week of fighting in Holland. Graf's men had paid a terrible price to gain time and slow down the Allies. He wondered if the time they had bought with their blood was worth one life, let alone the lives of his men.

"What are you grumbling about, Weise," Graf countered. "You still have your health."

Weise laughed and then coughed. Living on the wet ground in the damp air had given Weise a cold. "It has been a week of continuous fighting since we were assigned to these SS bastards. When are we going to leave this lot?"

"*Generalfeldmarschall* Model's order is clear. All soldiers will remain in their designated *kampfgruppes* until further orders," Graf explained. "I don't like it any more than you do, but we couldn't make it to the Sixth Regiment even if we knew where they were. There are a lot of Americans between us and west of the highway."

Weise shook his head. "From what I have heard, you never let that stop you in Russia."

Graf looked at his friend. Weise was dirty, unshaven, and the rings under his eyes were testimony to the fact that he hadn't caught a good night's sleep in days. Weise looked like hell itself, but he was right about one thing. In Russia, Graf had lived behind enemy lines most of the time. It became the natural condition of the Russian front. In one situation, he had helped move an entire company of sick and wounded Wehrmacht soldiers out of a trap right under the noses of a Russian tank division.

In Russia, self-reliance was the key to survival.

Graf thought about another time and place, a distant battlefield. The thought made him shudder. Late in November 1942, nearly two years ago, he was in Russia leading a team of the Brandenburg Commandos, the elite special forces of German military, and he found himself trapped behind enemy lines.

On November 24, Graf Commandos arrived at the town of Velikiye Luki, just as the Russian Red Army attacked. The town is located nearly 450 kilometers south of Leningrad, which was the target of Graf's commando operation. The massive Soviet attack changed those plans. The Russians attacked in waves, took tremendous losses, but kept coming. After intense fighting, the Russians succeeded in trapping the Wehrmacht troops in the town. Surrounded in the snow, it was similar to Stalingrad, but on a smaller scale.

Hitler ordered the garrison at Velikiye Luki to stand fast and wait for a relief force to break through to the garrison. The vital rail and road network in this area of Russia converged at Velikiye Luki. Most important, the town was the point of conversion from the east European rail gauge to the wider west European rail gauge. As a result, Hitler demanded that they hold the city. The German garrison along with Graf and his men were forbidden to attempt a breakout operation.

Throughout the icy-cold weeks of December, Graf and

his Brandenburg Commandos fought with Wehrmacht and *Fallschirmjäger* units to hold off continuous Red Army attacks. In the bitter cold days and nights the German defenders held off the well-equipped Soviet Third Shock Army. Outnumbering the defenders five-to-one, and with almost constant air support from the Soviet air force, formations of Red Army tanks and infantry units smashed against the German defenses. The Germans tenaciously held on, killing thousands of Russians in the process. At one point, Russian bodies were stacked so high, and frozen so stiff, that Graf had to withdraw his men half a kilometer to clear fields of fire.

Christmas passed. The German relief force still could not break through to the besieged defenders. As ammunition, food, and medical supplies ran low inside the cauldron, Graf and his men ate horse flesh and bravely fought on. The wounded were quickly patched up and returned to the front to fight. Burned-out Soviet tank hulls littered the terrain, but the Germans were running out of antitank guns and German casualties were proportionally worse as replacements were not available. Many units lost up to eighty percent of their men and almost all of their officers.

Finally, on January 5, 1943, the relentless Red Army attacks succeeded and the Soviets broke though the German defenses, splitting the town in two. There was no chance of relief or rescue. If anyone was to survive, they needed to fight their own way out. At this point, Graf realized that a successful defense was no longer possible. Graf made a decision to disobey Hitler's orders.

The battlefield looked like a page torn out of Hell. The wounded lay about unattended, moaning and pleading for help. Frozen bodies of Russians and German soldiers dotted the white landscape like maggots on a rotting corpse. The atmosphere was as black as those bodies.

Surrender was out of the question. The Russians seldom took prisoners.

In a blinding snowstorm and freezing cold conditions Graf led anyone who could carry a rifle in a breakout from the cauldron. Everything was white and frozen. Graf could barely see a few feet to the front, but he led them forward. What was not white was black from the blasts of grenades, *panzerfausts,* mortar shells, and artillery. The dead were scattered everywhere.

Graf led the way through the icy storm, avoiding the Russians when possible and fighting them when necessary. Without food, sleep, or hope, they fought for days like wild animals to escape. Somehow, in the chaos of the battle, they found the seam between the boundaries of two Soviet infantry units, exploited this gap, and fought their way out. On January 14, Graf and two of his surviving commandos made it to the German lines with 147 frozen, snowblinded, and bloodied survivors.

These 150 were the only survivors of the entire German force.

When the snowstorm ended and the Russians surveyed Velikiye Luki in the daylight, the snow was colored red. The German defenders lost seventeen thousand killed or wounded and three thousand captured at Velikiye Luki. Blood and courage were not enough. Such was the balance of life and death on the Russian front.

"Graf, are you okay?" Weise questioned.

"How's your hand?" Graf replied, snapping out of his darkest memories.

"Healing nicely," Weise offered as he raised his left hand to show Graf his bandaged hand, still bloodstained and dirty. "I'd report to hospital, but then who would take care of you and the youngsters?"

"*Ja,*" Graf grunted. "Besides, they will only take you if your arm or leg is missing, or you have a big hole in your chest. Walking wounded are returned to the front and usually sent as fillers to the units with the most urgent need for replacements."

"In that case, I will take my risks with you," Weise smiled a toothy grin. "If I must die here, I'd rather die surrounded by my friends."

A lot had happened in seven days, Graf thought as he scratched the stubble of beard on his face. As part of the SS *Kampfgruppe,* he and his men, without rest and with little resupply, had battled American paratroopers from the 101st Airborne Division since the initial attack along Hell's Highway on September 17. The Americans and British had split the German forces east and west of Hell's Highway. The reality of this geometry had kept him separated from von der Heydte's command. Instead, he and his diminished platoon had to suffer under the leadership of SS *Obersturmführer* Carl Kodritz. Kodritz needed everyone who could hold a rifle, and he was not willing to let any man leave the unit.

Up north, the American 82d Airborne Division had seized the bridges over the Waal River and the high ground near Grave and Nijmegen. Allied tanks, slowed but not stopped, had marched steadily up the N69 toward Arnhem.

The only happy story for the Germans was the fighting at Arnhem. There, the British 1st Airborne and an independent Polish Brigade were stopped and chopped up piecemeal by hastily organized *kampfgruppe* from the 9th and 10th SS Panzer Divisions. To support the battle against the veteran British and Polish paratroopers, General Model had brought in reserves, even arranging for some of the monstrous King Tiger tanks to join the assault.

Two nights ago, in a coordinated effort of two mixed armored groups to block Hell's Highway, his *kampf-*

gruppe attacked simultaneously from the east and west side of Highway 69. The corridor that the Allies held was very narrow near Veghel, only fourteen kilometers north of the American landing zones at Son. *Generalfeld-marschall* Model picked this point as the target for the counterattack.

Graf and his men had been part of the attack that hit Hell's Highway from the east. In spite of their best efforts, the attacks to take the town of Veghel failed, but they were able to cut Hell's Highway for a day. The situation was not going well for the Germans, but every minute they blocked Hell's Highway in the south denied the American 82d Airborne at Nijmegen and the British 1st Airborne at Arnhem vital supplies that were needed to sustain the fighting to the north. The Allied advance on Arnhem was now impossible until Hell's Highway was reopened. Accordingly, the British sent a brigade of the Irish Guards back from Nijmegen to Veghel to clear the road and support the 101st from the north.

Then, last night, enemy paratroopers from the 101st Airborne Division and British tanks and infantry from the Irish Guards attacked in force, throwing the Germans back. If the surviving British at Arnhem were to be smashed and a great victory won, Hell's Highway would have to be blocked again.

"Did you hear what Kodritz did this morning?" Weise asked.

Graf shrugged.

"He found three Dutch civilians begging food off his SS men," Weise replied solemnly. "He said they were spies and took out his pistol and shot them. Right in front of the men, right on the spot without as much as a word said. And one was an old woman."

Graf's jaw tightened; his eyes narrowed. By the rules of war, resistance fighters were not eligible for consideration as soldiers. Graf had little pity for partisans who fought with weapons. They were condemned to death automatically, without trial, but ordinary civilians begging for food was another matter. "We will have to account for all this someday."

"Yes. We are the masters today and no one can judge us, but tomorrow?"

SS *Hauptscharführer* Gunter walked up to Graf's position, two SS men with rifles following behind him. "*Oberfeldwebel* Graf, we will move southeast before nightfall. Order your group to assemble at the farmhouse in fifteen minutes."

Graf nodded. "Message received. Be careful, we found land mines in this area this morning."

Gunter glanced at Graf in shock. "Where?"

"At least a dozen of them, in a circle just about where you are standing," Graf explained seriously. "You know the type of mines they are?"

Gunter shook his head but kept his feet perfectly still.

"They are the kind of mines that pop up when you step on them and then blow up about chest level," Graf announced. "Bouncing Betty, I think the *Amis* call them. Nasty things. Will blow your nuts clean off."

Weise's eyes grew wide, and he stared at Graf in disbelief, but didn't say a word.

Oberjäeger Küster smiled, but refrained from laughing out loud. The other *Fallschirmjägers* watched silently.

Gunter whined, "But why didn't you mark the area? What are we to do now?"

"Raise your rifles high, over your heads to avoid trip wires and then back up, carefully, one step at a time," Graf recommended. "But don't worry, if they explode and splatter your body all over the field, we'll report to Kodritz that you died fighting bravely for the Fatherland."

Gunter ignored Graf's last comment but took the warning of the mines to heart. Slowly, Gunter raised his weapon high over his head and ordered the other two SS soldiers to do likewise. Carefully, with deliberate movements, the three SS soldiers backed up, trying to rest their boots in the exact same place where they had stepped while coming forward.

A flicker of glee formed in Graf's eyes as he struggled to hold back a smile. He watched patiently for five minutes while the SS soldiers painfully moved back a few feet the way they had come.

Then, checking his watch, he picked up his PPSh submachine gun.

"*Feldwebel* Weise, inspect the men's weapons while I am gone," Graf ordered. "When I return in thirty minutes, be prepared to move out."

Weise stood at attention in mock discipline for the SS men to see. "*Jawohl, Herr Oberfeldwebel!*"

Graf shook his head smiling. He trotted forward right through the "mined area" passing Gunter and the SS men.

"But the mines?" Gunter exclaimed as his face contorted in fear.

"*Fallschirmjägers* are not afraid of mines," Graf replied with a chuckle, and headed off to the farmhouse.

Weise, Küster, and the other *Fallschirmjägers* burst out in wild laughter.

Gunter, suddenly realizing the ruse, lowered his rifle and stormed off, following Graf.

Graf reached the farmhouse, passed by the SS soldiers on guard in a trench near a stone wall, then entered. Kodritz and an SS major, or *Sturmbannführer* in the SS rank structure, stood over a map table.

The *Sturmbannführer* looked up when Graf entered

the room. "So, you are the *Fallschirmjäger Oberfeld-webel* I have heard about?"

"*Oberfeldwebel* Graf, reporting as ordered, sir."

Red faced with anger, Gunter entered the room ready to approach Graf for the trick he had played on him. Gunter saw the *Sturmbannführer.* Instantly the SS sergeant's demeanor changed, and he remained silent.

The *Sturmbannführer* studied Graf for a moment, gazing at his Russian submachine gun, focusing on the Knights Cross that was barely visible at the neckline of Graf's camouflaged fighting smock. "We have no time for pleasantries. Join us at the map. I have limited time to issue orders."

Graf moved forward and looked at the map. The red arrows depicted separate attacks under way by the Americans and British. The blue arrows indicated the German counterattacks. Graf took particular notice of a blue line that depicted a route of march to the southeast and a blue bridge symbol designating a special operation to counterattack into the Allied flank.

"*Obersturmführer* Kodritz, you will move down this route and secure the western side of the canal here," the *Sturmbannführer* ordered. "Sappers will prepare the crossing. This crossing was destroyed by Allied aircraft a week ago. They will not suspect that we have repaired it."

Kodritz nodded.

"Once the crossing is ready, you will prepare it as we discussed, and I will move the *kampfgruppe* across to the west," the *Sturmbannführer* continued. "We will raise havoc for a day hitting the supply trucks and depots the British have established near Eindhoven and then withdraw."

"Brilliant," Kodritz answered. "It will be a glorious attack and will block the route north for at least a day."

"Yes, but it must happen no later than Monday morning," the *Sturmbannführer* replied. "The British are already moving in the east on Deurne and Helmond. We have only a short window of opportunity, but we must seize it."

Graf took a deep breath. It looked like he and his men would be heading behind enemy lines one more time.

The air smelled of apples, and the temperature was comfortably warm for the first time in days. As the sun inched higher in the east, Mira and Alexander walked their bikes along a dirt trail that lead to the town of Sint-Oedenrode.

"There he is!" Mira announced as she pointed to a boy across the field.

Alexander waved to the teenage boy at the other end of the field. The boy jumped on his bicycle and headed southeast.

"Does Peter know what to do?" Mira asked.

"Yes, I gave him Melanie's instructions, word for word," Alexander replied. He walked a few more steps then stopped his bike and looked at Mira. "You could have told me, you know. Imagine my shock when I met Melanie and saw that 'she' was a man!"

Mira smiled. "I couldn't help it. It was a code name. I had orders not to talk about it."

Alexander shook his head. "You know you can trust me."

"That's not the point," Mira laughed as she poked Alexander in the belly.

Alexander chuckled. "I can never be mad at you."

Mira chuckled. Yes, "Melanie" was a man. As the leader of the Bicyclists, Mira had taken upon herself the dangerous duty of passing information to the Allies. She didn't want Alexander implicated if she was caught by the Nazis. Since the Allies landed in France in June 1944,

Mira had passed dozens of intelligence messages that the Bicyclists had collected to the Allies by placing written messages at a secret drop in a loose brick in the wall near Saint Catherine's Cathedral in Eindhoven. Until yesterday she had not known the contact who picked up those messages.

Yesterday, after meeting "Melanie" for the first time, she learned the name of her contact. It was the silver-haired lady in her forties who had opened her door for them during the bombing. The lady's name was Johanna Halse, and she had taken the information from the Bicyclists, passing it to the British using a TR-4 wireless telegraph. The information that Johanna collected was radioed directly to Melanie.

It troubled Mira deeply to think how many had suffered and died for the freedom of her country. So many good people had opposed the Germans, some in little ways and others, like Johanna Halse, in more substantial ways. If housewives and teenagers could find the nerve to oppose the Germans, then maybe someday, after the entire country was liberated, the Netherlands could be proud of its resistance against the Nazi conquerors.

As sad as Mira felt when she saw the lifeless body of Johanna Halse in the basement of her home on September 19, she was also proud. Johanna's sacrifice was testimony to Mira of the courage of the people of the Netherlands. They had been conquered and occupied, but never beaten.

Mira's thoughts quickly drifted to the task at hand and from Johanna to Melanie, who was actually a Dutch-born American officer named Lieutenant Jan Laverge. Five-foot ten-inches tall, blond-haired, and handsome, the twenty-five-year-old Laverge had responsibilities well beyond his years. He was as charismatic as he was effective at the game of espionage and became the leader of a small group of agents who formed the Netherlands Section of Special Intelligence (SI) of the American Office of Strategic Services, or OSS.

The OSS was an American intelligence organization that helped direct, train, and supply anti-Nazi resistance groups in German-controlled Europe. The OSS focused on special operations. They parachuted agents behind enemy lines, training resistance groups to engage in hit-and-run raids and guerrilla warfare. Less spectacularly, but as important, OSS operatives like Laverge recruited agents in Nazi-occupied Europe to gather information on German leaders, military resources, and troop movements.

Laverge arrived in Eindhoven on September 21, 1944, three days after the liberation of the city, establishing a base of operations in a house at Number 2 Vestdijk Street. He immediately contacted the various Dutch resistance groups using the excellent Dutch telephone system, coordinating and gathering information on the Germans. Laverge contacted Mira, and their reporting network began yielding excellent information almost immediately.

"Do you think Melanie will act on the information we provided?" Alexander asked.

"That is why we are here. This is our chance to do something important for the future of our families and the Netherlands."

Mira's soul swelled with pride as she thought about her Bicyclists and how they had passed on their findings to Lieutenant Laverge. This latest information was important enough to Laverge to cause him to drive to the village of Sint-Oedenrode. The American paratroopers had established their headquarters in the Castle at Sint-Oedenrode. Laverge wanted them to check Mira's report. He also asked Mira if she would volunteer as a guide.

Mira proudly accepted.

Mira and Alexander hopped on their bikes, pedaling a half kilometer down the road to the town of Sint-Oedenrode.

As Mira approached the town, the memory of her father filled her thoughts. It was at Sint-Oedenrode, in May 1940, that her father had fought with other Dutch soldiers to keep the Germans at bay. Her father was killed in a field near Sint-Oedenrode.

Mira pedaled harder, trying to hide the conflict burning in her heart.

She thought about what she had been taught about Sint-Oedenrode. Legend had it that the town was named after a Scottish princess called Oda, who was blind, but miraculously cured. As a result of this miracle, Oda became a Catholic, devoting her life to God. In search of prayer and solitude she traveled to Holland. Eventually she arrived in the little settlement called Rode, which was old-Dutch for "opening in the woods." Princess Oda was kind to everyone she met and beloved by the locals. When she died in AD 726 the villagers decided to call the place Sint-Oda-Rode in her honor. Eventually, the name was modernized to Sint-Oedenrode.

Mira wondered if this legend would bring her luck. If the Princess Oda could be cured of her blindness, maybe this was a sign that the Bicyclists could help the Allies to see what the Germans were up to.

As they rode into Sint-Oedenrode, Mira saw dozens of tough-looking American paratroopers positioned in trenches as well as in some of the homes. Signs of a recent battle were scattered all about, including a smoldering German halftrack.

The Americans had established several checkpoints along the roads. Mira and Alexander were stopped at a

checkpoint just outside the town by a well-armed paratrooper.

"Halt!" The paratrooper ordered, keeping his submachine gun pointed in the air. The man didn't look like
someone to be trifled with. "Speak English?"

"Yes, a little," Mira answered. She noticed that there
was a small white heart painted on the side of the soldier's helmet.

"What do you two want?" the gruff paratrooper
quizzed.

Mira smiled and turned to Alexander. Alexander took
his red notebook from his haversack and Mira retrieved
a special pass and handed it to the American.

The soldier read the paper carefully.

Mira looked to her left at the activity in a nearby field.
A group of American paratroopers guarded eight German prisoners who were digging graves. A line of dead
German soldiers lay next to the wood line. The mounds
of a dozen freshly dug graves were nearby.

"Okay, I guess you can pass," the American announced.

"What happened in this field?" Mira asked.

"The Krauts launched an attack on the town on
Thursday," the soldier replied, "but we held them off.
We killed quite a few and are just now getting around to
burying 'em."

At that moment, a young German soldier, wearing an
unbuttoned jacket and no hat, stopped digging and
looked up at Mira. The boy was no more than nineteen,
probably younger. His face was thin. His cheerless eyes
gazed at Mira in humiliation.

Mira shivered at the sight of the boy digging a grave
for his dead comrades. In spite of the occupation, coupled with her determined opposition to the Nazis and

what they stood for, she could not hate this young soldier, but instead felt sorry for him.

The American paratrooper passed the papers back to Alexander and sent them on their way.

As Mira and Alexander bicycled along the road, they passed a long line of British trucks and jeeps idling bumper to bumper in the road. They continued their trek to the fifteen-century castle that was the temporary home of the 101st Airborne Division Headquarters.

Mira and Alexander stopped at another checkpoint at the road junction near the castle. Once more, Alexander presented the special pass that Melanie had given to the guard. This time, a smiling American paratrooper scanned the pass and without a word, quickly waved them on.

A young, athletic-looking American soldier was waiting for them at the entrance of the castle. The soldier, who worked for Lieutenant Laverge, looked at the two Dutch teenagers. "Miss Vogel? Alexander van Janssen?"

"Yes," Mira answered.

"My name is Corporal Weber. Please park your bikes near the entrance and follow me."

Mira and Alexander moved their bicycles to the side of the castle entrance and followed Weber past two guards standing at the doorway and into the castle. Weber ushered them into the anteroom of a dining area that was now serving as a military planning room.

"Wait until I can get their attention," Corporal Weber whispered.

Mira and Alexander could see inside the room. Lieutenant Laverge stood with his back to Mira, looking at a large map of Holland that had been tacked to the wall. Large red and blue arrows designated the movements of German and Allied units in Operation Market Garden.

An American major chomping on an unlit cigar, with his arms folded across his chest, stood to the right of Laverge. The major listened intently as the OSS officer explained the most recent intelligence scoop from the Bicyclists. Three soldiers, a British officer, a British sergeant, and an American paratrooper, stood silently to the major's right.

Mira and Alexander waited patiently, overwhelmed at being a part of this, the liberation of their country.

"That bridge was destroyed two weeks ago, along with every other crossing along that canal," the major protested, taking the cigar from his mouth and pointing to the area on the map. "I've personally double-checked the photos. There is nothing there. Air recon doesn't show a damn thing."

"Yes sir, but they didn't see the Ninth and Tenth SS Divisions in Holland when we started this operation," Laverge replied, reminding the major of how the unexpected discovery of German armored units in Holland had upset the Allied Market Garden plan. "The Bicyclists saw these enemy units. They reported precise unit locations to us before the start of the operation. We didn't believe them then; however, we'd be fools to disregard them now."

Mira glanced at the soldiers standing next to the major. Mira recognized the American paratrooper as the same American she had kissed on the cheek in Eindhoven near Saint Catherine's Cathedral on the second day of liberation.

"Well, we don't have enough rifle companies to send on wild-goose chases," the major announced.

"Sir, then at least send a reconnaissance patrol to check it out," Lieutenant Laverge offered. "The Dutch resistance has risked their lives to get us this information."

"All right, I'll send a patrol," the major responded. "But it will have to have both an American and a British component. We have responsibility for this area right now, but by Monday that terrain will be handed over to the British to control."

"That makes perfect sense," Lieutenant Laverge replied.

"The question is, where are the main German tank reserves that can reach Hell's Highway?" the major asked. "If what your Dutch resistance folks are telling you is true, then we should expect a major attack soon."

"That's right, Major. From what the Dutch have told me, and from my study of the terrain, I think you should send a patrol to check out the canal from both sides." Laverge answered and waved his arm to show the approach the patrols might take. "And, Major, are these the three you have in mind to lead the patrol?"

"Yes," the major answered as he turned to the men waiting patiently to the side. "This is Lieutenant Palmer of the Fifteenth Hussars and Colour Sergeant Gilchrist."

A thin, tall officer about twenty-three years old snapped to attention and offered a proper British salute. "Second Lieutenant Palmer, at your service."

Laverge nodded. "Excuse me, Major, but why three leaders for two patrols?"

"Palmer will lead a patrol on the eastern side of the canal toward Erp and report any activity he finds," the major announced. "The area on the east will become part of the British Eighth Corps area of responsibility. I have been ordered to keep my 101st boys inside the Thirty Corps area."

"I see," Laverge replied.

"Staff Sergeant Baker is the leader of one of our jeep-mounted reconnaissance squads. Colour Sergeant Gilchrist will be with Baker's team, but because this part of the terrain is still in the 101st area of responsibility, Baker will be in charge."

Baker nodded. Gilchrist snapped to attention.

"Sir, before we begin, could you give us the overall picture of what is going on?" Palmer replied.

"Fair enough," the major answered. "Yesterday was a very bad day, our worst so far. Bad weather delayed our resupply while the Germans attacked in our sector to cut Hell's Highway from the west and from the east. The Krauts seized a largely undefended part of the road between Uden and Grave. In the east the Germans cut the 69th Brigade of the British Fiftieth Northumbrian Division in two and ran down the highway shooting up trucks and supply vehicles."

Palmer, Baker, and Cat studied the map as the major explained the situation.

"With warnings of the German movement provided by the Dutch resistance, we counterattacked and managed to block the German attacks with the 506th Parachute Infantry near Uden and the 502d Parachute Infantry to Veghel. General Horrocks, commander of Thirty Corps, sent a force to clear the road at Veghel. In short, with the help of the Dutch resistance and some tough fighting, we stopped the Krauts cold yesterday, but they blocked Hell's Highway and stopped supplies and equipment from traveling beyond Veghel.

"North of our sector the Eighty-Second Airborne is holding all the bridges along Hell's Highway and fighting off heavy German attack. The lead elements of Thirty Corps are advancing north of Grave. North of Thirty Corps, near Arnhem, the British 1st Airborne is holding on by its fingernails. If Thirty Corps doesn't reach them soon, they're done for.

"I don't think I have to tell you that Hell's Highway is the lifeline for the men of the Eighty-Second in Nijmegen and the British First Airborne in Arnhem. We have to stop the Germans from cutting this route again."

"This is where you come in," Laverge announced. "According to the plan I have worked out with the major, Team One, led by Lieutenant Palmer, will scout the east side of the canal and report any German activity. Team Two, Staff Sergeant Baker and Colour Sergeant Gilchrist, will move to Lieshout, contact the resistance cell there, gather the latest intelligence input from this cell, and then scout the canal from the west side. If either patrol finds anything, you will radio us, and we can respond with a unit to counter the Germans."

The major nodded. "Any questions, gentlemen?"

"I understand we'll have guides from the resistance?" Palmer asked.

"That's correct," Laverge answered. "They'll be of immense help to you as they know the terrain and have contacts in the area who are scouting for German units."

"The important thing is that we check out this report," the major interjected. "If the Germans can cross the canal at this location, we could be in for a very tough time."

"Exactly," Laverge said.

"Both teams will have to move out right away," the major added.

"But can these resistance folks be trusted? I understand they're just kids?" Palmer asked.

"Ahem . . ." Corporal Weber coughed, trying to get Lieutenant Laverge's attention.

Laverge turned around and looked at Mira and Alexander. "Well, why don't you ask them yourself, Lieutenant?"

Lieutenant Palmer turned and blushed.

The major smiled. "Hello, I'm Major Danahy, Division G-two. Please don't take offense at the lieutenant's comment. When my men are at stake, we all have to be confident in who we are betting their lives on."

Mira smiled. In halting English she tried to respond. "We took no . . . offense from . . . your words. We are happy to guide you."

"Well, we're glad to have your help," Major Danahy replied. "Especially since Lieutenant Laverge has told me so much about you."

"We are . . . honored to help," Mira explained, taking time to be sure of her English. "My cousin, Alexander, will go with Lieutenant Palmer. I will go with Sergeant Baker."

Baker stared at Mira for a second.

Lieutenant Laverge smiled. In perfect Dutch he explained to Mira and Alexander that the intelligence information they had provided was important enough to verify and thanked them for their courage. He took them to the map and explained the operation he had planned with the major. Then he introduced Mira to Staff Sergeant Baker and Colour Sergeant Gilchrist.

"We meet . . . before," Mira said as she smiled at Baker. "In Eindhoven."

Baker looked dumbfounded, not recalling how he had met Mira. He turned to Major Danahy. "Sir, please tell me you're joking. You want us to take these kids with us? They should be in school, not riding with us on a combat patrol."

"That's an order, Baker," the major responded without hesitation. "These two know the terrain, and they know where the Krauts are hiding. Besides, this mission is a piece of cake. You'll be back tomorrow morning with a jeep full of apples and schnapps."

"But sir—" Baker protested, but was cut off as Major Danahy raised his hand signifying silence.

"It's a hell of a war, Baker, and we'll use every card in the deck to win it," the major announced. "I've arranged for two demolitions experts from the 326th Airborne Engineers to join your team. They will meet you in about thirty minutes."

"Yes sir," Baker responded.

"Colour Sergeant Gilchrist, you will be under Baker's command until the mission is complete or the British units advancing in the east take control of the area."

"Understood, sir," Cat replied.

"All right, Baker, that's all," the major ordered. "Get cracking, you're already late."

Baker's patrol lined up along a dirt trail beneath a row of poplar trees not far from the castle at Sint-Oedenrode. Colour Sergeant Cat Gilchrist whistled his tune as he leaned against the side of the lead Bren Carrier. His men were loaded up in their vehicles and ready to go.

Guardsman Avery sat in the driver's seat of Cat's Bren Carrier smoking a cigarette. Mira Vogel sat with Guardsman Roy and Guardsman Gaines in the back of the armored vehicle.

Behind this Bren Carrier was Corporal Ackers's Carrier. Alexander van Janssen sat quietly in the back of this carrier, next to Guardsmen Friskin and McNevin. Their bicycles were lashed to the back of their respective vehicles.

Guardsman Roy, a squat, mustached, heavyset Irish Guardsman in his late twenties sat next to Mira, eating a piece of SPAM from a tin can with a pocket knife. He poked a piece with his knife, offering a slab of the meat to Mira. "Missy, care for a bite to eat?"

Mira grinned and nodded. "*Ja. Dankjewel* . . . thank you."

"It's not much, but it will keep your strength up," Roy offered.

Mira took the piece of meat and nibbled on it. "The American sergeant . . . Baker . . . is not happy with me?"

"Don't rightly know, Missy. It's hard to tell with Yanks."

Corporal Ackers climbed down from the Bren Carrier and walked over to Colour Sergeant Gilchrist. "Cat, do these bloody bastards have any idea what they are doing?"

Cat stopped whistling and smiled. "Ask me that question tomorrow."

Baker's jeep was in the front of the three-vehicle column with Corporal Zanovitch in the driver's seat. Baker had left the rest of his reconnaissance squad behind, willing to risk only himself and Zanovitch on a mission he considered a waste of time.

"So where are they?" Zanovitch asked.

Baker shrugged and shook his head in disgust. He checked his watch for the third time. It was already past 1000. "How the hell should I know?"

A few more minutes passed. Formations of C-47 aircraft flew high overhead, traveling north.

Zanovitch pulled a pack of Lucky Strikes from his breast pocket, brought the pack to his mouth, and pulled out a cigarette. Placing the pack back in his pocket he pulled out a Zippo lighter and lit the tobacco. "I sure hope they show up soon. I would hate to miss out on this patrol."

Baker shot Zanovitch a cold glance.

"Sergeant Baker!" Cat shouted. "Look behind you. Our long-lost guests are headed this way."

Baker turned around. Two soldiers carrying heavy packs were trudging toward him from behind the last Bren Carrier.

The two American paratroopers cast curious looks as they passed the British troops and saw a pretty, dark-haired girl in the back of the Bren Carrier.

"You Baker?" A stocky private first class asked, huffing and puffing from the heavy load he carried.

"Staff Sergeant Baker to you," Baker replied. "You're late. What took you so long?"

The two soldiers dropped their packs in the dirt. The soldier replied angrily: "It ain't easy gathering up all the demolitions we were told to bring."

Baker stood silently looking at the two combat engineers. Every pocket of their uniform was stuffed with equipment, ammunition, or rations. The heavy packs at their feet bulged. Baker could see three sticks of TNT sticking out of the top of one of the packs.

"My name is Swanson," the private offered and then turned to his comrade. "This is Haynes."

"I've been waiting for you for two hours," Baker growled. "Did anyone brief you on this mission?"

"Hell no," Swanson answered defiantly. "We were just told to grab as much TNT and C-2 as we could carry and meet you here as soon as we could. Do you want us or not? I'd be happy to turn around and rejoin my unit."

Colour Sergeant Gilchrist stopped whistling and chuckled.

Annoyed, Baker shook his head again. "Nope, no such luck. You're with us. Store your packs on the side of my jeep and mount up, and be sure not to blow us up in the process."

The two paratroopers complied and started to tie a pack to each side of Baker's jeep.

Baker walked over to Cat whispering, "Look, I don't think this patrol will amount to anything, but let's get one thing straight. No unit can have two leaders in charge."

"No arguments from me, Staff Sergeant, my orders are clear," Cat replied. "Now why don't we cut the crap and get moving?"

Baker's face hardened as he returned to his jeep. He climbed into the right-front passenger side and placed his hand on the pistol grip of the .30 caliber machine gun mounted in front of him.

"Crank it up, Zano," Baker ordered. "Let's get this circus on the road."

Zanovitch smiled, turned the starter switch on the dashboard, and pushed down on the ignition button on the floorboard with his right foot. The jeep engine revved to life. The Bren Carriers behind Baker's jeep started their engines as well.

One of the soldiers in the back touched Zanovitch on the shoulder. "Buddy, you might want to put that cigarette out. There's enough explosives in the packs attached to the sides of this jeep to blow us all to Paris and back."

Zanovitch shrugged and took a long puff on his cigarette. "If we're going to die, what a way to go. I ain't never been to Paris."

Baker grimaced at Zanovitch's stubbornness, but he didn't order him to get rid of the cigarette. Instead, he reached for a map lying between the seats, unfolding it on his lap. He then leveled the barrel of the machine gun forward, looked behind to see if the two engineers who were crammed into the backseat were ready to roll, and with a wave of his hand, signaled Zanovitch to move out.

The jeep lurched forward. The Bren Carriers followed in turn with twenty yards between vehicles.

It's going to be a long day, Baker thought.

Baker's Reconnaissance Jeep

7: D+6

In war, all turns on the time factor.
—Sir Basil H. Liddell Hart, military theorist and author

Afternoon, Saturday, September 23, 1944, in a forest overlooking the road to the village of Lieshout:

"I hate the phrase 'a piece of cake,'" Baker said to Zanovitch as the jeep bounced down the narrow trail. "The last time someone told me an upcoming mission would be a piece of cake was just before the beginning of Operation Market Garden."

Zanovitch didn't respond, instead concentrating on driving the jeep.

The sun was high in the sky as Baker considered their plan. Avoid the main road and move through the forests to the village of Lieshout. Make contact with one of Mira's resistance members there. The contact would then give them the latest update on the situation along the canal south of Beek. Check out the area south of Beek and, if needed, blow up any parts of a bridge that could be used to cross troops and vehicles. It seemed simple enough, but in war the simplest tasks often become difficult.

Something about the operation made him uneasy. Maybe it was the haste with which the plan was thrown together, or possibly the issue of working with Mira's resistance group. Maybe it was Mira, or maybe it was just Major's Dahany's reference to "a piece of cake."

Baker remembered something that his father had once told him: something about a map and blocks and a story from the American Civil War.

To the southeast, Baker saw a small puff of black smoke rising above a clump of trees. Suddenly, he remembered the passage he was thinking about. His father had recited a passage from an epic poem by Stephen Vincent Benét. The gist of the passage was that if you take a flat map and moved wooden blocks upon it strategically, the thing looks well; the blocks behave as they should. The poem stated that the science of war was moving live men like blocks and getting the blocks into place at a fixed moment. But it took time to mold your men into blocks, and flat maps turn into country where creeks and gullies hamper your wooden squares. They stick in the brush, they are tired, they straggle after ripe blackberries, and you cannot lift them up in your hand and move them. . . . It is all so clear in the maps, so clear in the mind, but the orders are slow, the men in the blocks are slow to move; when they start, they take too long on the way. The general loses his stars, and the block-men die in unstrategic defiance of martial law because they are still used to just being men, not wood blocks.

Baker's three blocks moved slowly along a narrow logging trail through the woods.

Baker had a funny feeling that his blocks were about to find a gully in their hastily contrived plan. The puff of smoke bothered him. "Zano, pull over there and stop."

Zanovitch drove the jeep to the side of the trail, cutting the engine. Baker climbed out of his jeep, grabbing the map and his Thompson submachine gun. Carefully he crouched forward to the tree line.

To his front was an open field of fire and a macadam

road that led from Lieshout in the southeast to Sint-Oedenrode in the northeast. He could see about four hundred yards.

The Bren Carriers parked in the trees behind Baker's jeep. Swanson and Haynes jumped out, took up firing positions by the side of the jeep, and pointed their M1 rifles to cover the trail.

Cat's Irish Guardsmen deployed next to their vehicles as had the Americans. Cat signaled for his men to wait and slid forward through the trees to Baker.

Baker and Zanovitch lay on the ground, looking to the southeast.

"What do you see?" Cat whispered as he reached Baker and Zanovitch.

Baker pointed to the southeast. "Germans."

Three hundred yards to the southeast two German *panzergrenadiers* sauntered nonchalantly down the road, walking as calmly as if they owned the area. One German carried a submachine gun, the other a rifle. They strolled down the road to the southeast, toward a clump of trees away from Baker and his men.

"I wonder what they're doing out here all by themselves?" Zanovitch offered.

"Probably a reconnaissance patrol," Cat replied.

"We'll leave them alone," Baker answered. "No telling how many there are."

Baker, Zanovitch, and Cat watched patiently as the Germans walked southeast.

"This road leads to Lieshout," Cat announced, looking intently at Baker. "How are we going to get there if we leave these Jerries behind us?"

The two Germans were a hundred yards away from the point where the road entered a clump of trees when the German with the submachine gun signaled to someone. A German halftrack suddenly pulled out of the trees and onto the road. The halftrack drove up to the two German soldiers. The German with the submachine gun yelled some instructions. Then the two men climbed into the halftrack.

"Well, we won't be able to avoid them now," Cat asserted. He pointed to the road and designated the way the Germans would approach their position. "If they follow that road, they'll pass right next to us. If we let them pass, they will end up in Sint-Oedenrode at your division headquarters. What do you want to do?"

Zanovitch nodded. "He's right. If we let these Krauts by us and we carry on to Lieshout, they may turn around and get behind us."

Baker listened and took in the situation. Advice was wonderful, but the decision rested on his shoulders. He knew he had to decide quickly. The enemy would be passing by them in a couple of minutes.

"Deploy the men on line here," Baker ordered decisively. "Zanovitch, get the bazooka."

Cat signaled Ackers to bring the men up. Zanovitch backed up and then ran to the jeep. The bazooka was strapped to the rear of the jeep, and Zanovitch, Swanson, and Haynes worked together to unload it. Zanovitch enlisted Swanson as his loader and handed him three rockets to carry.

The halftrack moved north on the road with a puff of black exhaust smoke shooting out from the rear of the armored vehicle just as Cat's men and Zanovitch reached Baker.

"The road they are on comes toward us and then turns northwest. Wait for them to pass us. Once they take the bend in the road, hit the rear of that halftrack when they are about twenty yards away," Baker ordered. "Think you can make the shot?"

Zanovitch smirked. "At this range, I never miss."

"Everybody down and quiet," Baker ordered. "Hold your fire until I give the word."

The seconds ticked by as the German halftrack slowly moved forward. Baker feared that the Germans might see his men or his line of vehicles in the woods. He waited and watched as his heart pounded loudly in his chest.

The Germans traveled down the road toward Baker and his men. The halftrack had truck tires in front and a track with four road wheels in the rear on each side. The top was open. Baker could see three men in the open troop compartment. One of the men manned a machine gun.

The halftrack clanked by as Baker lay on the ground, concealed from view by the cover of the trees. The vehicle picked up speed, coming within fifteen yards of where Baker and his man hid in ambush. As the vehicle turned at the bend in the road, Baker peeked through the foliage, staring straight into the face of the commander of the halftrack.

Whether the German sergeant saw Baker or not, Baker would never know, but the German saw something and started shouting. The halftrack continued down the road as Baker screamed. "Zanovitch! *Now!*"

Zanovitch jumped out of the woods, ran ten yards, and then knelt on the side of the road.

The halftrack picked up speed and the Germans in the back scurried to turn the machine gun back to the rear.

Zanovitch placed the fifteen-pound launcher on his shoulder, aimed, taking a moment to sight the enemy vehicle in the stadia reticle of his rocket launcher.

Flames shot out of the front and rear of the bazooka as the 2.36-inch rocket grenade jetted from the tube. In a flash of fire and smoke the rocket impacted the rear of the halftrack, a perfect shot. There was a loud ear-popping sound as the round detonated against the rear of the halftrack and the high-explosive shaped charge seared through the halftrack's metal rear doors.

The vehicle lurched forward, as if it had been pushed by a giant hand and stopped. In the smoke and flame, two Germans who survived the initial blast struggled out over the sides. One man's clothes were on fire.

"Fire!" Baker ordered.

His men opened up with rifle and machine-gun fire. The rounds pinged off the metal of the burning halftrack. The two Germans who slid off the left side of the halftrack were easy targets. Every British and American weapon fired at them. The two men fell, riddled with bullets.

In less than twenty seconds it was over.

"Cease-fire!" Baker ordered and then stood up, waving his right hand in front of his face as the signal to cease-fire in order to make sure everyone understood his command.

The men along the ambush line stopped firing. The only sound now was the crackle of the flames and screams from a man inside the halftrack.

Baker heard those screams and guessed that they must be from the driver, who was somehow pinned inside the vehicle.

Thick, oily black smoke formed in a column above the flaming German vehicle.

Cat calmly stood up, walked up to the open compartment of the burning halftrack, and dropped a grenade inside. He dove to the ground, next to the dead German who was still on fire. The grenade exploded with a dull, hollow sound that echoed inside the armored vehicle. There was no more screaming.

Cat walked back to the line where Baker was now standing.

"Was that necessary?" Baker asked.

"If I'm ever trapped inside a burning Bren Carrier," Cat offered icily, "I hope some Jerry will do the same for me."

Baker looked at Cat and then ducked as the ammunition aboard the flaming wreck detonated. Everyone hit the dirt as a shower of sparks flew skyward.

After a minute the fire died down. The shower of sparks ended.

Baker stood up. "Check the bodies. Look for maps or papers. Collect the Kraut weapons and dump the weapons in the forest."

The men moved out and checked the bodies of the dead Germans.

After a few minutes searching, the German weapons were collected and then thrown into the trees.

"No maps or documents, Baker, other than pay records," Zanovitch reported.

Baker acknowledged Zanovitch's report. "Let's mount up. Move back to the vehicles."

Baker walked back to the jeep and found Mira standing in the logging trail, observing the action.

"Everyone . . . is all right?" Mira asked.

Baker ignored her question. "Get back in the vehicle."

"I will pray for them," Mira offered.

"For the Germans?" Baker argued.

"Yes, even for the Germans," Mira answered as she looked into his eyes, as if she was searching for something.

Baker turned away. "All right men, let's move it."

The men collected their gear and moved to their vehicles.

Swanson and Haynes helped Zanovitch tie the bazooka to the back of the jeep.

"That was a damn good shot, Corporal," Swanson offered Zanovitch.

Haynes laughed. "Yeah, Swanson bet me five bucks that you would miss."

"You're wasting your money betting against me, Swanson," Zanovitch chided the engineer. "I told you, at this range, I can't miss. That makes two kills in as many days."

"Impressive," Haynes replied. "Okay, Swanson, pay up."

"How about a Kraut watch instead," Swanson said with a grin. "The last owner doesn't need it anymore."

Haynes shook his head. "No dice. Pay up. Cash."

Swanson pulled a wallet out of his left pants pocket and reluctantly handed Haynes five dollars.

"That is my last dollar," Swanson said sadly.

"So where are you going to spend it here?" Haynes chided.

Baker listened to the banter but felt hollow. He realized that but for the luck of seeing a puff of black vehicle exhaust above the trees, it could have been his men on fire and lying dead in that field. He recognized that in combat, life and death turned on the blink of an eye.

Cat came up behind Baker. "That was a reconnaissance patrol and the Jerries sent them this way for a reason. We should be careful how we enter Lieshout."

Baker turned to face Cat. "Okay, what do you suggest?"

"We should approach the town from two directions," Cat suggested.

"Split up?" Baker questioned.

"Yes, temporarily. I'll take my Bren Carriers down the road, the same way the Germans came at us. We'll spread out and be ready for a fight," Cat offered. "You take your jeep south, through the trees, and come in from the west. They won't see you coming. If there are any Jerries in the town, we'll hold the blokes by the shirt while you kick them in the pants."

Baker considered the plan and smiled at the analogy. "Agree. If there is any firing, we will both move to the sound of the guns to support the other and flank the enemy. If there is no contact, I'll meet you in the town square."

Cat nodded. "You'll need to move out first, since it will take you longer to go through the woods. I'll move from here in twenty minutes. In the meantime, I'll report this incident to headquarters."

Baker checked his watch and nodded. "Zanovitch, Swanson, Haynes! Mount up, we're moving out."

Baker's jeep moved south, along another narrow logging trail.

Oberjäger Küster put his finger on the trigger of his FG-42 automatic rifle. He heard someone talking in English up ahead. He waited patiently, listened some more, and then crawled toward the sound. Moving as carefully as he dared and ready to fire at a split-second's notice, he inched forward on his belly until he could see his prey.

Fifteen meters in front of him were two British Bren Carriers, parked one behind the other. A helmeted British soldier stood to the right side of the nearest Bren Carrier. The man was talking on the radio. Two British soldiers knelt near this man with their weapons pointed down at the ground. In the second Bren Carrier, a British soldier and a Dutch civilian sat in the troop compartment.

Küster smiled. He had caught the British with their guard down. There wasn't any security posted away from the Bren Carriers, plus there were no signs that the British expected contact.

Küster inched his way back five meters behind some thick vegetation, careful not to give himself away. When he felt that he could move unobserved, he ran at a crouch about thirty meters to a wall of cut wood that lined the logging trail.

The young corporal sprinted behind the logs and found *Oberfeldwebel* Graf, *Feldwebel* Weise, and the seven other *Fallschirmjägers* who were the survivors of the squad.

"Report," Graf ordered.

Sweat rolled down from Küster's forehead. The youngster was worn out from his exertions to return safely and quickly to the squad, not to mention the fatigue of a week of desperate close combat, yet his eyes were eager. "There are six to eight British soldiers and two Bren Carriers parked along the logging trail, fifty meters . . . due northwest of here. The leader is on the radio, making a report."

"A vehicle-mounted reconnaissance patrol," Weise offered. "The Tommies must be getting ready to move into this area to widen the route to the north. We'll have to act fast if we expect to catch them before they move out."

Graf nodded and patted Küster on the shoulder. "Good work, *Oberjäeger* Küster."

Küster offered a slender grin and beamed with pride at his sergeant's compliment.

"Attention men," Graf ordered. The *Fallschirmjägers* turned toward the *Oberfeldwebel*. He looked at their tired faces. Graf knew he was going to ask them to obey him one more time. He knew they all would, without question, and hoped that he would not lose any in the process. "We hit them hard and fast. Küster, you lead me and the rest back to the position where you saw the Tommies."

Küster nodded.

"Weise, form an oblique firing line with the machine gun. Once Küster brings us to the position I will deploy you and Stöhr to the left to set up the MG42. You will have Henning and Wigand as support."

Weise assented.

"How many rounds do we have for the MG42?" Graf questioned.

"Three hundred," Stöhr replied.

"Short bursts," Graf ordered. "Just as *Feldwebel* Weise has trained you."

Stöhr nodded. "*Jawohl, Herr Oberfeldwebel.*"

"The rest of you will be with me. I will initiate the attack with a grenade. No shooting," Graf explained. "Weise, when the grenade goes off, you open fire. When I throw the second grenade, you and your men will cease-fire."

"It will be done," Weise replied.

"Then we will rush in and finish them off," Graf explained. "None of them must get away."

"Prisoners?" Weise asked.

"If any survive the assault, take them prisoner," Graf replied. "Prisoners are secondary to safety. I will not lose any more men for the sake of a Tommy prisoner."

The *Fallschirmjägers* listened intently. In a few seconds, they would be in combat again.

"*Oberjäger* Küster, you will lead," Graf ordered. He looked down at his PPSh-41 submachine gun and clicked the safety to "fire." "Safeties off."

All the *Fallschirmjägers* complied and each soldier switched their weapon safety mechanism to "fire."

"Surprise is with us. No one gets hurt," Graf declared. "Patrol formation. Move out."

*   *   *

The jeep drove down the logging trail lined with tall evergreens, the air filled with the scent of pine. The sun was shining. If it wasn't for the war, Baker thought, this would be a beautiful day.

Zanovitch was at the wheel with Baker riding shotgun with the .30 caliber machine gun fixed to the hood of the jeep. Haynes sat behind Zanovitch with a Thompson submachine gun. Swanson sat behind Baker with an M1 rifle.

The four Americans were ready for a fight, but Baker hoped to avoid one.

The sun was pleasantly warm as the jeep drove on. Baker tried to keep alert, but his thoughts jumped from Cat, who he considered an arrogant Irish son-of-a-bitch, to the look on Mira's face as she said she would pray for the Germans.

Baker couldn't understand Mira's comment and, at the same time, he wanted to. His experience since D-Day in Normandy, nearly four months ago, convinced him that there was no sense to life, It was all random chance. Life and death, love and hate, past and future were all lies that we convinced ourselves to believe. Praying for the Germans, the people he was trying to kill, didn't make sense.

The only thing that mattered was the here and now. The only thing that mattered was to kill the enemy and keep his own men alive. If he was the only one killed in an entire army of a million men, in one of the greatest battle in history, the victory would have no interest to him. He'd be dead. The rest was idealistic crap.

But he knew that isn't what his father would tell him or his friend George Risner. His father had been a true soldier. He saw things with a clarity that Baker never understood. His friend George was an idealist. George and Mira would have gotten along well together, he mused.

A year ago he might have felt the same way. A year ago, he might have fallen for a girl like Mira, even though she was a few years younger than he was. But that was a year ago. A lot had happened since then.

Both of these people, the father he never understood and the best friend he couldn't save, were dead, and for what? The war went on, as if they had never existed.

The thought of the men he had seen die flared through his mind like a meteor shower burning across the midnight sky. He had seen so much death, so many bright lights that had turned black and cold.

He didn't want to die in Holland, or have any more of his men die, for just a trifle, for something as simple as looking up to see a bird singing in a tree as a sniper found his mark. He didn't see the logic in it, but then figured that war had no logic; if it did, it had a dark, impenetrable logic all its own.

The important thing, he had learned, was to stay focused on the task at hand and not to think too much about it all. His mind had to focus on the next tree line or the next possible location of a German ambush, not on thoughts of dead men or, for that matter, women.

"Baker, you okay?" Zanovitch asked.

"Yeah, slow down as we approach those trees," Baker ordered.

Zanovitch turned the wheel as he followed the winding trail at ten miles an hour.

Baker aimed the barrel of the .30 caliber machine gun to the front. His finger wasn't on the trigger, but the weapon was locked and loaded, with safety off, and in an instant he would be ready to send a short-belt of fifty .30-06 bullets at anything that looked like a German.

The radio in the jeep crackled. Baker reached for the

earphone of the radio headset. He could hear Cat giving the report of the ambush of the German halftrack to the intelligence section at 101st Airborne Division Headquarters.

Ahead, the trees began to thin. Baker put down the earpiece and raised his left hand to signal Zanovitch to slow down.

The jeep slowed as the church steeple of Lieshout appeared in the distance. Baker raised his left hand in a clenched fist, signaling Zanovitch to stop.

As the vehicle rolled to a stop, Baker grabbed his Thompson submachine gun and stepped out of the jeep.

"Zano, come with me," Baker ordered. "We'll move to the edge of the trees and see what we can see. You two stay here. Monitor the radio."

Baker signaled for Zanovitch to follow him to the edge of the woods. As they reached the edge, they crawled on their bellies.

In front of them was an open field that had been freshly harvested. The furrows were dug in long, even lines paralleling the edge of the village. Lieshout was two hundred yards ahead.

Baker looked at the terrain. The ground was completely open. Whoever crossed that field was at the mercy of any guns that might be in the town.

There was no sign of enemy activity.

Baker took out a pair of binoculars from the leather pouch on his left side and scanned the town from left to right. The church, the tallest building in the town, was near the center. He carefully searched the church tower and then followed the outline of the town to the southeast, going over every house. He saw one elderly woman hanging laundry out of a second-story window.

He inspected the town again, looking for the telltale

glitter of a sniper scope or the reflection of the sun in a set of field glasses.

Nothing.

A line of telephone poles led along the road in and out of the town. He observed the exit to the town. An old man walked along the southeast approach to the town, herding a cow. Everything looked routine.

"See anything?" Zanovitch asked.

Baker shook his head. "I don't see any Germans, only a farmer herding a cow and a lady hanging laundry. Looks peaceful enough."

"Do you think that halftrack was on its own, like us?" Zanovitch asked.

Baker shrugged his shoulders. "That's my guess."

"They were from an SS unit. They must have been up to something," Zanovitch announced.

"You're right," Baker replied. "But I don't see anything in the town."

"Well, what do you want to do now?" Zanovitch questioned.

Baker checked his watch. "The Brits will be moving out. Let's get back to the jeep and push into town."

Baker and Zanovitch crawled back a few feet, then rose to a crouch and ran back to the jeep.

It was a demoralizingly beautiful day. If Graf was prone to pray, he would have prayed for rain and fog.

High above, a formation of Allied planes flew east to bomb the Fatherland.

Graf looked up at the formation of bombers and observed the tops of the trees gently swaying in the breeze.

Oberjäger Küster signaled to Graf that they had arrived near the enemy position. Without a sound, Graf signaled for Weise to deploy as they had planned.

Graf waited for several tense moments as he listened to the enemy talking.

Finally, Weise and the machine gun were set and the signal was passed up the line to Graf.

It was time to fight.

Graf listened for another moment to the voice talking in English.

Unbeknownst to his men, and especially to the chattering "professor" Weise, Graf was an educated man. In 1932, he graduated from the University of Berlin with a degree in English. From 1932 to 1936 he lived and studied in the United States at the University of Chicago. In 1936, fluent in English, he returned to Germany and mastered Russian.

Since then, his studies were all martial. The days when he was a student in America seemed like a distant dream. His language abilities came in handy during his time in the Brandenburg Commandos, but his reason for joining them was something altogether different.

Since those long, lost days, Graf had suffered a great deal in the war. To survive, he had steeled his soul. He could no longer conceive of a life without duty, responsibility, and battle. He promised himself he would think about other things after the war.

The way the war was going, however, he believed he wouldn't have to worry about life "after the war."

Graf raised his hand and signaled for the men behind him to move forward, one section to the right and one to the left of his position.

Six *Fallschirmjägers* crawled quietly forward, two to the right and three to the left of the *Oberfeldwebel*.

The confident English voice continued to talk, unaware there was danger so near. Graf could hear the conversation and realized that the British soldier was making a radio transmission.

Graf placed his PPSh next to him and reached for an M39 grenade in his pocket.

He checked one more time to his left and right to make sure his men were ready. The *Fallschirmjägers* to his left and right lay on their bellies with their weapons pointed in the direction of the British.

Graf held the *eihandgranate* in his right hand, unscrewed the cap with his left, and then jerked the pull lanyard, igniting the fuse.

The grenade puffed a whiff of smoke and the fuse sizzled. Graf held the grenade for a second and then lobbed it over the foliage toward the voice making the radio call.

"Grenade!" a voice shouted in English and a millisecond later, the grenade exploded.

There was a piercing blast, followed by the deadly ripp . . . ripp . . . ripp sound of the MG42 machine gun.

Graf smiled as he pulled the second grenade from his pocket. Stöhr was doing as ordered. Short bursts.

"I'm hit," a voice shouted in English.

The machine gun continued its killing tune: ripp . . . ripp . . . ripp. Bullets ricocheted off metal and more voices shouted in English.

Graf threw the second grenade a bit to the left of the first and reached for his PPSh.

The grenade detonated in a shrill blast. A man screamed.

"*Fallschirmjägers* up! At them! Assault fire!" Graf ordered.

The line of *Fallschirmjägers* stood up as one and opened fire. They walked forward like a wall of death, keeping on line so as not to mask one another's fire.

As he broke into the open ground Graf could see three dead British soldiers lying in the mud. A man inside one of the Bren Carriers popped up from behind the protection of the armored sidewall and fired a quick shot at Graf. The shot missed. Graf turned his PPSh on the man and riddled him and the Bren Carrier with bullets.

A British soldier and a Dutch civilian who had been hiding behind the Bren Carriers ran off into the woods. Graf ran forward, took aim, and dropped them both with a quick burst of his submachine gun.

The skirmish was over. Graf stood in between the two Bren Carriers. "Cease-fire! Security perimeter! Küster, three o'clock. Berna, six o'clock. Merckel, nine o'clock. Dörnefeld, twelve o'clock. Check the bodies. I want all their papers and maps. Gather supplies, especially food, water, and medical."

The *Fallschirmjägers* responded immediately to Graf's orders. Security was posted at all four points of the compass. The men not pulling security searched the bodies of the dead British soldiers. There were seven dead soldiers and one Dutch civilian.

"Recon Team this is Kangaroo. Say again last message," the radio speaker announced.

Graf stepped over the dead British leader and looked into the Bren Carrier for the transmitter. He grabbed the transmitter and pushed the talk button. In English he responded: "This is Recon Team. All is well. I must get off the radio now. Out."

Weise looked at Graf. "What did you tell them?"

"I told them that all was well and that I couldn't talk to them right now," Graf explained. "Do you think you can find two of our lads to drive these things?"

"You know I can," Weise replied. "I'm tired of walking."

Graf pushed the magazine release on his PPSh forward

and removed the drum. Slowly, he sat down against the side of the Bren Carrier, took out a bag of ammunition from the pocket of his camouflage smock, and started refilling the magazine with bullets.

As he filled the magazine he stared at the dead British soldier who had been talking on the radio. The man lay facedown in a wide pool of thick, brownish-colored blood. In his left hand, the dead soldier gripped a British Sten submachine gun.

Weise walked up to the dead British leader and started checking his pockets.

"You should take that British Sten gun," Graf proposed to Weise and pointed to the weapon lying next to the dead British leader. "It's better in a fight than the MP40 you carry."

Weise shrugged. "Maybe so, but I like my submachine gun. It's a good German-made weapon."

Graf snorted. "You can lay low and fire from the prone position with a Sten. The magazine feeds to the side. With an MP40 you can lay no lower than the length of the magazine."

"That could be," Weise replied with a look of disbelief, "but I'd rather find more of that medical sulfur powder for my hand."

"Good luck," Graff offered. "That's an American luxury. You won't find it on the Tommies."

Weise continued to rifle through the dead man's pockets. Finally he looked up at Graf and smiled, as he displayed two packets of sulfur powder.

Graf shook his head and laughed.

"*Feldwebel* Weise! Food rations!" *Jäger* Henning announced. "An entire squad ration box!"

"Do you hear that, Graf, at least we will not go hungry tonight," Weise said with a smile.

"Distribute the rations among the men," Graf ordered. "Pick up anything you think you can use. Hurry, we must move out quickly."

At that moment, young *Oberjäger* Küster came from the woods, dragging the dead civilian by the heels. He stopped near Graf and laid the body at Graf's feet. The body was riddled with several bullet holes in the back. The civilian had died instantly. Graf looked down at the dead civilian without remorse.

"What a pity," Küster announced with a hint of regret, as he turned the body over. "*Herr Oberfeldwebel,* how old do you think this partisan is?"

"Old enough," Graf replied as he glanced at the body and then continued loading shells into the PPSh drum magazine. "Any documents?"

"No papers on this one," Küster replied.

"I took this off their leader," Weise said as he handed Graf a brown-covered British military identity card. "He's from a British reconnaissance unit. His name is Second Lieutenant Palmer."

Zanovitch gunned the engine racing the jeep across the dirt field.

Baker attempted to aim the barrel of the .30 caliber machine gun forward as the jeep bounded across the plowed field, but he was having a tough time of it. Swanson and Haynes held on for dear life as the jeep jumped skyward hitting each successive furrow.

Baker pointed to a side alley entrance to the left. Zanovitch turned the jeep and stopped when they reached the side of a tall, gray house.

"Damn Zanovitch! Did you have to hit every bump in the field?" Haynes complained. "My ass will never be the same."

Zanovitch spit on the road. "You're ass might have been full of holes if the Krauts were in this town and hit us in that open field. Consider yourself tenderized but unwounded."

Swanson laughed. "I told you we'd make it to the town without getting shot. You owe me five bucks!"

"We ain't in the town square yet," Haynes countered.

"Do you guys bet on everything?" Zanovitch asked.

"Most things," Haynes replied. "We've been swapping those five dollars back and forth since Normandy."

Baker shook his head. "Let's focus on the mission, boys. Dismount."

Baker snatched his Thompson submachine gun and walked to the corner building. He peeked out at the main street and slowly searched the narrow lane for signs of danger.

Haynes and Swanson lined up behind Baker with their backs to the cold, stone wall, their weapons ready.

"See anything?" Swanson asked.

Baker shook his head and then looked back at Zanovitch. "Follow us in the jeep about ten yards behind. Haynes, you take the lead on the left side of the street. Swanson, you follow me on the right."

Baker raised his Thompson to fire as Haynes crossed the alley. Haynes made it across without incident and Baker signaled for the patrol to move out.

Slowly, they advanced down the winding alley with Zanovitch trailing behind. The alley opened into a street.

As Baker walked forward a window suddenly opened above him.

"Take cover!" Baker shouted as he swung to the ground and pointed his Thompson at the open window.

An old man looked down on him and smiled. *"Bevrijding!"*

Baker's heart stopped for a moment, and he breathed a heavy sigh. "I almost shot you, you fool."

The man continued to smile at Baker, and then his head popped back inside.

Baker stood up as Haynes and Swanson smiled.

"You're fast on the draw," Swanson offered.

Baker shook his head. "The old coot's lucky I didn't blast him."

The old man reemerged from the window and hung out a long orange sheet. *"Bevrijding! Bevrijding!"*

Windows opened across the street. Anxious faces appeared and curious looks turned to joy. Orange-colored cloth started to appear everywhere.

"Liberation!" a gray-haired lady shouted from her window. "The Americans are here!"

The word must have spread through the town like fire in a paper mill. In minutes, every window and door was opened and people started pouring outside. Dutch men, women, and children greeted Baker, Swanson, Haynes, and Zanovitch like conquering heroes.

Baker smiled to keep up appearances but was upset by the disruption. "You're welcome. Yes, liberation. We are happy for you, but we have a mission to complete."

A thin, gray-haired lady stepped forward and kissed Baker on the cheek.

"I think she likes you, Sarge," Haynes joked.

Baker shot Haynes a malevolent look and gently pried the woman away. "Excuse me, ma'am. We have to go to the village center. . . . The village center."

The woman smiled. *"Dank u wel!"*

Zanovitch grinned from ear to ear as men patted him on the back and women reached over to kiss him while he slowly drove the jeep down the street.

Baker and his men traveled through a small sea of

joyous people, down the narrow street toward the village center. When Baker turned the corner, he saw Cat and his Irish Guardsmen surrounded by jubilant, cheering townsfolk.

The village square was filled with nearly a hundred people. There was a small stone fountain in the center of the square with people singing and laughing.

Baker was annoyed. This was not in the plan. The blocks that were supposed to move across the map were getting stuck again. The Bren Carriers were lined up in front of the fountain, facing southeast, but the crowd was all around them, and Cat's soldiers were totally consumed in the celebration.

"Where did all these people come from?" Baker asked as he walked toward Cat.

Cat shrugged. "Must be full of refugees from the fighting in other villages. Any sign of Jerry?"

"No. Not a lick."

Some of the people had orange bands of cloth on their left arm to show the colors of their country. A few of the townsfolk handed out wine, apples, peaches, pears, and tomatoes to Baker and his team.

Haynes stood next to Baker, who was next to an old man pouring wine from a bottle into a small glass.

"Hey, Baker, you should try some of this. It's really good." Haynes offered.

"Maybe later," Baker replied.

Mira was standing behind Cat and stepped forward. She had a wide smile on her lips. "This is my hometown. Everyone is happy that the Germans are gone!"

"Hey, Swanson, where's that five bucks?" Haynes shouted.

"All right, you win," Swanson replied.

"Mira," Baker asked. "When do we meet your contact?"

"He should be here, somewhere," Mira answered happily as she searched the faces in the crowd.

Baker turned away. Something made the hairs on the back of Baker's neck stand up. He hated this feeling, but he had learned to trust it. In the center of the commotion he looked up to scan the buildings surrounding the square. A flash of light from the reflection of the sun on a piece of glass caught his eye.

Before he could react a shot rang out that echoed in the town square.

Haynes dropped the glass of wine and jolted backward, falling into Swanson's arms.

"Oh my God!" Swanson yelled.

The celebration stopped as the Dutch civilians panicked and ran for cover in every direction. Many fell to the ground or took cover behind the fountain. A few stood there in shock, looking around.

A woman who lay next to Haynes's lifeless body started screaming. Most of Haynes's face was gone.

Mira was one of those standing motionless with a look of terror disfiguring her attractive face.

In a flash, without thinking, Baker lunged toward Mira and pulled her down to the ground. As he pulled her to the ground, his Thompson shuddered violently in his left hand. He looked at his weapon and realized that a round had struck it in the butt, shattering the wood, and missing Baker by inches.

"Sniper, church tower!" Baker shouted.

Cat took cover behind a Bren Carrier. "Covering fire!"

The British soldiers rushed behind the nearest Bren Carriers and blasted away at the bell tower.

Baker pulled Mira behind Cat's Bren Carrier. "Stay down and stay here!"

Mira looked at Baker with a face full of fear. "Yes."

Shots echoed in the square as the British and American soldiers fired at the church tower. Dust and pieces of red brick fell from the tower as the bullets tore away at the belfry. Somehow, in spite of the overwhelming amount of fire, the sniper managed to fire again.

The round struck inches away from Colour Sergeant Gilchrist.

"Bloody hell!" Cat shouted as he ducked behind the protection of the Bren Carrier. "Roy, get that Bren Gun firing!"

Guardsman Roy reached over the side of the armored vehicle, pulled the Bren light machine gun off the front of the vehicle, and quickly put the gun into action.

Baker looked for a new weapon. He glanced at Haynes's body, which lay out in the open, and saw the dead soldier's Thompson lying on the ground. The Thompson was just out of Baker's reach. Baker crawled out to grab the weapon. Just as he did, the sniper fired, again barely missing Baker's hand.

Baker drew back for a second, then lunged forward, and caught the web sling of the Thompson in his right hand and pulled it in. Rolling back to cover, he crawled back behind the Bren Carrier next to Mira. He checked the magazine of the Thompson and charged the weapon.

"At least one in the church tower!" Baker shouted. "Anyone see any more?"

"No," Cat yelled back. "But the bloody church could be full of 'em."

Baker hesitated. He needed a rallying point, a rallying point from which to draw confidence and courage, a rallying point that would get him and his men through this Hell.

He was afraid that his rallying points were vanishing.

He knew what must be done but wondered if his well of courage was deep enough. His father had done it and made it look easy. Mac had done it and had provided him with a rallying point to hang on to when he was staring into the abyss near Carentan at Bloody Gultch. These men and others had given him courage and examples.

In Normandy, somehow, he had done it, but he didn't know how he did it, or worse, if he could do it again.

At that moment, a bullet snapped by his ear. It came so close that he felt it whizzing past.

Suddenly, he found his rallying point.

"Cover me!" Baker shouted as he jumped up, running toward the church.

Cat saw Baker run forward. "Covering fire. Damn it, covering fire! Church tower!"

Zanovitch and Swanson popped up from behind a Bren Carrier, plastering the church belfry with bullets. The British did the same and fired a mad volley at the openings to the bell tower.

Baker ran like a football fullback, zigzagging left and right toward the church, until he reached the front doors.

The sniper fired again, hitting the Bren Carrier where Cat was crouching.

"Damn it. Cover me!" Cat screamed as he sprang up and raced behind Baker, reaching the church entrance a moment after Baker.

The two men stood near the church doors, their backs to the brick wall.

"You trying to be a hero?" Cat asked angrily.

Baker didn't answer. He kicked open the door, leveling his submachine gun as he quickly scanned the inside of the church for Germans. "Bloody hell," Cat exclaimed and followed to Baker's left side.

Not seeing anyone inside, Baker walked forward aiming his Thompson at an open door situated to the left of the altar.

As the two men moved toward the altar, Baker heard the sound of someone coming down the stairs. Suddenly, a German burst through the door to the left of the altar. The German stopped at the opening when he saw Cat, pointed his MP40 at him, and fired.

Cat fell backward as Baker fired.

The German was thrust against the wall of the church as a dozen bullets from Baker's submachine gun struck the German in the chest. As the German fell, he fired a long, wild burst from his weapon. The bullets fired inches above Cat's head, shattering a large stained-glass window.

Cat looked up and then looked behind at the window, breathing a sigh of relief.

"You okay?" Baker asked, nonchalantly.

"Yeah. I slipped."

"Looks like you're running out of lives, Cat," Baker chided.

"Twenty pounds says I'm not," Cat replied.

"Make it ten. I'm only a poor sergeant," Baker said.

"And I thought all you Yanks were rich," Cat answered as he rose from the floor and checked his weapon.

Baker cautiously moved toward the dead German. There were four large holes in the man's chest and a pool of blood forming on the wooden floor. The man's eyes—Baker thought he looked as if he were nineteen or twenty—were wide open, staring at nothing. Baker saw that the German had an SS emblem on the side of his helmet.

He looked up and saw the metal spiral steps that led to the belfry. He took a moment to reload his Thompson submachine gun.

Cat moved up behind him. "If that sniper is still in the tower, he probably knows we're coming for him."

Baker nodded and started up the metal stairs. Cat shook his head in disbelief and followed close behind.

Baker heard the sound of the firing outside. His men and the British were keeping up a continuous covering fire on the church tower. The steady sound of a British Bren Gun was reassuring.

Baker climbed up the spiral stairway to the level just below the belfry. The trapdoor to the belfry was open.

Baker looked at Cat and pointed to the left and right of the ceiling and whispered: "You fire left. I'll fire right. We both fire, on three."

Cat nodded.

Suddenly a stick grenade fell down through the open door and clanked against the metal steps.

The grenade landed at Cat's feet. The grenade hissed as the fuse burned.

Baker quickly kicked the grenade down the stairs with the toe of his right boot.

The grenade bounced down the metal stairs with a sinister sound. Baker and Cat hugged the walls of the stairway as the grenade detonated on the ground floor.

Steel fragments ricocheted off the metal stairs. Smoke and dust rose from the explosion, but when the dust cleared, Baker and Cat were still standing.

Cat looked at Baker and breathed a sigh of relief.

Baker pointed back at the ceiling. "One, two, three!"

Baker and Cat fired though the floorboards at the same time and kept firing until the magazines of their submachine guns were empty. When his weapon's magazine was through, Baker dropped his Thompson and quickly drew the .45 caliber pistol from the holster on his right side. He took a deep breath and rushed up the final flight of stairs screaming at the top of his lungs.

There were five shots, some from a loud American .45 caliber pistol and others from a German 9mm pistol.

Cat reloaded his Sten gun. As he snapped the magazine in place, he heard the sound of a body above him hit the floor with a loud thud.

"Baker?" Cat shouted.

U.S. M1A1 Thompson Submachine Gun

8: D+6

According to The Hague Convention (IV, 1907) the following are considered as soldiers: All armed persons wearing uniforms or a badge which can be clearly distinguished from a distance.
—Printed in German on a surrender leaflet dropped
by Allied aircraft in September 1944

Afternoon, Saturday, September 23, 1944, in the village of Lieshout:

In the war movies, they make death look heroic. In reality, it isn't that dignified.

Baker was on the floor of the belfry staring at the man he had just killed.

It all happened in an instant. When he had rushed up the stairway, he lunged forward, drenched in adrenaline, firing his .45. Sailing through the air as he fired, Baker flopped onto the hardwood floor, landing on his right side.

The German sniper had already been hit from the shots that he and Cat had fired through the floorboards, but when Baker came up the stairs, the German was still alive and sitting with his back against the redbrick wall of the belfry, wounded in the leg and abdomen. Unwilling to surrender, the German sniper had pulled out a Luger pistol, aiming it at the opening in the floor, ready to fire at anyone who might emerge.

The German fired as Baker appeared, but the German's aim was off.

Baker's aim was true.

As Baker lunged through the opening, he fired fast and hit the German in the chest with his first shot. In rapid succession, Baker finished him off with three more shots as he crashed to the floor.

A .45 caliber pistol makes big holes in people.

When it was all over, Baker sat up and looked at the dead sniper. The German's *Stahlhelm* helmet was adorned with the white lightning bolt insignia of the SS. The man looked to be in his early twenties. The German's chest, dripping with brown-red blood, was ripped open from the slugs from Baker's .45. The German lay on his right side, the Lugar still in his lifeless right hand.

Blood covered the floor.

To the sniper's left was a K-98k bolt-action rifle with sniper scope. Several long, 8mm brass shell casings from the sniper's rifle lay on the floor and seemed to connect with the blood.

"Baker!" Cat yelled.

"All clear," Baker replied.

Cat poked his head up from the opening in the floor, Sten gun first, ready to fire. He saw the dead German and then looked over to Baker. "Bloody hell, are you all right?"

Baker gave a weak nod of his head.

At that moment, a burst from a Bren Gun struck the outside of the brick wall of the belfry, sending red dust and brick chips flying though the air.

"Cease-fire!" Cat bellowed. "Damn it. *Cease-fire!*"

"Cease-fire men!" Corporal Ackers shouted from below. "Cat, is that you? Are you all right?"

"Damn it! I'll be a might better if you stop shooting at me," Cat growled back. Cat climbed up the remaining stairs and crouched over to the tower wall. "I'm standing up now, and if any of you bastards fires at me, I will personally kick your bloody asses all the way back to Donegal!"

"Weapons down, on safe," Ackers ordered. "Everyone cease-fire."

Cat cautiously peeked over the edge of the belfry and then stood up. He looked down at his men and waved. After a moment, Cat turned to Baker offering his hand. "Thanks . . . for saving my hide down there."

Baker didn't answer, but took Cat's hand and pulled himself up.

For a moment the two lions were face-to-face, eye-to-eye. Any animosities they had felt toward each other in the past were now forgotten. Now, through the crucible of combat, they were brothers in arms.

Baker turned and looked down at the village square. Haynes's body lay near the right of the fountain. A Dutchman lay prone to the left of the fountain, facedown in the road. The sniper had claimed two victims.

The townspeople came back to the street, standing around the two fallen men.

"So why did you do it?" Cat asked.

"What, save your life?"

"No, I assume you did that because of our deep friendship," Cat mocked. "Why did you rush the church by yourself? Are you trying to get yourself killed? Who do you think you are? You're a squad leader, not a one-man army."

Baker glanced at Cat for an extended, silent moment before answering. "I'm very, very tired of seeing my men killed."

Cat didn't reply. The look in Baker's eyes said volumes.

Baker looked down to his side and fumbled with the binoculars from the leather case at the left side of his web belt. Bringing the binoculars to his eyes he searched the area to the southeast for the enemy. He didn't realize that his hands were trembling.

Cat noticed, but didn't say anything.

Mira would be seventeen in another month, but she felt much older. You have to grow up fast when your father is killed when you are twelve and your mother is bedridden with grief, Mira thought. War ages you more than any other event or experience.

Mira wore a knee-length gray coat over her simple gray dress and white blouse. Her shoes were sturdy black leather, made for walking and good for bicycling, but not very fashionable. She realized that everything about her was practical except her idealism. She believed in a free Netherlands and had decided to do all she could to hasten the day when the Germans would leave Holland and the Netherlands would be free again.

But idealism was difficult when you were a few feet from the body of a boy who was alive only a few minutes before. Mira looked at Haynes. She couldn't stop staring at his face, or rather, the place were his youthful, good-looking face had once been.

Mira felt drained. The sight of Private Haynes, spilling his life's blood on the cobblestones of the town square, flooded her emotions. After the shooting had ended, she had sensed the normal exhilaration of surviving a brush with violent death. Now that the excitement was over, she felt the guilt at having survived when others did not.

When the shooting ended, the townspeople returned to the village square to see if anyone was wounded and to remove the dead. Their mood was somber and respectful, utterly different from the elation that had filled the air when they had rejoiced at the news of their liberation. A woman sat on the ground next to the dead

Dutchman and sobbed. Friends helped her up as other people carried the body of the dead man away.

Mira thought about her Bicyclists and how young and innocent they were. Each one of the teenagers burned with the same youthful idealism that fueled Mira's dreams of liberation. This past week had been a roller coaster of emotions. Some towns and villages had been liberated, while others were left in the hands of the Germans. Some homes, farms, and villages had become battlefields as the deadly give-and-take of combat scraped over these places like a huge, blood-drenched glacier, scarring the land, destroying homes, and killing human beings. Some cities, like Eindhoven, would experience the devastation of aerial bombardment and fire during their time of greatest happiness. All of the Netherlands would suffer. Liberation would not be free but would exact a terrible price.

In spite of the knowledge of all this horror, Mira knew in her soul that her cause was worthy and that this sacrifice was the cost of liberation. She had no internal contradictions concerning her belief that she would pray for all people, yet work hard to free her country.

Swanson walked over to his dead friend, falling to his knees. He picked Haynes up in his arms and sobbed. "Chuck, no! Chuck!"

The British soldiers stood nearby and watched Swanson, unwilling to interrupt his sorrow.

Mira walked over to the Bren Carrier and retrieved a wool army blanket that was lying on top of the wooden bench in the troop compartment. She asked a man in Dutch to help with Private Haynes's body. She walked over to Swanson, gently placing her hand on his shoulder.

"I am sorry, Private Swanson," Mira said softly, keeping her hand on Swanson's shoulder. "I will pray for him."

Swanson looked up, trying to hide his emotion, then held Haynes in his arms for a minute, covering Haynes's face in his embrace.

Mira continued and knelt down next to Swanson. Gently, she pulled him away. Swanson slowly lowered Haynes to the ground.

"You must let him go. You must. . . . These people will bury him."

Swanson nodded.

Two old men and a fourteen-year-old boy stood near the fountain waiting for Mira to give them the word to pick up the body.

Swanson breathed a deep sigh. Tenderly, he placed Haynes's hands on his chest. Respectfully, he ran his right hand across Haynes's bloody face and closed the one eye that was still there and open. He paused, as if in a silent prayer. He then took Haynes's wristwatch, wallet, and removed a letter from Haynes's breast pocket. Finally, as if to complete the act of saying good-bye to a close friend, Swanson took the dead soldier's metal identification tags. "I'll send this to his parents in Oregon. It's not much to show for a man's life."

"He has everyone here to testify to that life," Mira answered. "He has you to testify to that life."

Swanson looked at Mira. "Chuck's from Oregon . . . Woodburn, Oregon. He used to tell me stories about playing basketball, football, and track for his high school. He was quite an athlete and a good friend. We've been friends ever since we entered the 326th back in forty-three. . . ."

Mira handed him the blanket. "Cover him. These men will take care of him."

"I'm okay now," Swanson answered. He took the wool blanket from Mira and covered Haynes's body. He glanced into Mira's big brown eyes. "Thanks."

Mira nodded.

They both stood up and Swanson walked back to the Bren Carrier.

"Here mate, have a cig," Corporal Ackers said softly as he offered Swanson a cigarette.

Swanson nodded, taking the cigarette from Corporal Ackers.

The two Dutchmen and the boy gently picked up Haynes's body and carried him off to bury him in the town cemetery.

Mira picked up Haynes's helmet. The helmet had a white "E" for "Engineers" painted on both sides, as did Private Swanson's helmet. Haynes's helmet, however, was spattered in blood. Mira didn't recoil from the blood. She carried the bloodstained helmet to the fountain and placed it on the stone ledge that retained the shallow pool of water. She faced the helmet to the southeast, facing the enemy, as if it were a memorial in Haynes's memory.

As she set the helmet, she saw a portrait of queen Wilhelmina lying on the ground. The Queen had always been a symbol of Netherlands' independence and resistance to the Germans. The glass in the frame had shattered, but the picture was whole. Mira clutched the photo, tapped the broken glass to the ground and placed the image of Netherlands' queen against the fountain wall just below Haynes's bloodstained helmet.

Mira turned and saw a boy standing nearby, holding a bicycle. "Peter!"

Mira and Peter embraced as friends.

"I saw what happened," the boy said.

"Yes, it was horrible."

"I've come from Beek-en-Donk," Peter announced.

"What did you find out?"

"The Germans plan to cross the canal early tomorrow morning. Sometime before dawn," Peter replied.

Mira hugged Peter. "I am proud of you. This information is very important. Now go back to your mother and stay at home. I will tell the Americans."

Peter took a step back. "I am not a child. Some of us want to fight. There is a group in Beek. They are not afraid and they have rifles."

Mira searched Peter's face and saw anger and defiance. The village of Beek was just north of the area where the Germans would create a crossing site. "This is not the time to do something rash. I know that group. They are hotheads and impatient."

"No, they are resistance fighters," Peter said, shaking his head. "They are not cowards, and I am not a coward either."

Mira looked at Peter and saw the determination in his face.

Peter put his hands on the bicycle handlebars, ready to push off. "You have your information. I must be getting back."

"Peter, promise me you won't do anything! It's too dangerous. Too many youngsters have been killed already. Let the soldiers do the fighting, they know how."

Without answering, Peter climbed on his bicycle and pedaled away.

"If there is one thing I hate more than anything else, it is retreating," *Oberfeldwebel* Graf hissed as he walked along the side of the road.

Ten *Fallschirmjägers* followed behind Graf with Feldwebel Weise close enough behind to carry on a conversation.

"My feet are killing me," *Feldwebel* Weise whined.

"We must have marched five hundred kilometers since we arrived in this damn country."

"Maybe so," Graf answered, "but at least it is flat."

Weise laughed. "Yes, flat, wet, and muddy."

"I thought you liked it in the *fallshirm* infantry?"

"Yes, it's absolutely grand, and I am still tired of walking and walking," Weise replied. "When the war is over, I will ride everywhere. I will refuse to walk, even a mile. I will not even walk to the store."

Graf laughed at the thought and then looked at the sun low on the horizon. "It will be dark in two hours. We must pick up the pace."

"It is just like that bastard Kodritz to take our new vehicles from us," Weise complained. "Riding in those carriers, even for just an hour, almost made me wish I was a *panzergrenadier*!"

"He had two antitank guns that had to be towed and ammunition to haul," Graf argued. "What else could he do?"

"You are defending him? What would he have done if we hadn't come across the British in the first place? So he shows his gratitude by confiscating our vehicles and ordering us to walk to the rendezvous point. That's not how a *Fallschirmjäger* officer would treat us."

"Stop complaining. We'll hitch a ride on the next vehicle that passes."

"Of course," Weise snorted.

The German paratroopers trudged along in silence. As they marched, the sound of their boots on the macadam road sounded a soldier's rhythm that was as ancient as war itself.

Graf turned his head and spied a column of trucks heading their way. The trucks looked like moving bushes as they were heavily camouflaged with tree branches and pine boughs. Without stopping, the trucks streamed down the road past Graf's string of tired *Fallschirmjägers*. The trucks were all different shapes and makes, one German, two French, and another of Belgian or Dutch manufacture. The proud Wehrmacht had been forced to steal vehicles from wherever it could.

"Well, at least the SS have trucks," Weise announced.

As the trucks passed, Graf saw that each one was filled to capacity with SS infantrymen.

The tired *Fallschirmjägers* continued hiking for another kilometer, silent in their own thoughts.

The sun was shining and the air was fresh. As he marched, Graf thought about the long road he had traveled since he enlisted. When he was young, he never dreamed he would be a soldier, but dreams had a funny way of twisting in Hitler's Germany. In 1938, while studying the Russian language in Berlin, he was involved in a brawl with three hooligans who had decided to beat up an old man. Graf went to the man's aid, and in the process of defeating the hooligans broke the nose of one of his assailants and the collarbone of another. The man with the broken collarbone nearly died in the hospital. The old man scurried away, afraid even of his rescuer, as Graf finished the fight by booting the third attacker in the ass and hurling him into the Spree River.

Somehow his antagonists learned his name and reported him to the authorities for anti-German behavior. The man they were beating was Jewish and the Berlin police sided with the three hooligans. To make matters worse for Graf, it turned out that the thug with the broken collarbone was the brother of a high-ranking local Nazi official. When the police started coming around asking friends and neighbors questions about Graf, his travels, and his political preferences, Graf decided to lose them by joining the Luftwaffe and volunteering for the *Fallschirmjägers*.

In spite of his disgust for the Nazi Party, Graf considered himself a patriotic German. He felt that the Nazis were a temporary blight on Germany and that, with time, real Germans would put a stop to their madness. In the interim, he found the *Fallschirmjägers* to be a select breed of soldier, different from many of the other units in the Wehrmacht. The *Fallschirmjägers* were part of the Luftwaffe, not the army, so their training, equipment, and supply were different from the army or the Waffen SS. Most important, the *Fallschirmjägers* considered themselves the elite of the German military and their leadership reflected the very best in Germany. *Fallschirmjäger* leaders were expected to be the toughest, smartest, and most tactically competent that Germany had ever produced, and the sergeants and officers of the paratroop corps lived up to that reputation.

In units of the Wehrmacht, commanders were often in the lead, with their men, sharing their soldier's hardships. In the *Fallschirmjägers,* this was a rule, not an exception. Much more was expected of *Fallschirmjäger* leaders and the common saying was that "the front is where the commanding officer is."

This elite ethos appealed to Graf, and he soon thrived in the paratroops, finding that he excelled as a leader. His superiors recognized his leadership talents as well. After initial training, he was placed in a special pioneer (engineer) unit of 7th Flieger Division and trained to use the latest explosives.

In August 1939, the world held its breath as Germany, Poland, France, and Great Britain teetered at the precipice of war. On September 1, 1939, Hitler told the Nazi Reichstag and the people of Germany that Poland had tried to invade Germany. With that announcement, the war started and the Germans launched a well-prepared invasion of Poland. The French and British declared war on Germany, but did nothing but hurl threats. The Poles courageously fought alone against Germany's modern army and air force, but were quickly outclassed by the Wehrmacht.

At the time, Graf was still in training, and a week into the Polish fighting was transferred to a highly secret training facility in Czechoslovakia. To Graf's dismay, instead of getting into the action, he missed the entire campaign, his time filled with one difficult training exercise after another. German troops occupied Warsaw, the capital of Poland, on October 1, and organized Polish resistance ended on October 6, 1939.

For Graf, however, the end of the war in Poland did not mean an end to his special training in Czechoslovakia. Instead, Graf's training intensified and included several practice glider landings behind mock enemy lines.

During this time a war of words, not steel, continued between Germany and the French and British. This situation was called the *Sitzkrieg*, or Phony War. Although France and England had declared war on Germany, there were no significant battles.

As Graf and his comrades kept up a relentless pace of drills, live-fire combat exercises, and glider operations in Czechoslovakia, he began to wonder why he and his comrades were training so hard.

Then, in May 1940, all his questions were answered. His unit of specially trained glider-borne *Fallschirm-jägers* was alerted for action. The war of words between Germany and France and England would soon turn into a war of flesh and steel.

The German plan of attack called for an armored thrust through the Ardennes forest. The plan relied on the right flank of the panzer attack being covered by the infantry of the 6th Army. This army would need to cross the Albert Canal, and blocking their way, defending the bridges over the canal, was the Belgian fortress at Eben Emael.

Graf's mission was top secret and strategic. The select group of specially trained *Fallschirmjägers* was to fly by glider and land directly on top of the Belgian fortress of Eben Emael. An assault of this kind had never been attempted before in history. The fortress was reputed to be impregnable, with numerous cannons and machine guns. Most impressive, the fortress was manned by a garrison of over a thousand of Belgium's best soldiers.

On May 10, 1940, Graf and seventy-three *Fallschirmjägers* landed their DFS 230 gliders directly on top of the diamond-shaped fortress just as they had practiced in the secret training in Czechoslovakia. The *Fallschirmjägers* knocked out the guns with the use of specially designed demolitions called shaped charges and captured the top of the fortress. The Belgians fought back, but the heavily outnumbered German *Fallschirmjägers* beat back repeated attacks. One day later, the *Fallschirmjägers* were reinforced by the German 151st Infantry Regiment; the 1,200 Belgian soldiers inside the fortress came out of the deep tunnels and bunkers to surrender. With the Belgian guns knocked out and the fortress in German hands, the route through Belgium was opened for the tanks of the Wehrmacht.

The assault landing on Eben Emael was an important victory for Germany. Graf served as a private in a squad, but earned the respect of his leaders and fellow *Fallschirmjägers* and proved his potential as a combat leader. He fought with distinction during the battle, personally destroying a Belgian machine-gun bunker and saving the lives of many of his comrades in arms. As a result, Graf was cited for bravery by his commander and awarded the Iron Cross Second Class.

After the decisive capture of the great fortress of Eben Emael, the rest of Belgium and the Netherlands quickly surrendered. After a few more weeks of fighting, the French capitulated. The British managed to evacuate most of their men from the French port of Dunkirk, but none of their heavy equipment.

What had not been possible in four years of combat in the First World War had been accomplished by this new German war machine of tanks, Stukas, and paratroopers in a matter of weeks. The blitzkrieg had succeeded beyond the Wehrmacht's wildest dreams. Germany was triumphant. All of western Europe was now occupied by German troops.

But the war continued. In 1941, Graf found himself leading a *Fallschirmjäger* rifle squad in the German airborne campaign to capture the island of Crete. The fighting on Crete was bitter and the *Fallschirmjägers* were stretched to the breaking point to win an uneven campaign against much heavier British and Australian forces. In spite of this imbalance, the *Fallschirmjägers* prevailed, and Graf again distinguished himself and was decorated as a hero once more.

The war changed dramatically when Hitler ordered the Wehrmacht to attack Russia. On June 22, 1941, the greatest invasion in history occurred when Hitler's legions, nearly a million men, attacked Stalin's Russia. Surprise was complete, and entire Soviet formations were smashed into the summer dust. Millions of Soviet soldiers were killed and captured in huge battles on the Russian steppe. The Germans won victory after bloody victory in 1941, and German *panzers* moved within fifteen kilometers of Moscow, nearly able to see the spires of the Kremlin.

Then the Russians, with their backs to the wall, counterattacked. The Germans, at the end of their supply line, were hurled back. Moscow, the great prize, would remain just out of reach of the Nazi grasp.

The fighting changed. Cold. Bitter. No quarter. Desperate. The battles in Russia consumed the German army. In 1941, Graf was sent to the area south of Leningrad. There, in October, during a horrific battle in the snow, he earned Germany's highest military honors, the Knight's Cross to the Iron Cross, for his leadership during one of the greatest defenses in modern military history on the Neva River.

It was shortly after the battle of the Neva River, however, that he got into trouble. His "old-fashioned" sense of German honor was the cause.

"Did I tell you that *Leutnant* Hanzer was killed?" Weise suddenly announced.

Graf thought back to his platoon leader, young Lieutenant Hanzer. He remembered a week ago, when he had counseled Hanzer on an officer's ability to know when to disobey orders. "I didn't know . . . when did it happen?"

"I saw the casualty reports when I was trying to arrange transportation for us from that idiot Gunter. It seems he died during the attack at Sint-Oedenrode a few days ago."

Graf shook his head. "Hanzer was a good man."

"Yes, he deserved better. We deserve better."

"We all die, Weise. What counts is how we die. At least he died leading his men, surrounded by his comrades."

"Your sentiment is touching, if somewhat bourgeois. Are you trying to write your own epitaph?"

"I'm afraid that all your education, professor, has turned you into a communist or a philosopher. I'm not sure which is worse," Graf joked.

"You are right; better to remain simply a cynic," Weise suddenly turned and looked back and saw three squat armored vehicles moving south, toward them. "Graf, there are StuGs headed our way. Let's hitch a ride with them."

Graf turned and looked down the road. Three assault guns, camouflaged with pine branches, were barreling down the road at twenty kilometers an hour. Graf stopped in the middle of the road, waving to the lead vehicle.

The lead StuG rolled to a stop and the two following assault guns slowed and halted in turn.

The lead assault gun commander, a veteran sergeant, took off his headset and shouted down to Graf. "I'm *Feldwebel* Schmitt. What can I do for you, my friend?"

"Oberfeldwebel Graf, Sixth *Fallschirmjäger* Regiment, now with the SS *kampfgruppe* heading south," Graf announced. "We could sure use a lift."

"I'm heading there as well," Schmitt answered. "Have your men hop on."

"*Danke!* All right, men, climb aboard the first two StuGs."

Graf's *Fallschirmjägers* quickly complied, clambering up the squat, tree-branch-laden armored vehicles. Graf climbed aboard the lead StuG and gave a hand to Weise and three others as they scrambled up, searching for handholds on the armored vehicle. In a few minutes all the men were seated on top of the StuGs. Graf took a position near Schmitt.

"With any luck we should be there before dark," Schmitt announced to Graf. "Maybe they will have some hot soup for us?"

"That would be good news. My men are worn out and hungry."

Feldwebel Schmitt put his earphones back on and adjusted his throat microphone. "Driver, move out!"

The StuG jerked forward and, in turn, the other assault guns clanked down the road.

Weise sat next to Graf and smiled. "This is the way to go to war. Why walk when you can ride. Why did I ever join the *Fallschirmjägers*?"

Graf smiled. "You liked the uniform."

The column continued south for nearly fifteen minutes. The air was cool and the sky was clear. The drive was enjoyable.

As the StuG's rolled down the road they passed a column of refugees. About twenty Dutch civilians trudged along the side of the road, heading northwest, carrying their belongings. One old man pushed a wheelbarrow that carried an old woman. The children looked up at the German soldiers as they passed. The adults did not.

Weise gazed at the victims of war. "I hope this never happens to Germany."

Graf didn't answer but merely turned away to look straight ahead.

The assault guns clanked on for another kilometer when suddenly, with a loud roar from the west, came a flight of American P-47 Thunderbolt fighter-bombers.

"*Jabos!*" Graf shouted as the first aircraft flew over their heads. The aircraft was so close that Graf could see the face of the pilot.

Graf grabbed Schmitt on the shoulder, pointing out the danger. The StuG commander screamed into his throat mike, and the armored vehicle picked up speed as the two P-47s circled around to make a strafing run. Schmitt shouted over the radio and ordered the three StuGs to disperse into the nearby woods. Before the assault guns could slow down to exit the road, a P-47 howled down from the heavens on a strafing run at the column.

The four 50-caliber machine guns in each wing of the first aircraft fired furiously as it dove at the trail StuG. As Schmitt's assault gun left the road, Graf could hear the gut-wrenching sound of the bullets from the P-47's guns hitting the StuG.

"Fire at that *jabo*!" Graf ordered as he turned and fired a long burst of shells from his PPSh at the attacking American aircraft.

All the *Fallschirmjägers* fired, but the first P-47 soared over them without a scratch.

The armor on the roof of the StuG was thin, and although the last StuG in the column was still moving, it was belching black smoke from its engine compartment.

"Here comes the second one!" Weise screamed.

Graf and his men blasted away at the onrushing aircraft as the StuG they were riding on tore across an open field toward the safety of a nearby forest. The *Fallschirmjägers* held on for dear life as the assault gun bumped across the terrain, firing with one hand and holding on with the other. The second P-47 pummeled the trailing StuG with a flood of lead, then shot some rounds at the second StuG.

The trailing StuG erupted in a ball of fire. As the second StuG exited the road, Graf looked back and saw one of his men fall off the top of the assault gun. Unwilling to stop and halt in the open terrain with the P-47s overhead, the StuG raced after Schmitt's vehicle and the safety of the forest.

Schmitt's StuG arrived at the forest unscathed and hid under a thick canopy of green. The second StuG rumbled into the woods while the *Fallschirmjägers* on top fired uselessly at the enemy aircraft. The third, caught on the road, became a feast for vultures as the P-47s attacked it in earnest and tore it to pieces.

Then, as if in spite, the P-47s flew low over the burning StuG and waggled their wings to symbolize their victory. As the *jabos* flew away, the third StuG burned—there seemed to be no sign of life from the crew.

Schmitt climbed out of the turret and walked to the edge of the forest to check on the crew of the burning StuG.

Graf climbed off as well, running toward his *Fallschirmjäger,* who had fallen off the assault gun. He reached the motionless body of *Jäger* Eckolt and saw that the enemy's machine guns had done their work. Eckolt was dead with half his side blown off.

Graf picked up the boy's body and weapon and carried him to the woods.

Weise stood at the edge of the trees as Graf returned. "Dörnefeld, Merckel, Wigand. Grab your entrenching tools. Burial detail."

Graf carefully lay the body down in the trees. He opened the dead boy's uniform collar and bent the bottom portion of his metal identification tag until it detached. Graf then placed this portion of the ID tag in his pocket. He moved over to a tree and sat down, disconnected the drum magazine from his PPSh, and began reloading the drum with bullets from his haversack.

Feldwebel Schmitt returned empty-handed from the burning StuG. He looked at Graf and then at the body of the dead *Fallschirmjäger.*

"At least you have something to bury," Schmitt said. "We'll wait here until it gets dark, and then we'll head out for the *kampfgruppe.*"

Continuing to push bullets into the magazine, Graf nodded.

Darkness covered the town of Lieshout like a candle snuffed out in a room with no windows. With the darkness, came exhaustion.

Inside a wooden barn on the north side of the village, Colour Sergeant Cathal Gilchrist finished a cigarette in the dim light of a kerosene lamp. The vehicles were parked outside, camouflaged and guarded. The men lay sprawled out on the hay. This past week had taken its toll on the limits of human endurance. Everyone was dead tired. Most were already snoring. Only Cat, Mira, Corporal Zanovitch, and Guardsman Roy were still up.

Roy had the first watch as he stood outside the barn, guarding the vehicles. The rest sat next to Cat while he studied a map of the area.

Zanovitch was boiling water in a tin ration can over a small metal stove. Baker was sleeping in a corner of the barn with his Thompson submachine gun at his side.

"I noticed you didn't like it when I called you 'sarge.' How come? We call Baker 'sarge;' it means no offense."

"In the Irish Guards the rank of 'staff sergeant' is called 'colour sergeant,' never 'sarge' or sergeant. It's an insult to do otherwise."

"Noted," Zanovitch replied. "So explain that to me again. You don't have to be Irish to be in the Irish Guards?"

"Well, we're mostly Irish or at least of Irish blood. I lived in England most of my life. The regiment was formed in 1900 by Queen Victoria. We're known as 'The Micks.' I joined in 1939 when it looked like there was no way out of this bloody war. Since then we've fought in France in 1940—we ended up leaving at Dunkirk—and then trained in England for the invasion. We landed in Normandy in June, fought with the Guards Armored Division in France at Caen and Mount Picon, and were one of the first units into Belgium."

"I heard about Caen," Zanovitch replied. "Operation Goodwood?"

"There was nothing good about it."

Cat sat back for a moment as he remembered a sunny July day near the French city of Caen. The Allies had landed in Normandy but were held up by a stiff German opposition. Operation Goodwood was supposed to change that by punching through the German defenses.

It was the largest tank battle that the British army had ever fought. Three armored divisions, nearly 900 tanks, 8,000 other vehicles, and 10,000 infantry were used for the battle. A tremendous preparatory air and artillery bombardment from 700 artillery guns and over 900 heavy bombers launched tons of shells and bombs at the German defenders. It should have been an easy victory.

Instead, it turned into a nightmare. The Irish Guards, part of the Guards Armored Division, was ordered to drive around the towns of Cagny and Vimont, but everything went wrong. Hundreds of tanks jammed the roads. When the assault began, the Guard's Armored Division had to drive through a British minefield and was pummeled by German artillery. Once through the minefields the attackers moved out into a fairly open plain; then the Germans smashed them with long-range 88mm fire from cannons placed in well-concealed positions.

The enemy antitank fire was accurate and lethal. The Germans started firing at the British tanks from nearly two thousand yards. The best British tanks, the Sherman Firefly, had to race forward to within a thousand yards to return fire. The result was a slaughter as the German 1st SS Panzer Division plastered the attackers from a web of well-fortified hamlets. Dug-in German 88mm cannons wrecked havoc with the British tanks. Dozens of British tanks were hit and immediately caught fire.

Cat remembered seeing palls of oily, black smoke as tanks blew up with orange-red fire belching from their turrets. Sherman after Sherman went up in flames. He saw the crews climbing out of tank turrets, on fire like torches, rolling on the ground, trying in vain to douse the flames. Soon, Cat's unit was pinned down and unable to advance.

That's when Cat earned his nickname, demonstrating that he truly had nine lives. With infantry support in short supply and tank casualties mounting, Cat led a platoon of riflemen against the German antitank gunners. While the Germans concentrated on destroying the tanks, Cat found a way to flank a line of 88mm guns and charged.

He started with twenty-one men and overwhelmed the defenders of the first gun. Without stopping, he led his men to attack the second. The fighting was sharp, brutal, and rifle butt to bayonet. By the time he had knocked out the third gun, he had only six men left.

Nevertheless, heroism was not enough that day. The German panzers counterattacked. The battle became a seething cauldron of burning and exploding armored vehicles. In moments, entire companies of British tanks were destroyed. Cat should have been killed a half-dozen times, but the hand of fate seemed to protect him. He scrounged German *panzerfaust* antitank grenades and his men destroyed two Mark IV tanks. After two days of terrible casualties and no-holds-barred fighting, the battle ended in a British defeat and Cat's platoon was reduced to only three survivors.

Yes, there was nothing good about Goodwood.

Zanovitch looked up. "Water's ready. Miss Vogel, Sar . . . I mean Colour Sergeant Gilchrist, how about some American coffee?"

"Sure, Yank. Thanks," Cat replied as he handed his empty metal water bottle cup to Zanovitch. "It seems that I'll educate you yet on the niceties of the British enlisted rank structure, but please, ladies first."

Mira smiled and nodded.

Zanovitch pulled his own metal canteen cup from its pouch on his web belt, tapped it against his hand to knock out the dirt, and then filled it by dipping it in the hot water. He then took out a brown packet of coffee, poured the contents in, and stirred it with the remains of the packet. Afterward he handed it to Mira.

Mira grasped the metal handle and took the coffee cup in both hands, savoring its warmth and aroma. "I have never tasted real coffee, only chicory."

"You never tasted coffee?"

"No, we could not buy coffee since the Germans arrived."

"Well, this is instant coffee, but it is pretty good."

"I have heard of this instant coffee. It is remarkable to think that you can make coffee from powder."

"Yeah, you just pour it from the packet, stir, and you have a good cup of Joe."

"Joe?"

"Yeah, that's American for coffee."

Mira sipped the coffee and closed her eyes for a moment. "It is very good. Thank you."

"Your English is very good," Cat offered.

"No. I understand better than I speak."

"You are doing fine, missy, just fine," Cat added.

"It must have been rough . . . the occupation," Zanovitch offered.

"We managed," Mira answered. "The Germans drafted men over eighteen and younger than forty-five as forced labor to work in German factories. They took everything from us for their war effort, and many things we were used to having became scarce. With the adult men gone, we had to work to feed our families. Food was often hard to come by. Bread was rationed, but we could grow vegetables in our gardens and in August and September the trees are filled with apples."

"What kept you going?" Cat asked.

"Hope. Hope that one day you would arrive."

"Thank you for helping us find this place to stay for the night, missy," Cat said as Zanovitch filled Cat's metal cup with water and passed Cat a packet of coffee. "It was kind of the townspeople to take us in."

"It is the least they can do. You have done so much for us."

"Tell me, why do you do this?" Zanovitch interjected. "You don't have to be with us. We can handle this mission."

"Yes, I do. It is my country. I must help."

There was a quiet moment while Zanovitch made his own cup of coffee. Then all three enjoyed their warm drink.

"Tell me about Sergeant Baker," Mira asked as she held the metal cup in her hands. "What kind of man is he?"

Cat shrugged. "I've only known him a few days, but after what I saw today I know that he is one hell of a fighter."

Zanovitch smiled as if he knew some important secret. "I've known Baker now for nearly two years; ever since he joined the 101st Airborne Division in 1942. I'm afraid he's a bit of a puzzle."

"What do you mean, 'puzzle'?" Mira asked.

"Well, it's hard to say. Sometimes he's the man you want to be with. He knows what to do and then does it. That's what keeps you alive. It's as if he was born to fight. Other times, well, he gets on your nerves."

"But what is he like as a person?"

"That's a bit more complicated. That's why I said he's a puzzle. Baker's not the easiest man to get to know. He holds a lot inside."

Cat looked at his watch. "Tomorrow will be a busy day. We should all get some rest."

Mira smiled. "Colour Sergeant Gilchrist is right. I will say good night now."

"Zanovitch, you are in charge until zero two hundred. Wake me up then."

"Will do, Colour Sergeant."

Just then, the door to the barn opened and Guardsman Roy entered. "Colour Sergeant Gilchrist. I made the twenty-three-hundred-hours radio check. They sent me this message. I wrote it down for you."

Cat nodded taking a small piece of paper from Roy.

"I'll get back to my guard post," Roy announced and then glanced at Zanovitch's metal cup. "Is that coffee I smell?"

Zanovitch nodded with a grin. "I was just going to bring you a cup."

"Thanks mate, that's awfully considerate."

Zanovitch handed Roy his canteen cup, and the Irish Guardsman pulled out the metal cup of the water bottle, transferring half of the contents to his cup.

"Well, I'm headed back out," Roy answered.

As Roy left the barn, Cat slid over to the kerosene lamp and read the message.

"What's the message?" Zanovitch asked.

"They haven't heard from Lieutenant Palmer's team. They are presumed missing in action."

Mira dropped her canteen cup on the floor. "Alexander . . ."

Zanovitch looked up at Mira. "Don't jump to conclusions, Miss Vogel. Missing in action doesn't mean they're dead. There could be a hundred reasons why they have not been able to report in on the radio. It's standard procedure to report recon teams as 'missing in action' when they don't report as scheduled."

"He's right, missy. First reports are often wrong. I've been reported missing in action a dozen times."

Mira looked at Cat with wide, teary eyes. "I never should have let him go. Alexander was just a boy."

Cat put his arm around Mira and ushered her to the side of the barn where a blanket was laid out on a pile of straw. "Get some rest, missy. We'll know more in the morning."

British Bren Carrier

Colour Sergeant Cathal Gilchrist

9

Untutored courage is useless in the face of educated bullets.
—GENERAL GEORGE S. PATTON JR., U.S. Army

Lieshout, Netherlands, 11:30 a.m., Sunday, September 24, 1944:

Baker glanced at his watch. The morning was passing fast.

The land was shrouded in a thick, gray fog so dense that Baker couldn't see more than five feet away. He knew that moving in this fog and bumping into an enemy ambush would be suicide. He decided to wait until the haze burned off and visibility improved.

Baker and Cat stood outside the barn staring at a map laid out on the hood of Baker's jeep. Baker held a canteen cup in his right hand and sipped lukewarm coffee. Cat smoked a cigarette.

"What the hell are we doing here?" Baker asked, more from frustration than from any hopes of an answer. "My reconnaissance squad is somewhere back near Koevering, doing God-knows-what, while I'm miles away chasing shadows in this damn fog."

Cat took a long drag on his cigarette, stared at the map, and said nothing.

"Do you have any idea where she went?" Baker asked.

"No. When Avery woke me up he said that the girl

was gone. He said she told him that she was going off to use the 'necessary,' but she never came back. Maybe she had enough of this shit and went home?"

Baker shook his head.

"Look, Baker, we received a radio message last night and learned that Lieutenant Palmer's team was missing in action. Mira was probably worried about her cousin. My guess is that she left to find out about him."

"Or she is off to tell the Germans about us."

"You don't believe that," Cat replied. "She's not a traitor."

"No, I know she isn't," Baker answered and then was quiet for a moment. "I can't believe she left without telling me."

Cat finished his cigarette, dropped the burning butt to the ground, and ground it out with his boot. "So what do you want to do?"

"I guess we'll carry on without her. Did she tell you anything more about what she learned from her resistance friends regarding the German crossing in this area?"

"Only that it was south of Beek, but then there's this note."

"Note?"

Cat offered Baker a folded piece of paper. The words *For Baker* were written on the outside. "When Avery went to look for her, he found this note. It's addressed to you, so I didn't read it."

Baker took the note, visibly annoyed at the turn of events and read:

Dear Sergeant Baker,
Do not be mad at me. Last night I learned that my cousin may be dead. I cannot let any more young boys die. I must go to Beek. If I do not see you again, please

*know that I am thankful to you. I hope we can be
friends.
Mira*

"Damn! This message makes no sense. She says she is
going off to Beek to save someone."

Cat looked at the map and pinpointed Beek several
miles to the northeast. "Look, Baker, we need a plan.
Our mission is to report the possibility of a German
crossing in this area. We no longer have a guide, but we
know that if the Jerries are going to cross the canal south
of Beek, it can't be far from here."

Baker bit his lip as he studied the map and considered
the possibilities. "Yesterday, I was able to see most of the
canal from the church tower. As soon as this fog lifts, you
and I will head up there and have a look at the crossing
site. If we don't see anything, we'll radio headquarters
that this was a wild-goose chase and a false report. Then
we can get the hell out of here."

"Okay, if that's how you want to play this, you'll get
no arguments from me. I'll get the men ready to move."

The air was thick as soup as *Oberfeldwebel* Graf
walked in the dense fog with his PPSh submachine gun
hanging from a sling around his neck. In his right hand
he had a compass. As he crossed a plowed dirt field he
checked the compass heading. Satisfied that he was on
course, he placed the compass back in his pocket and
looked back to the man behind him. "Keep moving and
keep sight of the man in front of you."

"At least this fog will keep the *jabos* off our backs,"
Feldwebel Weise offered. "Do you think we're going in
the right direction?"

Graf smiled. "Yes, Weise. You know, you chatter like a
woman. How is your hand?"

"I changed the bandage yesterday. It will be fine. Worry about yourself."

Graf suddenly felt the earth beneath his boots turn hard. He looked down and saw the road that he was looking for.

"Turn half right. Follow this road," Graf ordered and continued walking. "Pass the message back and send up a head count."

Weise repeated the message, ordering the men to quietly count off and pass the number back to him. After a moment he touched Graf on the shoulder. "All our rabbits are in line and accounted for."

"Good, it won't be long now until we reach the assembly area."

The line of *Fallschirmjägers* carried on. As the hour passed, the fog began to lift.

An outline of a soldier appeared up ahead.

"Halt!" a voice in the fog shouted. "Erika!"

"Munich," Graf answered, replying to the challenge with the correct countersign. "Weise, we have arrived, pass this back to the men. All weapons on safe. German troops up ahead."

Weise passed the information back to the man behind him who whispered it back to the man behind him.

Graf moved face-to-face with a *Feldgendarmerie* (military policeman) carrying an MP40 submachine gun.

"Halt!" The *Feldgendarmerie* ordered.

"*Oberfeldwebel* Graf with a squad of *Fallschirmjägers* to report to Obersturmführer Kodritz's group."

The *Feldgendarmerie* waved Graf forward. "Follow the road to the canal, then cross the canal to the house on the opposite bank."

"*Danke*," Graf answered. "There are nine of us, all *Fallschirmjägers*."

Graf marched on and followed the road. The road was

a narrow path in a forest of tall fir trees. As he walked down the road, he saw the outline of several tanks, half-tracks, and assault guns. Each vehicle was covered in fir branches. The armored *kampfgruppe* had found a very good place to hide.

Finally the trees ended and the road stopped at the canal. There was no bridge, but a rope was strung across the canal from one end to the other.

Graf stopped and knelt down. His men would cross using the rope. He checked the rope, saw that it was secure, and could take the weight of a man.

"Weise, tell the men to gather round. It looks like we are going to do some rope work."

The men arrived slowly, huddling around their leader. Graf looked down into the canal. The water was deep and cold, and the sides of the canal at this site were straight down and concrete, but the current was not too strong.

If they wanted to build a bridge, this location provided the perfect crossing. It was narrow, with reinforced banks at both ends.

"This is how we will cross this canal. You will sling your rifle over your shoulder, Cossack style. Then you will move headfirst and hold on to the rope with hands and feet until you reach the other side."

The men nodded that they understood.

"Who can't swim?"

Three men—Berna, Merckel, and Wigand—raised their hands.

"Damn," Weise swore. "And who said all good things come in threes? What are they sending us these days?"

"No matter," Graf answered. "You won't have to swim if you do exactly as I have told you. You three, wait with me until the end. Weise, you start and show them how it's done."

Graf placed his submachine gun on the ground and took off his web gear and helmet, piling them next to the submachine gun. He then looked at Weise and nodded.

Weise slung his MP40 submachine gun over his back and buttoned his pockets. He then walked up to the rope and grabbed the rope with his hands. The left hand was still bandaged. Graf saw it begin to bleed as Weise pulled himself across.

Weise pulled and crossed half the distance when his weapon shifted on his back. With his good hand he reached for the MP40 so that it would not slip into the river. When he did this, his injured hand was on the rope and he lost his grip. For a moment he held on with his feet; suddenly he gave way, and he plunged into the water. His weapon and gear pulled him down.

Without hesitation Graf leaped into the water. For a moment, there was no sign of either man. All the *Fallschirmjägers* on the east bank of the canal were on their feet searching the water for the two men. Then Graf came to the surface with Weise and all his gear in his grip. Weise took a deep breath and Graf managed to swim both of them to the west side of the canal.

On the west bank Graf grabbed a steel ring embedded into the wall. He waited there while signaling for the next *Fallschirmjäger* to cross over with Graf's equipment.

Oberjäger Küster was next in line and quickly climbed on the rope. He swiftly pulled himself across. Once to the other side he leaned over the concrete side of the canal and pulled up *Feldwebel* Weise.

Graf climbed up the wall and signaled for the rest of the men to cross over. In short order, Henning, Stöhr, Wigand, Merckel, Berna, and Dörnefeld made it across the canal.

After gathering their gear, Graf pulled Weise aside and inspected his hand. The wound was badly infected.

"I am sending you to hospital, as soon as I can," Graf announced.

Weise nodded. "I botched that up pretty badly, eh, and in front of the rabbits."

Graf shook his head. "Don't worry about that. You are a veteran of the Sixth Fallschirmjäger Regiment. They'll follow you to the gates of hell and through the fire if need be."

Weise stood up and shook Graf's hand. "Again you save my life."

Just then, SS *Hauptscharführer* Gunter arrived at Graf's side. "Graf, you are late. We are short of infantry on the west bank. We only hold a narrow perimeter along the canal. There is less than a company of SS men. Get your men into position before the fog lifts."

"Don't worry Gunter; my eight *Fallschirmjägers* and I are here to protect you."

Baker hesitated for a moment before taking the final step to the church belfry, then he moved forward. Cat followed right behind him. The fog was lifting. Baker hoped to conduct a quick surveillance and call the mission complete.

He glanced around. The body of the dead German sniper was gone and the blood had been scrubbed away. The church's Catholic priest had done his best to erase the carnage of war.

The only thing that remained of the previous day's struggle was a bloodstain on the floor and a single .45 caliber shell casing that was wedged against a crack of the belfry wall.

Baker stared at the shell casing, momentarily reliving the struggle. He remembered the instant when his eyes locked with those of the SS sniper. For that instant, they were both on the edge of fate. In that split second, the action could have cut either way. The German's face was indelibly stamped onto his memory. Baker was faster and, therefore, still alive. Had the German been faster . . .

He looked away and focused on the present, as all soldiers must. Death is an exquisite teacher, he thought. It throws life into sharp perspective, reminding us of just how limited our time is.

Baker reached into his left breast pocket and pulled out a cigar.

"Cigar?"

"Don't mind if I do," Cat said with a smile, as he thankfully took the cigar. "You Yanks must be well supplied to have fresh cigars."

"Not really," Baker replied. "It was a gift from a Dutch priest a couple of days ago."

"A generous man."

"Yeah. Unfortunately, he was killed just a few minutes after he gave these to me."

Cat put the cigar in his mouth and bit off the end. "Then it would be a sin to let them go to waste."

"I suppose so."

Cat pulled out a stainless-steel lighter and lit Baker's cigar. Once the stogie was burning bright, Cat lit his own cigar.

The two men were quiet for a moment savoring the taste and aroma of the tobacco.

"Where do you think she went?" Baker asked.

Cat shook his head. "Beek? Home? Who knows?"

Baker unbuttoned the leather binocular case at his side and brought the field glasses to his eyes to scan the terrain to the east. He had a clear view from the church tower. The Willemsvaart Canal traveled roughly northwest to southeast and connected with the wider Wilhelmina Canal. If the Germans were to attempt a bridging operation of the Willemsvaart Canal, they would have to do it between Beek in the north and the junction with the Wilhelmina canal.

"No bridge, or any sign of a bridge," Baker announced. "One thing's for certain, though, they can't cross tanks without a bridge."

Cat stood next to Baker gazing out over the quiet countryside with his own pair of field glasses. "Those woods, due east of us, would be a perfect place to hide armored vehicles if you were going to cross the canal."

Baker searched the woods with his binoculars. "You're right, but if anyone is there, they're concealing themselves very well."

The two men carefully searched the trees near the canal.

Baker put down his binoculars and took a puff of the cigar. "I think we're looking for Krauts that aren't there."

"Well, you may be right. On the other hand, if the Jerries wanted to cross in this area, they would probably cross right there and probably at night. With all the fighter-bombers we have in the air, it makes sense to cross after dark and make a dash for Hell's Highway while our planes aren't in the sky."

"Over what bridge?"

"You've got me there," Cat said. "They have to have a bridge."

"Well, I've seen enough," Baker said. "I think we report that we have observed the area, didn't find a bridge, and saw no enemy activity. If headquarters agrees, then we can leave this place."

"I'm not so sure. I've been thinking about this and have changed my mind. I was impressed with Mira; I have to admit that she was convinced that the Jerries were up to something."

"She's just a kid," Baker replied.

"She may be sixteen, but she's hardly a kid."

"Okay, so you think we should stay?"

"Consider this. If the Jerries were able to cross here, then there would be no one within miles to stop them."

Baker studied the road from Lieshout to the canal. "It's a straight shot from the woods to Lieshout and from here to Eindhoven."

"If the Germans retook Eindhoven, or just got tanks into the city, there would be such a fuss that the entire operation might fail."

"It may fail anyway."

"Yeah, but I'll be damned if it fails because I didn't do my job," Cat snapped.

Baker thought this over for a moment. "If the Germans did find a way to cross tanks, we certainly couldn't stop them, not with what we have."

"True, but I think we should give it one more day. This is a good observation post. We can observe the area from here without taking any further risks; besides, this town will offer us a place to defend from if we need to. We can set our machine guns in the south of the town to discourage anyone coming up the road from the southeast. At least it would slow the Jerries down long enough for us to get away."

Baker didn't answer. He scanned south of the bridge, saw the area where the Willemsvaart Canal connected with the Wilhelmina Canal, and observed nothing. He then worked his way up to the north.

Cat brought his binoculars back up. "Hold on, I see some activity. Look due east."

Cat pointed to an area north of the junction of the two canals. Baker brought the field glasses to his eyes and saw a group of civilians walking down a road parallel to the Williamsvaart Canal. The road was lined with trees spaced every twenty feet or so, but Baker could make out that there were about fifteen civilians. They looked as if they were carrying guns.

Baker's binoculars were only magnified to three-power, so he couldn't make out much more than that the civilians looked armed and were headed southeast. He glanced over at Cat's binoculars. "Can you make out those people walking down the road?"

"I'm already on it. I count seventeen civilians and some with rifles. They're wearing orange armbands. Probably resistance fighters. Most of them look pretty young."

"Orange armbands won't protect them," Baker announced. "Is Mira with them?"

"I can't tell."

With his binoculars, Baker scanned several roads that led to the group. "There, I see someone on a bike southwest of the group."

Cat adjusted his search and identified the person on the bike. "That's her. She's headed to join them."

"Let me see your binoculars."

Suddenly the distinctive and terrifying sound of a German MG42 machine gun erupted in the east.

The sun was shining. The air was warm, smelling of fragrant pine and ripe apples.

Graf and Weise sat with their backs to the brick wall. The four-foot-high brick wall surrounded a large brick-and-stone house situated between the canal road and the canal. The sturdy, two-story building was a water pumping station used to raise and lower the water level in the canal. It now served as Kodritz's headquarters.

Graf smoked a cigarette while he wrapped a clean bandage around Weise's left hand.

"You're going to lose that hand if we don't get you to a doctor soon."

Weise nodded. "There is no hospital here. What do you suggest?"

"I'll talk to Gunter and see if you can be evacuated tonight with the logistics team when the supplies arrive."

"*If* the supplies arrive, you mean."

"There is no other option."

"And if I do go with the resupply team, I will travel where? You know there isn't a field hospital for many kilometers. The nearest hospital is probably in Arnhem."

Graf didn't answer. He sensed what was coming.

"No, I'm finished. I couldn't even cross that canal."

"Nonsense."

"It's not nonsense," Weise answered. "I've been thinking about this for the past few days. I could surrender. The Americans have good medical facilities, or so I've heard."

"Surrender? Out of the question. *Fallschirmjägers* don't surrender."

"You know that's not true," Weise replied.

"So what is your point?"

"You know the war is lost. We don't have one chance in ten of winning. Besides, you hate the Nazis as much as I do. Why should we fight for Hitler?"

"I don't fight for Hitler. I stay because of these," Graf pointed to the sleeping *Fallschirmjägers* lying behind the wall.

"I'm not sure I understand that excuse anymore. If you had the courage of your convictions, you would take these lads with you and surrender. If you don't, you are surely condemning them to death as much as if you shot them yourself."

Graf's face turned hard as steel. "Keep quiet. If the SS hear you talk like that, *they* will shoot you. Is that what you want?"

"No, I want to leave this insanity. The darkest places in hell are reserved for those who maintain their neutrality in times like these. It's time to stop being neutral to this madness."

Graf was silent for a moment as he considered Weise's comment. He fervently believed that ruthlessness and brutality were, in most cases, a clear indication of cowardice. Yes, he had never embraced the Nazi cause, yet he had fought all over the world to achieve a victory that, in the end, would be a Nazi victory.

He consoled himself with the belief that it was his duty to fight for Germany. He relieved his conscious of guilt by telling himself that he was a *Fallschirmjäger* and not in the SS. He mitigated his reluctance to do anything more to oppose the Nazis with his fervent belief that the duty of a soldier was to obey proper orders.

Yet there were moral limits to obedience. He, of all people, knew that not all orders were to be obeyed.

"Looks like we have company," Weise announced.

An SS soldier ran to Graf and knelt next to him. "*Obersturmführer* Kodritz directed me to tell you that partisans are moving down the road. You are ordered to prepare your men to attack."

"Partisans?" Graf questioned as the SS soldier ran back to the right side of the German line. "Weise, get the men up."

Weise roused the sleeping *Fallschirmjägers*.

Graf moved to a hole in the wall and lay down on his belly. He peered from the side of the broken bricks and looked out. To his right-front, about one hundred meters ahead, he saw two lines of people walking down the left and right side of the road.

He quickly scanned the approaching group. They were children, barely teenagers, all wearing orange armbands.

Graf looked back at his men. His *Fallschirmjägers* were up and had their weapons ready. He signaled for Küster to join him. "Küster, run over to Gunter. Tell him not to fire. It would be too stupid to be knocked off by a kid from the Dutch resistance. I can disarm this gaggle without a shot and without anyone getting killed."

Küster nodded.

Before Küster could move, a burst of fire from an SS MG42 machine gun broke the silence.

The lead two youngsters were hit and dropped to the ground.

A boy in the rear of the column immediately ran off to the west. The rest of the civilians knelt to the ground seeking cover in a small ditch on the west side of the road.

All the SS soldiers were firing now, blasting away with every weapon they possessed.

More youngsters were killed.

"Cease-fire!" Graf shouted as he stood up. "Stop shooting!"

Graf's *Fallschirmjägers* knelt behind the brick wall with their weapons ready but without shooting.

The Dutch youngsters did not have time to shoot back. They were too stunned to react.

The SS men continued to fire, picking off the Dutch as they cowered in the ditch. Three boys stood up to run. Two were immediately cut down; the survivor hid behind the body of one of the fallen. The rest of the survivors remained pinned down in the mud, too afraid to lift their heads.

"Damn it! Cease-fire!" Graf screamed angrily. Graf felt as if he were choking. He couldn't find the words to express his anger.

The SS finally stopped shooting.

"Surrender now or we will start firing again!" Kodritz ordered in German.

No one moved. Graf could hear a boy crying.

"This is your last chance," Kodritz bellowed. "Surrender now. Stand up with your hands held high!"

"We surrender," a Dutch boy shouted in German. "Don't shoot!"

Five boys and a girl slowly stood up with their hands in the air. One of the boys was wounded, his left arm dangling as if it were hanging by a thread.

Kodritz shot an evil glance at Graf. "*Oberfeldwebel* Graf, I will handle this."

Graf stood near the wall, fifteen paces to Kodritz's left. Kodritz then walked out to the road, followed by Gunter and three other SS men. The *Obersturmführer* signaled his men to line up the six civilians on the road and face the prisoners to the west.

The teenagers stood by the road quaking in fear. The wounded boy at the end of the line fell to the ground sobbing.

"By order of the *Reichsführer* Heinrich Himmler, all partisans who take up arms against the Reich are to be shot," Kodritz ordered loudly, as if he were an actor on a stage. He cocked his P-38 pistol, walked behind the first boy and shot him in the back of the head.

The boy recoiled and crumpled to the ground.

"*Obersturmführer*, stop!" Graf shouted.

Kodritz ignored Graf and shot the next boy.

"*Obersturmführer*, we should keep them as prisoners!" Graf screamed and strode toward Kodritz.

Kodritz turned toward Graf, his pistol pointed at him. Gunter leveled his MP40 at Graf as well.

"Gunter. Shoot the *Oberfeldwebel* if he says another word."

Gunter smiled a sinister grin. *"Jawohl, Herr Obersturmführer."*

Kodritz then moved behind the girl. She was a pretty brunette, probably fifteen or sixteen. The breeze blew gently, and her hair fell over her right shoulder.

Kodritz fired; the girl fell over into the ditch.

Kodritz's pistol smoked in the cool air as he walked behind the remaining three boys. He killed the next two and then stopped. The last boy was holding his arm as he lay on the ground sobbing. Kodritz paused, slowly reloading his pistol with a new magazine.

"This is the fate of partisans," Kodritz announced as he aimed and pulled the trigger.

The bullet splattered the boy's skull.

The boy stopped crying.

Kodritz then turned to Graf.

Graf stood perfectly still, stone-faced and breathing hard, his PPSh submachine gun in his hands. His *Fallschirmjägers* stood at the wall, ready, watching, and waiting for a signal from Graf.

Graf heard his men snap off the safeties on their weapons. The SS troopers turned to look at Graf. Gunter kept the barrel of his MP40 aimed at the tall *Fallschirmjäger*.

Kodritz sauntered up to Graf and stood inches from his face. Graf could see pure hate burning in the *Obersturmführer*'s eyes.

"Since your men did not join in the battle, they will bury these partisans!"

Graf didn't move or reply.

Kodritz abruptly turned and walked away toward the brick building, followed by his men.

Graf stood silent and completely still for a moment.

"Help me with these children, men," Weise ordered.

The *Fallschirmjägers* slung their weapons and slowly lumbered over to the bodies to bury them.

Graf was still silent, immovable, as his men dragged the bodies to the east side of the road. *Jägers* Dörnefeld and Merckel began digging graves while the rest recovered the bodies.

Küster walked to the west side of the road. Suddenly he looked up and pointed. "There is one in the bushes!"

A civilian in a gray coat ran from the bushes. Without orders Küster rushed forward and tackled the person. Holding the civilian by the neck he brought his prisoner back to Graf.

Graf looked at the sixteen-year-old girl. Her eyes were red with tears, yet her face was filled with defiance.

"Küster, did she have a weapon?"

"No, *Oberfeldwebel.*"

"Then let her go."

A voice shouted from the second floor of the pump house. "Bring that partisan to me."

Graf turned and saw Kodritz standing on the second-floor terrace.

Graf thought quickly, his brain teeming with the dire possibilities. "This one had no weapon or armband, *Herr Obersturmführer,* and is therefore not a partisan."

"We cannot risk letting her go," Kodritz answered. "Shoot her."

"*Herr Obersturmführer,* since we cannot let her go for fear that she may tell someone that we are here, I will take personal responsibility for her. She is a prisoner of the Deutsches Fallschirmjäger until we can arrange for her release."

Just then a soldier came out onto the second-floor terrace and handed Kodritz a message. "We will settle this matter later. I hold you personally responsible, *Oberfeldwebel* Graf, to see to it that she doesn't escape."

With that comment, Kodritz turned and walked off into the building.

Graf breathed a sigh of relief.

Graf looked at the frightened girl. She had tears in her eyes as well as hatred on her face.

"Miss, I cannot tell you how sorry I am for what happened here. What is your name?"

"Mira," the girl answered meekly.

"Mira, if you do as I say, we will hold you until tomorrow, and then I will let you go. You have my word."

Mira looked at Graf in disbelief.

"Küster, take this girl inside the first floor of the pump house, tie her hands, and guard her until I arrive. Keep her out of sight of the SS."

Küster nodded, ushering his prisoner into the pump house.

"They shot them. Right there along the road. It was an execution." Baker put down his field glasses. He had watched the entire massacre and execution from the belfry. He felt sick and angry.

"What do we do now?" Cat asked. "I saw her captured. We can't leave Mira with those bastards."

"At least she's alive. Did you see any of the others make it?"

"One," Cat said as he pointed to the road leading to Lieshout.

A boy was running to the town. Baker found him with his binoculars. The boy was without a weapon, but he had an orange band on his arm.

"Cat, we need to talk to that kid."

Cat nodded. The two of them immediately ran down the stairs, out the church, and through the streets. They raced down the cobblestone street to the east in order to intercept the boy. As they entered the main lane, the boy ran between them. Cat grabbed him around the waist, pulling him to the side of a brick home.

"Easy lad, you're safe now," Cat announced.

The sobbing boy held on to Cat as if the British colour sergeant were his father.

Baker waited as the boy cried. After a while, Baker placed his hand on the boy's shoulder. "We're not going to hurt you son, we're your friends. Do you speak English?"

The boy nodded. "We wanted to see if . . . see if there were any Germans at the pump house."

"Are you part of Mira's Bicyclists?" Baker asked.

"Yes, she warned me not to do anything," the boy said. "I should have listened to her."

"What's your name, son?" Cat asked.

"Peter."

"Well, Peter, what do you know about the Germans?"

"The Germans plan to cross the canal tonight, near the pump house. We didn't know they were already on the west side."

"How do they plan to cross?" Baker questioned. "There is no bridge."

"They plan to bring a barge down from the north."

"A barge?" Cat quizzed.

"Yes. There is a big, steel-bottomed coal barge hidden on the east bank of the canal near Beek. They have it well camouflaged, but we found it. They will float it down at night, as the current goes south, and when your airplanes cannot see it. Then they will use the metal sheets on the barge as planks to drive their tanks onto the barge and to the other side."

"Blimey, I hadn't thought of that," Cat announced. "It's brilliant. Like a bloody pontoon bridge."

"Yeah, and if the Krauts are hiding in those woods,

they lay the barge in fast and cross over as many tanks and armored vehicles as they want."

"You're a good lad, Peter, and very brave," Cat offered. "Where do you live?"

"Here in Lieshout. My mama and papa live up the street."

"Well, get back home to them now, and stay away from the Germans."

Cat let the boy go.

"God bless you," the boy said as he ran off.

"Well, that's a fine situation. What should we do now?" Cat asked.

"I believe the kid. Do you?"

Cat nodded.

Baker looked at his watch. It was already 1440 hours. "We need help. We must report this to Division Headquarters right away."

Baker and Cat hiked back to the barn and found Corporal Ackers, Guardsman Logan, and Guardsman Avery hunched over the engine compartment of Cat's Bren Carrier.

"What's the problem?" Cat asked as he reached the group.

Guardsman Logan shrugged. "Colour Sergeant Gilchrist, I started her up, just like procedures say to do, and the engine caught on fire. We've lost all power."

"Aye, it looks like the electrical system shorted and burned up," Ackers said.

"I don't know why this happened," Logan offered. "I can't fix it either."

"What about the radio?" Cat asked.

"It's not worth cuckoo-spit, unless we can hook it up to another source of electricity," Ackers replied.

"What about your Bren Carrier?"

"It's no use boiling your cabbage twice," Logan offered.

"He's right," Ackers answered. "We'll probably do more harm than good. None of our men are radio technicians."

Cat shook his head. "Baker, let's try your radio."

Baker nodded; they walked over to Baker's jeep. Zanovitch sat in the driver's seat and Swanson sat in the front seat next to him.

"Are we moving out?" Swanson asked.

"Not yet," Baker replied. "Zano, crank up the jeep and turn on the radio."

Zanovitch turned off the radio, started the jeep, and turned the radio back on. Zanovitch took off his helmet, and put on a headset and tried to reach 101st Airborne Division Headquarters. After several tries he switched to the alternate frequencies and tried again.

"There's some kind of interference," Zanovitch announced. "We're picking up a very strong signal. The Krauts must be jamming us."

"Try to reach any station," Baker replied. "Maybe we can get someone to relay the message through to headquarters."

"I've tried that, too, no dice," Zanovitch answered. "Here, I'll put it on the speaker. Listen to this."

German military music blared from the speaker.

"Not a very catchy tune," Swanson joked.

"It's jamming for sure," Zanovitch added. "I hear the same shit on most of the other channels."

"If they are planning an attack," Cat remarked, "it makes sense to jam our frequencies right before the operation starts."

"Yeah, that's what I was thinking," Baker replied. "Sure as we're standing here, they're going to cross tonight."

Cat rubbed his face in his hands and thought for a moment. "It looks like it's up to us, then. There's no one else here. Even if we rushed back to get help, we couldn't count on any of your paratrooper lads getting here until the morning."

"You're right," Baker replied. "Now all we have to do is figure out how in the hell we're going to stop the Germans from getting tanks across that damn canal."

"Do you have any ideas?" Cat asked. "How do we sink a coal barge?"

Baker looked at Swanson. "How many explosives did you say you have?"

The sun was setting and the air was turning cool.

Graf was tired. His weapon, helmet, and web gear were placed to his left side. Like all veteran soldiers he had learned to grab short moments of sleep whenever he could. He simply stopped thinking and lapsed into unconsciousness, but not now. The unwarranted killing of the Dutch children had affected him and reminded him of his worst nightmares from Russia. As a result, he didn't want to close his eyes.

Weise moved into the first floor of the pump house and sat down next to Graf.

"Security is posted and all the partisans have been buried."

Graff nodded. "Good. Now rest. I will need you alert in the morning."

Weise nodded. "Yes, I look forward to another glorious blitzkrieg. We will advance for the honor of the Fatherland and push the Allies back to the English Channel."

Graf shook his head. "Maybe not that far."

Graf's squad, minus Dörnefeld and Merckel, who were outside providing security, were sprawled out on the floor resting. Stöhr slept silently while Henning was snoring loud enough to wake the dead. Wigand and Berna ate the last of the rations they had taken from the British patrol the other day. Küster sat in a chair, guarding the girl and smoking a cigarette.

Mira sat in the northeast corner, her hands tied with a rope.

Graf looked at Mira and then at Küster. He grabbed his water bottle, stood up, and walked over to Mira.

Mira looked down at the ground, not wanting to make eye contact with the tall German sergeant.

Graf knelt down and gently pulled her chin up with his right hand. He looked her in the face. "I'll untie your hands, if you give me your solemn word that you will not try to run away."

"You have my word," Mira answered in German.

Graf pulled out his long fighting knife.

Mira's eyes widened.

"Don't be afraid. I promised not to hurt you. I keep my promises."

Graf cut the rope. Mira undid the bindings and rubbed her left wrist.

"Would you care for some water?"

Mira nodded, took the canteen that Graf offered, and took a swig.

"*Danke,*" Mira said in German.

"You speak German well," Graf offered.

"Four years of occupation gave me many opportunities to practice," Mira replied. "We Dutch pride ourselves on speaking other languages. That's why so many of us speak English."

"I speak English as well," Graf said, switching from German to English.

"Yes, I can hear that you do," Mira answered in English. "Where did you learn English?"

"I studied in the United States, in Chicago, before the war," Graf offered. "Where did you learn English?"

"From my father and in school. English was mandatory study until you and your army came to Holland. After that, German became mandatory. I was able to learn both."

"And where is your father?"

"Dead. Killed by Germans in the invasion of 1940."

"And your mother?"

"She is ill and with my grandmother in Lieshout."

"Are you a partisan?" Graf asked.

"If I tell you that I am, will you shoot me?"

"No. I won't shoot you, even if you are a partisan," Graf said with a smile.

Mira didn't answer.

Graf nodded and walked back to his place along the wall.

"Keep an eye on her, Küster," Graf said in German. "I am going to grab a few moments rest. We will be busy tonight and stand-to is just after midnight. The barge should be here about oh one hundred, and with luck we will start crossing the tanks, StuG's, halftracks, and the rest of the *kampfgruppe* by oh three hundred. By noon tomorrow, we may be in Eindhoven."

Küster smiled. "That will be a sight to see."

Weise turned to Graf. "Do you think we will make it all the way to Eindhoven?"

"It's possible."

"So you will not consider what I was talking about earlier today. About the Americans?"

"No. If you mention it again, I'll be very angry with you."

"So tell me one thing, and I'll stop bothering you and let you rest."

"Anything to stop your chattering," Graf replied.

"Why were you arrested in Russia?"

"Who told you I was arrested?"

"That pig, Gunter, mentioned it. He said that Kodritz was checking on you, and that you were no better than the traitor Stauffenberg."

Graf didn't answer. He had never personally known Colonel von Stauffenberg but knew that he was one of the leading figures who had tried to kill Hitler last July. Stauffenberg had arranged an elaborate plot to kill the Führer and transfer power to anti-Nazi officers of the Wehrmacht. Stauffenberg placed a briefcase with explosives next to Hitler at the Führer's headquarters in East Prussia. Just before the bomb was to explode, Stauffenberg left the room. At the very last moment, someone in the room moved the briefcase away from Hitler. When the bomb went off, four senior officers were killed and everyone in the room was wounded, but Hitler survived. By the end of the day the plot had failed. Stauffenberg was arrested, put up against the wall of the German army headquarters building in Berlin, and shot.

Secretly, Graf had wished Stauffenberg had succeeded. If Stauffenberg had killed Hitler, everything might be different now.

But Stauffenberg had failed. Hitler was not dead. The Nazis remained in control and the war and the bloodletting ground on.

The reason for Graf's arrest was nothing as strategic as Stauffenberg's attempt on Hitler.

In Russia, after the terrible battle along the Neva River in 1942, Graf and his *Fallschirmjägers* halted a column of Russian refugees that were moving down the road behind their defensive position. The refugees were starving and merely wanted to go to another village down the road. Graf gave the refugees permission to pass, but an SS colonel arrived with a truck full of SS soldiers. The colonel ordered Graf and his men to execute the Russians as partisans.

Graf protested. The group consisted of old men, old women, and children. There were no military-age men or women in the group and, more important, the refugees had no weapons.

Still, the SS officer insisted that his orders be obeyed and that the refugees be executed immediately.

Graf hesitated.

He and his men had just fought a desperate battle against some of the best soldiers in the Red Army. He was a soldier who fought the enemy's soldiers. He was not an executioner. He was not about to kill civilians, especially children and old men and women.

Graf refused.

The SS colonel ordered his men to shoot the refugees. The SS soldiers obediently piled out of the truck and started shooting. The elderly died where they stood. The children tried to run away, but the SS men hunted them down, laughing as they finished them off.

Graf tried to stop the killing and struck an SS sergeant in the process. The SS men went for their weapons and so did the *Fallschirmjägers*. For a moment, there was a good chance that a battle would erupt between Graf's *Fallschirmjägers* and the SS. Both sides stood with weapons aimed at the other. Graf quickly saw the folly in this course of action and didn't want any of his men killed, so he ordered his men to stand down, and he surrendered.

Graf and three of his sergeants were arrested for disobeying orders in the face of the enemy. They were summarily transferred to service in a penal battalion. Service in a penal battalion was a death sentence. Penal units were considered highly expendable and were often placed in the most desperate situations with little support, supplies, or proper leadership. It was only by the interven-

tion of one of his officers, Major Friedrich August Frei-
herr von der Heydte, that Graf was spared from certain
death.

"Go to sleep," Graf ordered. "My history is none of
your business."

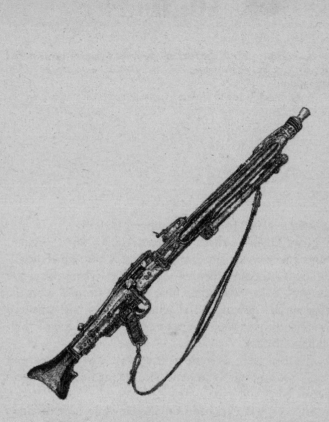

German MG42 Machine Gun

10: D+7

Sunday, 0140 hours, September 24, 1944.

Nine Allied soldiers huddled around Staff Sergeant Matt Baker inside the dimly lit barn. A kerosene lamp illuminated the barn just enough to allow them to see the diagram Baker was scratching into the ground with the edge of his bayonet. The Allied soldiers had smeared black soot over their faces to conceal the shine of their skin in the dark.

The men were as tense as taut wire. They were about to go into combat again, and the odds against them were fierce.

All eyes were focused on Baker while he explained what he intended to do. Cat, Zanovitch, and Swanson stood to Baker's front. The rest of the Irish Guardsmen, Ackers, Roy, Avery, Logan, McNevin, and Friskin stood around behind Baker.

Outside, the air was thick with water as the fog enveloped the land. Visibility was less than five feet.

Cat smoked a cigarette to the butt and then dropped it on the ground, smashing the burning embers with the sole of his combat boot. If men, like metal, are hardened by fire, then Staff Sergeant Baker will surely be tested tonight, or killed, Cat thought as he snuffed out the cigarette.

Cat glanced at Baker with concern. He admired the American's intense courage. He realized that Baker was also a solid combat leader and knew his tactics, but this course of action seemed almost suicidal.

"The problem is mathematical," Cat offered. "How do you separate one barge from a couple of hundred Germans and end up with two live Yanks?"

"I agree, there are risks, but do you have a better idea?"

"When you blow that bloody barge, you'll be in the middle of the anthill, and Jerry will know that you're the one who kicked the hill over."

"That's why this has to work," Baker insisted. "It's a choice between force and stealth. There are too many Germans to fight. You said yourself that it's up to us, and you know there isn't time for anything else."

Cat nodded. "You can be a dagger or a hammer. We could still move down there in this fog, get close, hit them all at once with guns blazing, then hammer the hell out of 'em. If we surprise them, maybe they'll lose their nerve and pull out."

"Or maybe they'll cross with everything they have? They wouldn't plan this crossing unless they have some power behind it. I'm guessing it's a company- or battalion-sized unit hidden in that forest. If so, they could outnumber us ten or twelve to one."

"Okay, you're probably right, but going in there with just you and Swanson is a hell of a risk."

"I don't see any other way. This is the one way we can even the odds."

Cat didn't like the idea of splitting up their small force, but Baker's battlefield logic was sound. If Baker and Swanson could blow up the barge, then the entire enemy force hiding in the woods on the other side of the canal didn't matter.

"Agree?" Baker asked.

"Agree," Cat conceded.

"This is the plan, then," Baker announced. "Swanson and I will move to the southeast, enter the canal, move upstream, and place the explosives at the crossing point. Swanson has rigged the demolitions to explode simultaneously once we activate the detonator."

"I've double-primed four bags of C-two explosives with det cord," Swanson added. "The det cord links all the charges, and once I set them off, they will go off all together."

Baker drew a line in the dirt showing the relative location where Cat and his men should be in relation to the pump house. "When you hear the explosion, open up with everything you have. Not before."

"And if anything goes wrong, you want us to wait?" Cat asked.

"Right. If you don't hear the explosion, then you should consider our attempt a failure and wait for the first enemy vehicle to cross. If they don't know you are here, you may still have a chance to hit them when they try to cross. That's where Zanovitch comes in."

"If I can get a clear shot, I can hit the lead vehicle with my bazooka," Zanovitch announced. "If all else fails, I may be able to block their crossing by destroying the lead vehicle."

Cat shook his head. "Or they'll just push it out of the way and continue crossing."

"Well, we'll know for sure in a few hours, won't we?" Baker replied in a tone that ended the debate.

"Understood," Cat replied. "We'll move out in an hour and take up a firing line as close to the pump house as we can get without being seen by the Jerries. The rest is up to you."

"Okay, let's go," Baker announced.

Cat turned off the kerosene lamp and they all went outside. A light rain began to fall as the men huddled together not only to hear their leader, but also to share body heat.

In the distance, Baker heard the ominous sound of armored vehicles moving in the forest.

"Don't worry, this will work," Baker offered.

"Yeah, and when I get home a beautiful bird with a pint of Guinness in her mitt will be waiting for me at the door," Cat joked. "You just take down that barge, Baker, or I'll have to risk the last of my nine lives to save your ass."

"I'll consider your offer an insurance policy," Baker answered.

"I should be going with you," Zanovitch protested.

"No, I need you and your bazooka on the other side," Baker answered. "I'm counting on you if my attempt doesn't work."

Zanovitch nodded. "Good luck."

"Swanson, is everything ready?" Baker asked.

"I've rigged four pack charges. All four are wired with blasting caps and twelve pounds of M-2 Tetrytol blocks in each bag, so they ought to do the trick," the confident New Yorker answered. "Once we place the charges, we'll unwind the det cord and keep moving away until we can get far enough from the bridge to hook the wires up to the firing device."

There was silence for a moment. The tension was thick. The men in the circle all sensed what was at stake and wondered deep down in their own souls what the morning would bring.

Baker looked at his watch. "All right. It's oh one forty-five. It'll take us twenty to thirty minutes to move to the southern bank of the canal, a few minutes to swim across, and then about thirty minutes on the far bank. You should hear the explosion around oh three hundred. The rest is up to you."

Cat nodded as he stuck out his hand to offer Baker good luck. "Just make it back. I don't fancy having to explain why the Irish Guards couldn't bring back their American friends. It looks bad in the newspapers."

Baker shook Cat's hand and smiled. "Don't worry, we'll make it. Remember, Mira's in that pump house. When we sink the barge, if all else fails, you have to save her."

"Just make sure 'all else' doesn't fail," Cat replied.

Graf shook Weise's shoulder. "It's time."

Weise opened his eyes with a startled look, then quickly calmed down and nodded. "*Ja, ja.* I understand."

The first floor of the pump house was lit by a candle in the center of the room. *Jäger* Dörnefeld, who had just finished security duty, sat on a wooden chair next to a small metal stove that he had made from a British mess tin and heated water for tea.

Graf's *Fallschirmjägers* prepared for battle. They put on their combat gear, stuffed ammunition and grenades in their pockets, and checked their weapons.

"Weise, Küster, orders group, now," Graf announced.

Weise and Küster stepped over to Graf and stood in front of their leader.

"Weise, you will check all the weapons and make sure every man has a basic load of ammunition. Redistribute ammunition if we are short. Especially check the ammunition for the machine gun today. I want Stöhr to have at least three hundred rounds."

Weise nodded. "I will also check that everyone has full water bottles."

"Good. Küster, you will be our point man today and will scout ahead when we are deployed in patrol formation. You will take Berna with you. He has shown himself to be an alert and dependable solider. He will be a big help to you."

"Thank you, *Oberfeldwebel*. I will not let you down."

"I know you won't, Küster," Graf said as he placed a hand on the younger man's shoulder. "Just keep Berna alive for me, will you?"

"*Jawohl, Oberfeldwebel!*"

"Excellent, now get to work," Graf ordered as he brought up his wrist to look at his watch. "We depart this building in fifteen minutes."

Weise and Küster turned and went to their tasks.

In the center of the open room of the pump house, Dörnefeld was still at his tea. He poured some of the liquid into a metal cup as he walked over to Graf.

"*Oberfeldwebel,* this is not much, the last of the tea I took from the British the other day," Dörnefeld offered.

Graf smiled and nodded. "You won't mind if I offer it to our guest, will you?"

"*Nein, Oberfeldwebel.*"

Graf took the cup of steaming tea over to Mira. She was awake and sitting in the corner with her arms around her knees, shivering in the cold.

Graf knelt next to Mira and offered the cup. "Please. It's tea. Drink this."

Mira nodded a polite thank-you and took the tea. The warm beverage invigorated her.

Graf pulled a biscuit from his pocket and presented this to Mira as well. "This is good. It is a gift from the British."

"Danke," Mira took this second gift and nibbled on the cracker. "What will happen to me?"

"We are about to leave. If you promise to stay here and not leave this building until noon, you will be free to go where you please."

Mira didn't answer.

"If you leave here before noon, troops may be crossing here most of the morning, and I cannot vouch for your safety."

"I understand," Mira replied. She took a final sip of the tea, handing it to Graf. As she did, she noticed Küster putting a book in his knapsack. The cover was unmistakable. It was Alexander's red-covered notebook.

Mira turned ashen.

Graf noticed the dramatic change in Mira's demeanor. "What is it?"

"Where did that soldier get that book," Mira asked.

"He took it from a dead partisan," Graf explained as he stood up.

Tears rolled down Mira's cheeks.

"Did you know the partisan who had this book?" Graf demanded.

"This belongs to my cousin," Mira sobbed. "Are you sure he is dead?"

Graf didn't answer.

An SS soldier entered the room and stood next to Graf. "*Oberfeldwebel* Graf, *Obersturmführer* Kodritz orders you to report to his command post upstairs, immediately."

Graf turned to address the SS soldier. "Tell the *Obersturmführer* that I am on my way."

The SS soldier nodded and left the way he had come.

Graf walked over to where he had left his helmet, weapon, and gear. He quickly put on his battle gear, placing the leather sling of the PPSh over his neck.

"In war, people who are in battles are killed, Mira. I am sorry to hear that this Alexander was your cousin. He was with an enemy unit and we had little choice."

Mira looked away, placed her face in her knees, and sobbed.

Baker and Swanson hiked through the fog carrying their heavy satchels filled with explosives. The fog slowed their movement. The mud made the walking worse. Baker paused frequently, checking his compass to make sure they were headed in the right direction.

They entered a thick clump of woods. The trees were placed so close together that Baker couldn't move through them standing up. There was no way around, so Baker got down on all fours. On hands and knees the two men moved through the woods for about twenty yards. Finally, they found a break in the trees and came to a clearing.

The two men sat in the mud catching their breath. Baker pulled out his compass and took another heading.

"Are we close?"

"The canal should be right over there, about fifty yards," Baker whispered as he pointed to the southeast. "We better crawl from here, just in case."

Baker and Swanson crawled on their bellies over the cold, wet ground. Baker could hear the sound of his breathing, but nothing else. He stopped several times to listen. Finally, he heard the sound of flowing water.

They had arrived at the western bank of the Willemsvaart Canal.

"Are you sure we are at the right spot on the canal?" Swanson asked.

"Close enough," Baker answered. "Now it's time to take a swim."

Baker waited a moment as he looked at the water

flowing steadily in the canal. From the western bank he could see that the water was deep. The current flowed south, but not too fast for them to swim to the far side.

He couldn't see the far bank, but from his study of the map he knew that the canal was only about twenty-five yards wide.

Baker turned to Swanson. "Ready?"

"As ready as I'll ever be," Swanson whispered.

Baker slowly lowered himself down the steep wall and into the chilly water of the Willemsvaart Canal. A moment later Swanson slid into the water next to Baker.

"Now all we have to do is get to the other side without getting shot," Baker whispered as he tied a rope to Swanson's side.

Baker still couldn't see the other side of the canal because of the dense fog. He unwound a length of rope that was tied to his web belt and handed the rope to Swanson. "Take this so we don't get lost in the fog. I'll swim across. You wait here. When I tug on the line, follow the rope and swim across to me."

Swanson nodded.

Baker pushed off the western bank of the canal. The heavy load of explosives he carried made the swim difficult, but he carried on, reaching the wall of the eastern side.

Finding a metal mooring ring to anchor his position, he tugged on the rope and waited. Swanson appeared a moment later and the two of them rested for a bit, listening for the enemy.

Somewhere to the east a dog started barking.

Swanson moved up to Baker's left. "That damn dog is going to give us away."

"Nothing we can do about that now," Baker replied quietly. "The crossing must be right in front of us."

As he pushed against the current through the water

along the eastern wall of the canal, he heard faint noises. As he continued to move north he could make out the sound of German voices.

Swanson heard the voices, too, and pointed up ahead.

"Yeah," Baker whispered. "We must be close."

Swanson took a couple of deep breaths and squinted in the direction of the crossing point. "Damn if I can see it."

"Wait here."

Baker swam forward a few feet and suddenly noticed the dark outline of the coal barge. The barge was big and fit inside the crossing point with only inches to spare, creating the perfect floating bridge.

Baker quietly swam back a few feet and found Swanson waiting. "It's ten feet in front of us. Move forward and start placing the charges."

Swanson nodded and handed a spool of det cord to Baker. "Hang on to your pack charges. I'll be back after I place these two."

Swanson swam into the fog.

Baker waited. He pulled the pistol from his holster. The dog was barking louder now. Baker was sure the dog sensed that he and Swanson were in the water.

Baker heard more voices talking in German.

Swanson paddled back to Baker. "I placed the charges. Two more will do the trick. Hand 'em to me."

"I can hear Krauts all over the place, so be careful," Baker whispered.

As Baker handed Swanson the explosive charges, he heard the grinding of tracks against steel road wheels.

"Kraut tanks," Swanson offered. "They must be moving to cross the barge point."

Baker noticed that Swanson's teeth were chattering. A combination of cold and fear. Baker put his hand on Swanson's shoulder. "We're running out of time, but you can do this."

"Just hang on to that det cord," Swanson replied as he took the last two charges from Baker. Swanson then moved along the wall, into the fog, back to the barge.

Baker stood in the water, his right foot supported in a crag in the canal wall, with water up to his neck. He was all alone as he waited for Swanson. He felt his heart pounding hard. The minutes ticked by. The barking dog seemed to be somewhere just above him.

Then, very near, Baker heard another German voice. He couldn't see the German in the thick fog, but he was close. He heard footsteps sounding just above him on the eastern bank.

"*Schieben Sie hoch. Lassen Sie uns gehen!*" a gruff voice shouted from above.

Baker held his breath for a moment, grasping onto the mooring ring, and aiming his pistol toward the bank above him.

Tense minutes passed. Baker waited as he clicked down on the thumb safety of his .45 caliber Colt automatic pistol.

Suddenly, Swanson appeared.

Baker put his finger to his lips, signaling silence.

The two men waited in the water for a tense moment, then the voice moved away.

"Okay, they're set," Swanson whispered.

Suddenly, Baker looked up and saw a German soldier pointing a rifle down toward the water.

"*Wer ist dort?*"

Baker pulled Swanson under the water and pushed him back to the south, away from the barge.

The German screamed again and fired his rifle.

The bullet hit a yard north from Baker.

Baker and Swanson slowly swam away from the confused German sentry. Baker was sure the German had heard them, but in the fog he was shooting at shadows. It was just enough confusion for them to get away.

"Auf was schießen Sie?" a different voice in German screamed. *"Kein Schießen sie Dummkopf!"*

Baker and Swanson swam away, hidden in the fog.

"To the west side," Baker whispered as he rolled out the detonation cord from the spool. "We'll get over the west side of the canal and then blow it."

The two American paratroopers swam to the west wall of the canal as they heard the sound of armored vehicles approaching. Pushing through the water and lighter now that they weren't carrying the heavy packs of explosives, they quickly reached the western side of the canal. Groping for footholds, Baker climbed up the wall, reaching down to help Swanson up. Within seconds they were out of the water and up on the western bank.

The fog was less dense above the canal. Baker could make out the dark outline of the barge.

Swanson lay near the wall of the canal to make the final preparations to set off the explosive charge. He took a small wooden box out of his pocket and gently removed a blasting cap. He next pulled out a pair of pliers from the leather case on his web belt. Carefully, he primed the detonating cord with the blasting cap and laid out a two-foot-long length of variable time fuse pyrotechnic delay cord. Once the variable time fuse cord was laid out, Swanson attached a fuse igniter to the time cord and used the pliers to crimp the igniter to the time cord.

Baker heard the sound of a German armored vehicle moving to the barge. He waited anxiously as Swanson worked to prepare the demolitions charge.

"We're running out of time."

"Almost there," Swanson replied.

"Come on."

"There," Swanson answered and he placed the primed fuse on the ground. "If everything works, when I pull this igniter, we'll have thirty seconds before the variable time fuse ignites the blasting cap that will set the det cord and the explosives off. We should be safe here on this side of the canal, but there will be one hell of a fireworks display."

Just then a German halftrack crossed onto the barge.

Baker watched as the halftrack moved slowly across the center of the barge and then got stuck trying to exit the west side. German voices screeched curses, and a dozen men worked on the east side to fix the ramp.

"Now, before they get across the barge!" Baker ordered.

Swanson pulled the fuse igniter. The time cord fizzed and the seconds went by as the flame slowly traveled to the blasting cap.

Baker and Swanson lay on the ground. Baker could see the halftrack make another attempt at the western ramp of the barge. This time the halftrack made it across to the west side.

A dozen Germans cheered.

"*Fahren über!*" A German voice shouted from the western edge of the canal to the Germans on the east side.

At that moment the time fuse hit the blasting cap. In a flash faster than the blink of an eye, the detonation cord exploded and set off the four packs stuffed with demolitions.

A huge shower of sparks and flame shot up from the eastern side of the barge. Objects sailed through the air and men screamed. A thick black smoke filled the canal.

The explosion echoed against the walls of the pump house. Debris fell from the air. Baker and Swanson hugged the mud, covering their heads with their hands.

Then, for a brief moment, there was an eerie silence.

Just as suddenly, all hell broke loose. Bren machine-gun fire stuttered from the west. German soldiers shouted orders. A StuG pulled up on the east side of the canal at the crossing point, but stopped at the canal's edge.

Baker saw the outline of the barge and saw that it was tilting. Swanson had done it right. The eastern side of the barge was blown away. Baker watched as the barge rapidly filled with water, listed to the east, and sank.

"The bastards can't cross this canal now," Swanson said in jubilation.

Suddenly, Baker sensed that someone was behind them.

"*Hände hoch!*" a stern voice shouted in German.

Baker turned, gazing into the cold, steely eyes of a German paratrooper with an assault rife pointed at them.

The two Americans dropped their pistols and raised their hands.

Graf and his *Fallschirmjägers* manned the front windows of the first floor of the brick pump house. The SS men on the second floor blasted away at the flashes in the fog.

Stöhr opened fire with the MG42.

"Cease-fire!" Graf ordered. "Hold your fire until I tell you to shoot."

"Yes, *Oberfeldwebel*!"

Graf looked around the dark room. As soon as the firing started they had put out the candle. In the dark he could see his men. He could also see that Mira was still in the corner. The shooting outside continued, but Graf's men could only see a few flashes and no definite targets; so they held their fire.

It was amazing, Graf thought, how fast the tides of war shifted. A few minutes ago, he was ready to lead his men as part of an attack with tanks, assault guns, and halftracks. Now he was in charge of a squad defending an isolated outpost, fighting in the fog, and cut off from his main force by an enemy of an unknown-sized unit.

Küster entered the southern entrance to the pump house with his two prisoners in front of him. Just then, a bazooka fired from somewhere in the fog. The halftrack that was in the center of the road just to the north of the pump house erupted in flames.

Graf stood up. He cradled his PPSh in his arms. "What did you find Küster?"

"Two American paratroopers, *Herr Oberfeldwebel*. The barge has sunk. We will not be able to get any armored vehicles across the canal. These two must have placed the explosives. They are saboteurs. Should I shoot them?"

Graf looked at the two men in the glowing light of the burning halftrack.

"No, Küster, they are soldiers in uniform. You and I might have done the same thing. They are not saboteurs to be shot."

"Yes, *Herr Oberfeldwebel*."

Graf looked at Baker and Swanson then spoke to them in English: "Well, I must say, it is an honor to be up against some professional soldiers for a change."

Baker looked surprised. "You speak English? Now I am impressed."

Graf laughed. "I don't suppose you will tell me the size and composition of the force facing me outside?"

"Nope, not a chance," Baker answered.

"Well, in that case, I have a battle to fight. If you remain in the corner with our little partisan over there, I will treat you as soldiers, then you may live to see the hospitality of a German prisoner-of-war camp. Now move!"

Then in German, Graf said: "Küster, put them over there with the girl. If they try anything, shoot them instantly. Do not hesitate. These two are dangerous."

Küster nodded. Pointing with the barrel of his weapon, he herded the two Americans to the corner.

Graf returned to his squad, deployed in a line along the three windows that opened west along the wall.

"This is a fine mess," Weise replied. "We are pinned in this building. If the forces in the woods cannot cross the canal, then we are stuck here with only our squad and a handful of SS men."

The SS on the second floor blasted away in a wild fusillade of fire. One SS fighter fell from the balcony and landed in front of the building. In another moment, Kodritz, Gunter, and one other SS soldier rushed down from the second floor and entered the room.

"Why aren't you firing?" Kodritz demanded.

"We have no targets to shoot at from here," Graf replied. "What are your orders?"

Kodritz looked enraged. He stared at Graf and then looked around the room. In the reflection of the light from the flaming wreck outside he spied the Americans and Mira in the corner.

"Who are they?"

"We just captured them. Most likely, they are the ones who blew up the barge."

Kodritz went into a rage. He stomped back and forth screaming obscenities and then came back to Graf and stood inches from his face.

"I just received orders to evacuate to the eastern bank of the canal. We cannot cross the canal, thanks to these two spies. If we cannot use this crossing, our forces are useless here. The *kampfgruppe* commander has decided to move us north, toward Veghel and Koevering. The main fight is now there!"

Graf didn't reply or bat an eye.

"Your *Fallschirmjägers* and my two men are the only ones left on this side of the canal."

"What are your orders, *Obersturmführer*?" Graf repeated.

"Kill these three, and we will leave here immediately."

"These are my prisoners. I will not kill them."

Kodritz seemed ready to explode. He pulled his P38 pistol from its holster, aiming it at Graf's head.

"War moves people. It either moves them to our side or into oblivion. War is the most powerful force of change in human history . . . and the most demanding. Germany, led by the power of National Socialism, entered the war in 1939 with dreams of creating a new order. Our dreams have yet to be fulfilled, but only because the Bolsheviks, the capitalists, and their Jewish masters have tricked the world into opposing us. How can we win against such odds? I'll tell you how. By being ruthless. By being true believers. By crushing the weak with an iron boot. By showing no compassion for traitors."

Graf stood silent.

"You have opposed me from the beginning. You and your *Fallschirmjägers*. You are no better than the enemy."

Bullets struck the side of the building, sending brick chips and dust swirling inside.

"Kill these three. I will shoot you if you do not obey me!" Kodritz screamed.

Graf didn't flinch. He stood perfectly calm awaiting the bullet. "Shoot. Maybe it's time that I paid for my neutrality."

"That's it then," Kodritz yelled and pulled back the hammer of his pistol.

A shot echoed in the room.

The sounds of battle were winding down as there were few targets for anyone to identify in the fog. The German halftrack exploded for a second time as some ammunition in the back caught fire and detonated.

"Keep that Bren Gun firing on the second floor of that building," Cat ordered. "Short bursts. Just to keep their heads down."

"Aye, Colour Sergeant Gilchrist!" Guardsman Roy replied.

Cat looked out into the fog and liked what he saw. He couldn't see the barge, but from the size of the fireballs and the noise of the explosions he had no doubt that Baker and Swanson had accomplished their mission. The destruction of the German halftrack and the dozen or so dazed Germans who had walked into his Irish Guardsmen's line of fire after the big explosion were just icing on the cake.

"Good shot, Corporal Zanovitch," Cat shouted with glee. "That bastard is burning like a Christmas tree in January!"

"I told you, I never miss."

"The Jerries must not have many men on this side of the canal," Cat announced.

"No, if they did, you think they would have tried to rush us," Zanovitch answered. "Just let 'em try. We're in a good position here, and in this fog, we'll send 'em back a ballin.'"

Cat looked at his watch. It was nearly 3:45 a.m. Dawn would be on them in about an hour and a half. He was sure that his small group could hold out until then.

"So what are we going to do about Baker and Swanson?" Zanovitch asked. "Do we sit here until daylight?"

"That's a good question. They were supposed to make their way southeast and then approach us from the south. I think we'll just have to wait."

"Maybe they're wounded or captured?"

"No way to tell," Cat replied. "We'll wait. Ackers, keep a clear eye to the right for the Yanks!"

"Aye, Colour Sergeant, if I see the Yanks, I promise not to shoot 'em," Ackers yelled back.

The bullet blasted into his head and the body fell to the floor.

"*Scheiße!*" Gunter screamed, raising his weapon and firing his MP40 at Weise at point-blank range. Weise crumpled to the ground, his back falling against the wall. The blood trailed down the wall as he slid to his rump and landed in a seated position.

Graf turned, pulled the trigger on his PPSh, and plastered Gunter with lead. For an instant the SS sergeant twitched from the recoil of so many rounds hitting his body that he seemed suspended in midair, but he fell as well.

Instantaneously, Küster swiveled his FG42 to the right and fired a burst that killed the other SS soldier with two well-placed shots before the SS man could fire at Graf.

In a matter of seconds, it was over.

Obersturmführer Kodritz, Gunter, and the SS soldier lay dead on the floor. *Feldwebel* Weise had shot the SS officer from behind before he could kill Graf. Now, for saving his friend, Weise lay against the wall, dying.

Graf ran to Weise and knelt at his side. "Why?"

"I couldn't remain neutral. You are my comrade in arms."

Graf put his hand behind Weise's head in an attempt to comfort him. He quickly looked at Weise's wounds, immediately recognizing that Weise had only a few seconds to live.

"You were going to let him shoot you, weren't you?"

Graf shook his head. "I don't know. Maybe."

"You mustn't. You can't," Weise said as the blood came up in his throat and he began to choke. "You are the only one who can keep our rabbits alive."

And then, with a sigh, he leaned to his right side and died.

Graf gently placed him down on the ground.

The room was silent for a long while, broken only by an occasional short burst of Bren Gunfire directed at the floor above them.

"*Oberfeldwebel*, what do we do now?" Küster asked.

"We can't stay, and we may not be able to retreat. *Fallschirmjägers*, prepare to attack."

Graf's men checked their weapons before preparing to assault in the fog.

"There must be a better way," Mira shouted in English. "He intends to attack."

"You won't stand a chance," Baker offered.

Graf looked at his men and signaled for them to wait. He looked like a man ready to die as he strode toward the American sergeant. "I have been fighting this war since 1940. Who are you to tell me that we do not stand a chance?"

"You could surrender. Your war would be over."

"No, surrender is not in my vocabulary. My *Fallschirmjägers* do not surrender."

"I could arrange a truce."

Graf faced Baker and hesitated. He paced a few steps. "I'm listening. What do you suggest?"

"I can order the men outside not to fire. They will listen to me. I'll let you cross back to the eastern side of the canal and you set the girl and us free."

Graf looked at his ever shrinking band of *Fallschirmjägers*. His men were like rare gold coins to him; precious, scarce, and only spent after careful consideration. He would not sell his men without gain and he saw that there was no gain in dying in this stinking pump house in a battle that was already lost.

Graf looked back at his men and then at Weise. "You give me your word as a soldier and a paratrooper?"

"I give you my word as a soldier and a paratrooper."

Graf moved forward and stared into Baker's eyes. For a moment, wolf met wolf. "Then it is, as you Americans say, a deal. Call to your men."

Baker nodded and went to the window.

"Cat, it's Baker. Can you hear me?"

"Baker, yes, I'm right happy to hear you're alive. I just moved up another rifle platoon. We've got machine guns positioned on the flanks. We'll have you out of there in no time."

"Good work, Cat, but I want you to order the men to cease-fire. I'm arranging a truce. Here's the plan: We let the *nine* remaining Germans here cross to the east side of the canal, and they will let me, Swanson, and Mira go free."

"I understand. Can you trust them?"

"I believe so."

"Then we'll cease-fire," Cat yelled.

"Good. Don't shoot. Nobody fires. Clear?"

"Clear!" Cat replied.

Baker turned to Graf. "Done."

"What's your name?" Graf asked.

"Staff Sergeant Matt Baker, 101st Airborne Division."

Graf nodded. "I am *Oberfeldwebel* Wilhelm Graf, Sixth Fallschirmjäger Regiment."

Baker searched Graf's eyes, as if he had seen him before, on some far forgotten battlefield. "We ran up against the Sixth Fallschirmjägers in Normandy."

"Yes, I was there. St. Come du Mont. Also at Carentan and St. Lo."

Baker nodded. "I know St. Come du Mont and Carentan."

"Those were desperate days. We are much the same, you and I. Both *Fallschirmjägers*. Both leaders. We have even been in some of the same battles. In a different world, I might call you friend."

"Maybe in a different world, but what we fight for, in the end, makes all the difference."

Graf nodded. "Or maybe my curse is that I did not have the luxury to choose my place of birth."

"Your men killed those Dutch kids in cold blood yesterday. I saw it all from the church tower."

"Not my men, but this SS pig," Graf said, pointing to Kodritz's lifeless body. "In this war, I have watched many men cross the fine line from soldier to murderer. Once that thin line is crossed, the harm is severe."

Baker studied Graf, realizing that this man meant what he said. "I've always thought that the biggest challenge is to act as a soldier as well as a decent man."

Graf nodded. "My men will act as soldiers, not as murderers. I not only want my men to live through the fighting they must face, but also to have lives worth living after the fighting is done."

Baker didn't answer, but just stared at the tall German.

"So, we have more in common than you wish to admit," Graf replied as he placed the sling of his PPSh submachine gun over his neck and signaled for his men to get ready to depart. "I may see you again, Staff Sergeant Baker, and let us hope that it is in better circumstances."

Baker stood with Swanson and Mira, waiting patiently as the Germans collected their gear and prepared to leave.

Graf walked over to the soldier who had captured Baker and retrieved the red notebook. He then walked over to Mira and, without a word, handed the notebook to her.

Mira took the book, hugging it in her arms.

Graf glanced at Baker, as if he were going to say something more, hesitated, and then turned to his men. "*Fallschirmjägers,* move out."

Baker listened and watched as he waited in the pump house with Mira and Swanson. The bodies of the one German paratrooper and three dead SS soldiers lay on the floor.

In the east, on the German side of the canal, Baker heard the sound of armored vehicles moving in the forest, but he could tell that the sounds were moving away from the canal. With no means to cross, the German tanks had no choice but to head north.

Baker's mission had been a success, but with every success in war there is a cost.

Mira looked up at Baker and drew close to him, still holding the red notebook at her chest. "Is it over?"

Baker put his arms around her. "I think so. I am sorry about Alexander."

"He wanted so much to see his country free. Now he will never know."

"I don't know why things turn out this way. I don't understand much about this war, but when I meet people like Alexander and you, I realize why I fight. We must end this. We have to end this. And the Krauts will not give up until we make them."

"So much death. So many lives ruined. Sometimes I wonder how anything can be worth all this misery."

Baker didn't answer. He didn't know what to say. He didn't have the answer that would soothe Mira's loss.

"But, in my heart," Mira continued, "I know that Alexander believed that there was no choice but to oppose the Nazis. No one in my country wanted this war. No one wanted war except the Nazis. A lot of good people tried to deal with them, and a lot of them were killed for no other reason than because the Nazis wanted them killed. In the end, there was nothing else to do but fight them."

Mira looked up at Baker. Her eyes were red from crying, but her face was filled with determination. "Soon, we will all be free."

Swanson moved to the door. "Looks like the Irish are coming in."

The fog was dissipating as Colour Sergeant Gilchrist and Corporal Ackers carefully entered the pump house with their weapons at the ready, only to find Baker with Mira in his arms.

Cat grinned as Baker and Mira separated. The Irish Guards Colour Sergeant then looked around the room and knelt next to the lifeless body of *Obersturmführer* Kodritz.

"You, my friend, have the luck of the Irish," Cat said as he glanced at Baker. "And I suppose you and Swanson dispatched these Jerries?"

"No, but that's a story that I'm not sure I understand and I watched it happen."

Cat gazed at Baker, narrowed his eyes, and nodded. "I look forward to hearing that story sometime. And Mira, it is good to see that you are safe."

"Thank you. I am happy to see that you are unhurt as well, Colour Sergeant."

Cat strode over to Baker and the two men shook hands.

"I'm glad you brought an extra 'platoon,'" Baker chided.

"Aye, by brass and bluff. I thought that ruse might make the Jerries think we had a few more blokes that we really do."

"Looks like you still have some of those nine lives left," Baker offered with a tired smile. "We should move back to Lieshout, before the fog lifts and they see just how few of us there really are."

"Yes, and maybe we can make radio contact with headquarters," Cat added.

Guardsman Roy entered the room, carrying Baker's nickel-plated .45 caliber pistol in his hand. "I found this out back."

Cat took the silver pistol from Roy and held it in his hand, admiring the weapon.

Baker stared at the pistol. "This pistol was my father's side arm. Colonel Joe Baker. He died in Italy just before D-Day."

"Now I understand." Cat nodded and handed the pistol to Baker. "His father's sword he hath girded on."

Oberfeldwebel Graf moved his men through the woods in single file. They were dripping wet from their brief swim across the channel. After a short trek, they came across two StuGs, lined up in column with engines idling.

The assault guns were camouflaged with evergreen branches. Graf moved around the vehicles to the right until he arrived at the lead vehicle. He looked up and saw that the commander was Sergeant Schmitt.

The StuG commander waved and climbed down from the vehicle.

"Graf? Still alive?" Schmitt questioned. "What the hell happened to the barge?"

"It's a long story," Graf replied. "What are our orders?"

"You and your men are to come with me," Schmitt said. "I am to move my StuGs north and report to an *Oberstleutnant* von der Heydte who commands the Sixth *Fallschirmjäger* Regiment. I am sure you know him. I'm supposed to pick up any *Fallschirmjägers* from the Sixth that I meet on the way. It looks like you are going home."

"Home." Graf smiled. "We will ride with you."

Schmitt nodded. "Tell your men to hop on my StuGs and we'll move out before the fog lifts and the Jabos come back."

"Mount up *Fallschirmjägers*, we still have a war to fight," Graf ordered.

U.S. M9A1 2.36-inch Rocket Launcher (Bazooka)

11

The minstrel boy to the war is gone,
In the ranks of death you'll find him;
His father's sword he hath girded on,
And his wild harp slung behind him;
"Land of Song!" said the warrior bard,
"Tho' all the world betrays thee,
One sword, at least, thy right shall guard,
One faithful harp shall praise thee!"
—Verse from "The Minstrel Boy"

December 15, 1944, 2200 hours at Mourmelon-le-Grand, France:

Baker's nightmares were a swirl of faces, places, and tunes. The tune of "The Minstrel Boy," the song that Cat was forever singing, rolled around in his head. At the same time, stark images kept bringing his thoughts back to St. Come du Mont. He jolted awake, snapped from his dream by an internal demon.

For a moment, he didn't know where he was. He reached for his weapon, but realized in the same instant that he was safe, far behind the front lines, in the 101st Airborne Division base camp at Mourmelon-le-Grand.

Eyes open, he stared at the roof of the tent. His soul was filled with an eddy of emotions about the fighting in Normandy, his dead friend George Risner, and the tall German *Fallschirmjäger* in Holland. The dream didn't make sense, but few of his dreams did these days.

He remembered George Risner as vividly as if George had died only yesterday, rather than nearly six months ago. As hundreds of paratroopers walked by, they observed the grisly site of George's body burnt to a crisp standing upright in the turret of the tank, and the crossroads soon took on the infamous designation of Dead Man's Corner. He remembered how it took a day for the Graves Registration team to arrive and finally pull Risner's charred body out of the tank.

He remembered . . .

War isn't Hell; it's worse, Baker thought as he imagined his friend's burned torso stuck in the hatch of the destroyed tank.

In his soul, he knew that Risner was a better man and a better soldier than he would ever be. He also realized that in combat it was luck, more than anything else, that determined whether a person lived or died. Skill, technique, speed, or attitude often made no difference. It was a matter of time and place.

If he had been closer to Risner's tank, he might have saved his friend.

Then he realized, in a way that was beyond explanation, that he had met the man who had shot Risner.

He shook his head.

Impossible . . .

He must be imagining things, he concluded.

The action was so fast at St. Come du Mont. Everything had happened in a matter of minutes, as most combat actions do. In the action and reaction of combat, the give-and-take of life and death, how could he be sure?

But he was sure. As sure as the hot sun overhead on a humid August day at Fort Bragg. As sure as death.

The German he had met in Holland, the one he had arranged a truce with and let go at the pump house near the village of Lieshout, was the man who had killed George Risner. Baker was suddenly and absolutely sure, without any doubt, who had killed his friend.

He remembered the round-drummed submachine gun and the hunter's look of the German's face.

Baker sat up on his cot. He was bathed in sweat. The

stove inside the tent was off, the temperature outside was cool, but he was not.

Cold, wet, tired, and scared.

Why, Graf thought, is war always this way?

A Ju 52 transport lumbered forward on the snowy runway.

Oberfeldwebel Wilhelm Graf checked his watch and then took one last long drag on his cigarette. He savored the tobacco for a moment and stared at the deep white snow on the ground.

Feldwebel Küster approached Graf and reported. "*Oberfeldwebel*, the platoon is ready. Weapons, ammunition, and equipment have all been stored inside the aircraft."

"Good. Get all our rabbits aboard and prepare to take off. Check their parachutes one more time. I don't want any of these youngsters falling out of his harness."

"*Jawohl, Oberfeldwebel*," Küster said with a grin and then marched off to the plane.

The night was dark and the snow was falling in big, wet flakes as men with shovels struggled in the wind to clear off the tarmac at Padeborn, Germany.

Graf slung his PPSh over the shoulder of his white camouflaged battle smock and headed toward the Ju 52 Transport aircraft. As he reached the door, the hand of a young *Fallschirmjäger* shot out and grabbed Graf's hand to give him a lift inside. Once inside, Graf moved up to the pilot's cabin.

"This weather is shit! Shit I tell you!" the pilot cursed. "This is worse than Russia. How do they expect me to fly in this shit?"

Graf didn't reply. From his point of view, the entire operation was a gamble. Taking off in a blizzard with ten-foot visibility was just part of the package. Besides, it was not his job to fly the plane. His job started after they left the plane.

Graf sat down in the flight engineer's seat behind the pilot. The seat gave him a clear view of the cockpit and the windshield. Right now, all Graf could see was snow.

In spite of the horrible weather, the first three aircraft had taken off without mishap. The Luftwaffe, unable to gain command of the air from the overwhelming might of the Allied air forces, was only able to operate transport aircraft at night. The timing of the offensive demanded that the *Fallschirmjägers* take off no matter how bad the weather.

Graf watched in steady anticipation as the Luftwaffe officer nervously checked his instruments. Graf turned his head back to the cargo compartment to make one last check of his men. Seventeen fully armed *Fallschirmjägers* anxiously sat in cargo seats, waiting for the Ju 52 to take off.

The aircraft shuddered as the engines sputtered and came to life. The three-engined Ju 52 was the workhorse of the Luftwaffe and one of the few aircraft in the diminishing German air fleet that was suitable for parachute operations.

Memories of his last combat jump from an "Iron Annie," as the Junker 52 was called, flooded his mind. It had been in May 1941, during Operation Mercury, the invasion of Crete, and a lifetime ago. In those early days of the war, the Luftwaffe could fill the sky with aircraft. During the invasion of Crete, an entire *Fallschirmjäger* Division of eight thousand men had jumped into combat.

During Operation Mercury, the 7th Flieger Division had consisted of three parachute regiments with divisional artillery, engineers, and communications troops, as well an airborne assault regiment that had four battalions with three parachute and one glider battalion and supporting assets.

The *Fallschirmjägers* had fought hard in Crete, defeating the British and Australian defenders, but at such a terrible cost in casualties that the German High Command never again contemplated another airborne assault.

Those were the old days.

Now, more than three years later, everything was different. These were desperate times. Hitler had decided on one more roll of the dice for an all-or-nothing win. To secure this miracle, all options were employed, including the use of paratroops dropped behind enemy lines. Now, on the eve of a massive German counterattack into the snowy Ardennes woods of Belgium, focused on a quiet and unsuspecting sector of the Allied front, Graf and his men would be part of the first major German airborne operation since the fighting in Crete in 1941.

Only this jump was of a different scale. One regiment of twelve hundred men, formed into four infantry companies, plus a heavy weapons company, and a signal and engineer platoon, would parachute behind enemy lines. To make the operation more dicey, and for the slow flying Ju 52s to avoid destruction by Allied fighters, the parachute jump was planned for the dead of night.

The planners could not plan on the weather and, Graf mused, this blizzard did not bode well for the operation.

A red signal at the end of the field flashed three times.

"*Achtung!* Our signal to take off!" the pilot shouted.

A deep-throated roar enveloped the cabin of the Ju 52 Transport as the pilot pushed the throttle forward to full power.

The reverberation from the three BMW 132T nine-cylinder radial aircraft engines was deafening.

Graf looked out through the cockpit windshield. The

weather was appalling with the snow coming down furiously. He could barely see the dim lights illuminating the outline of the airfield.

"Here we go!" the pilot yelled.

The Ju 52 raced toward the end of the runway. Graf saw the three blue lights designating the take-off point grow closer and closer.

Then, just as the overloaded "Iron Annie" neared the blue lights at the end of the runway, the aircraft was suddenly airborne. The heavy plane began to slowly gain speed and altitude. With a steady drone the Ju 52 climbed into the snowy darkness.

The pilot looked back to Graf and yelled: "So far so good. If this beacon setting is correct, we are on course. One hour and thirty minutes to go. I'll give you the fifteen-minute warning when we approach the drop zone."

Graf nodded and stood up. Encumbered by his parachute and combat gear, he carefully moved back to the seat near the jump door.

As he moved to his seat *Feldwebel* Küster shot Graf a look of confidence as Graf sat down.

Graf patted Küster on the shoulder.

After the fighting in Holland, Graf had made sure that Küster was promoted to *Feldwebel*. The rest of his men, except for the few he had brought back from the Hell of the Netherlands, were new, young, and inexperienced. To his dismay, some of the newest recruits were not of the best quality.

More important, no one except Graf had ever parachuted before. These *Fallschirmjägers* would earn their wings on their first jump.

He looked out the side window into the blackness and saw the barely visible red glow from the exhaust of the port engine. Graf shook his head. The pilot was using a radio beacon and his odometer to dead-reckon navigate to the drop zone. If the pilot found the drop zone in this weather, it would be a major miracle.

Graf no longer believed in miracles.

He reached for the sealed envelope *Oberst* von der Heydte had given him before they took off. The current operation, code-named *Stösser,* was under the command of *Oberst* von der Heydte and on special instructions from the Führer himself.

He opened the letter, turned on his flashlight, and read. It was an important order that was to be read to every soldier prior to the attack:

**Regimental Order Number 54,
dated 16 December 1944.**

Soldiers, your hour has come!

At this moment strong attack armies have started against the Anglo-Americans. I don't need to tell you any more. You feel it yourselves. We gamble everything. You carry within you the holy obligation to give your all, to perform to the utmost, for our Fatherland and our Führer!

Signed: Field Marshal Gerd von Runstedt
Commander-in-Chief West

Graf shook his head. His men were briefed. They knew their orders. Their job was to conduct specific operations behind enemy lines near the Belgium town of Bastogne. *If* the Ju 52 pilot placed them on their designated drop zone, then he and his men would do their duty.

Graf folded the letter and put it back into his pocket. No additional encouragement to his men was needed.

* * *

Unable to sleep, Baker lit the candle that was placed on an empty ammunition box between his and Zanovitch's cots. Zanovitch was asleep, snoring.

That man never had trouble sleeping, Baker thought.

The air inside the tent was damp. Condensation covered the white winter-liner of the tent.

Baker searched his haversack and took out a pad of stationary and a pencil. Sitting on his cot, he blew on his hands to warm them, then placed the pad on his knee and addressed a letter to Mira.

He wasn't much of a writer. He found writing an extremely difficult task. He hardly ever wrote his mother, but he had somehow found the time to write several letters to Mira. Somehow, writing to Mira wasn't as difficult as writing to anyone else. He enjoyed her letters, and since he didn't have anyone special back home, Mira offered him the opportunity to think about something other than the war.

Mira had written five letters to each one he sent, but that had not seemed to bother her. Each letter from Mira was cheerful and full of life. He was able to put things in his letters to her that he couldn't tell anyone else.

Baker wrote a few lines then put down his pencil.

He watched the flame flicker in the candle for a moment.

He tried to conjure up the jumbled feelings in his heart.

Fear. In battle, he had not overcome it, but had learned to use it.

Hate. In combat he had not embraced it, but had turned its fire into action and had not stepped over the line from soldier to murderer.

Pride. In the thick of the fight, pride in his unit and his brothers in arms had caused him to love his men, but he had learned that to win in combat he had to risk the thing he loved.

Love.

A lot had happened since he had last seen Mira.

When the Germans had left the pump house, Baker brought Mira back to her mother in Lieshout. There they had an opportunity to talk. For a moment there was no war. For a moment he visualized a future he had never contemplated before, and they had promised to write each other—a promise Baker never thought would materialize.

Then it was time to go and Baker, Zanovitch, and Swanson returned with Cat and his men to Veghel.

Cat rode with Baker in Baker's jeep all the way to Veghel. Baker smiled as he remembered the crazy Irishman singing his damn song, "The Minstrel Boy," as they rolled up the road to Veghel. As soon as they arrived in the town, Baker and Cat reported the action at the pump house to Major Danahy, 101st Airborne Division G2.

The fighting for Hell's Highway, however, was not over. Baker and Cat, two soldiers from different armies who had become friends, said their farewells and returned to their units and new missions.

Operation Market Garden lasted two more days. It ended in an Allied failure. The British XXX Corps could not reach the surrounded British 1st Airborne at Arnhem in time. On Monday night, September 25, the survivors of the brave British 1st Airborne Division and the Polish Brigade withdrew across the Rhine River by rafts to the safety of the southern shore. Of the 10,600 men of the British and Polish force that landed north of the Rhine near Arnhem, only 2,398 were evacuated. By September 26 the bold Allied plan to end the war before Christmas 1944 had failed.

The fighting, however, did not stop. The Germans would not give up and defended stubbornly. The 101st Airborne was sent north to an area that soon became known to troops as the "Island." This strip of land was located between the Nederijn and Waal rivers with Arnhem to the north, Nijmegen to the south.

The fighting on the "Island" was one of constant skirmishing and patrols. The weather was cold and wet, and the Germans fought with snipers and mortars. After more than a month of constant fighting, the 101st Airborne Division was relieved in early November and left Holland for a base camp in Mourmelon-le-Grand, France.

There, the Division rested, received replacements, and trained.

The candle flickered and went out. Baker fumbled in his pocket for matches and relit the candle. He tried to gather his thoughts as he once again took up his pencil.

He started writing to Mira about George Risner. He hadn't talked to anyone about George in a long time. He didn't know why he felt it was important that she know about George, but he knew he wanted to tell her about him, and how he died.

"Baker, you awake?" A gruff and familiar voice sounded from outside the tent.

"Yeah. Mac? Is that you?"

First Sergeant Mac Hassay opened the tent flap.

Baker turned around, surprised to see Mac making a call so early in the morning. Mac was in full combat gear.

This was not a good sign.

"Grab your gear and get over to Headquarters ASAP," Mac ordered without any fanfare.

"What's up?"

"The shit is hitting the fan again. Something is happening along the Ardennes front. General McAuliffe wants you to take your recon boys up north to Belgium, as soon as possible."

"Where?"

"Hell, Baker, I don't know. Someplace called Bastogne."

Baker quickly grabbed his gear. Quietly humming the tune of "The Minstrel Boy," he left the tent for Division Headquarters and his next mission.

GLOSSARY

101st Airborne Division, "Screaming Eagles": Activated on August 15, 1942, the 101st Airborne Division became one of the most famous units in the European Theater of Operations during World War II. The 101st Airborne arrived in England on September 15, 1943, and received additional training in Berkshire and Wiltshire. On June 6, 1944, the Division was dropped into Normandy behind Utah Beach. Against fierce resistance it took Pouppeville, Vierville, and St. Come du Mont. On June 12, the stronghold of Carentan fell, and after mopping up and maintaining its positions, the Division returned on July 13 to England, for rest and training. On September 17, 1944, the Screaming Eagles took part in one of the largest of airborne invasions in history, Operation Market Garden, and landed behind German lines in the Netherlands (Holland). The Screaming Eagles took their objectives and then battled the Germans along Hell's Highway from September 17 to 26, 1944.

Amis: German slang for Americans.

Arbeitseinsatz: German term for the drafting of laborers from the occupied countries to fill the vacancies in Germany in arms factories, the farming sector, and community services. In 1942, Dutch civilians were drafted across the Netherlands for this forced labor. Every man between the age of eighteen and forty-five was obliged to leave his home to work in German factories. By 1945, nearly eight million workers were drafted from the occupied countries for forced labor in Germany.

Bailey bridge: A transportable, prefabricated truss bridge that can be carried in trucks and is strong enough to hold tanks. The Bailey was used very effectively by Allied combat engineering units to span gaps up to sixty meters wide during World War II. The Bailey is considered one of the great examples of military engineering as it requires no special tools or heavy equipment for construction.

Bren Carrier: A small, tracked, open-topped British-designed armored vehicle also known as the universal carrier; used by British forces during World War II.

Bren Gun: The Bren was an extremely effective .303 caliber, 22.8 pound, light machine gun used by the British Commonwealth forces in World War II. The word *Bren* comes from Brno, the Czechoslovakian city of design, and Enfield, the location of the British Royal Small Arms Factory.

C-47: An American made, two-engined transport aircraft also known as a Skytrain, Dakota, or DC-3. The C-47 was the workhorse of World War II and was used to drop paratroopers, tow gliders, and haul passengers and equipment.

Colour Sergeant: The equivalent rank of staff sergeant in the Irish Guards of the British army. The insignia is a crown over three chevrons.

D-day: The unnamed day on which a particular operation commences or is to commence. D+1 is the second day of the operation, D+2 the third, etcetera.

Det cord: Short for detonation cord. Det cord is an explosive cord that has many purposes but is primarily used to set off several explosive devices at once.

Division: An organizational combat unit generally made up of two or three regiments, or two or more brigades, and usually controlled by a corps. In general, a division would have between ten thousand and twenty thousand soldiers assigned.

DZ: Drop zone. Paratroopers jump into DZs.

Enfilade: A concept in military tactics used to describe a military formation's exposure to "flanking fire." The word comes from the French *enfiler*—to skewer.

Fallschirmjäger: German for paratrooper.

Feldgendarmerie: German field police. These military policemen directed traffic and maintained order and discipline behind the front lines.

Feldwebel: German for sergeant.

FG42: The Fallschirmjägergewehr 42 was an 8mm Mauser, 11.2-pound automatic rifle produced in Germany during

World War II. The FG42 was developed specifically for the use by *Fallschirmjägers,* hence its designation as Fallschirmjägergewehr. After the horrific fighting during the airborne assault on Crete in 1941, the *Fallschirmjägers* expressed the urgent need for a weapon with more range and firepower. The result was the FG42, which could fire in semiautomatic and automatic modes. A weapon ahead of its time, it was difficult and expensive to manufacture and only small numbers were issued during the war.

Firefly: A British Sherman tank that was upgraded from the standard American Sherman tank with a high-velocity seventeen-pounder (76mm) cannon. The standard M4 Sherman tank was woefully undergunned, armed with a 75mm cannon that could not penetrate the front or flanks of most of the German tanks in World War II. The seventeen-pounder cannon allowed the Firefly to defeat the German Panzer V (Panther) and Panzer VI (Tiger) tanks.

First sergeant: The chief noncommissioned officer of a company, battery, or troop in the U.S. Army.

Flak (*Fliegerabwehrkanone*): Antiaircraft artillery. The term *Flak* became known by Allied forces to mean anything shot into the air in an air-defense role against enemy air units.

G2: A staff officer responsible for intelligence collection and intelligence operations, normally at the division level. In the U.S. Army the G2 is the assistant chief of staff, G2 (Intelligence) at the division, corps, or army level of command.

Generaloberst: German for colonel general, a rank used by the German military in World War II and equivalent to general in the U.S. Army. It is the rank before *Generalfeldmarschall* (field marshal).

Hauptscharführer: German SS rank for master sergeant.

Hauptsturmführer: German SS rank for captain. Literally, "head storm leader."

Heer: The regular German army formally announced in 1935 and disbanded in August 1946 by the Allies.

Irish Guards: Originally formed in 1900, the Irish Guards are a unit with a proud heritage in the British army who are affectionately known as "The Micks." The Irish Guards fought in the early battles of World War II, and in June 1941 the 2d and 3d Battalions landed with the Guards Armored Division in Normandy and fought with the Guards Armored Division until the end of the war, taking part in the advance from the Seine to Nijmegen. It was just before Operation Market Garden that Lieutenant Colonel J.O.E. Vandeleur, commander of the Irish Guards Group, led an attack on the bridge over the Meuse-Escaut Canal at De Groote Barrier (as explained in the film *A Bridge Too Far,* with Vandeleur played by the actor Michael Caine). This bridge is known today as Joe's Bridge to honor Vandeleur and the exploits of his Irish Guards. During Operation Market Garden the Irish Guards worked closely with the 101st Airborne Division to keep Hell's Highway open for the British XXX Corps.

Jabo: A German term derived from the German *Jäger*-bomber, or fighter-bomber (literally, "hunter-bomber").

Jäger: German rank of private in the *Fallschirmjägers* (paratroops).

Jawohl: German for "Yes sir."

Kampfgruppe: The German term *kampfgruppe* refers to a flexible combat formation from company to brigade sized. *Kampfgruppe* were banded together temporarily to perform a specific task and formed from different types of military units that were required or available.

Leutnant: German for lieutenant

Luftwaffe: German air force. The *Fallschirmjäger* (paratroopers) were officially assigned to the Luftwaffe, not the Wehrmacht (German army), but received direction, combat support, and logistics from the regular Wehrmacht.

LZ: The military abbreviation for landing zone. Gliders landed in LZs.

Maschinengewehr 42: German for Machine Gun 42, or MG42. The MG42 was a superb, fast-firing machine gun that entered service with German forces in 1942. The 7.92mm (8mm Mauser) rifle-caliber weapon was one of the fastest firing (1200 rounds per minute) and most effective machine guns ever made.

MP40: The MP40, often called the Schmeisser, or "burp gun" by the Americans, was a highly effective 9mm submachine gun used by the Wehrmacht during World War II. The MP40 (Maschinenpistole 40, literally "machine pistol 40") was used extensively by *Fallschirmjägers,* squad leaders, and platoon leaders. The MP40 was very effective in close combat and had an effective range of about thirty meters. The MP40 had a folding metal stock and a thirty-two-round detachable magazine.

Oberfeldwebel: German for master sergeant, a senior sergeant who usually led a section (sixteen to twenty soldiers) or platoon (thirty to fifty soldiers). *Herr Oberfeldwebel* is the proper official greeting and literally means Mr. Master Sergeant.

Oberjäger: German rank of corporal in the *Fallschirmjäger* (paratroops).

Oberstleutnant: German for lieutenant colonel. A lieutenant colonel usually commanded a battalion or battle group of anywhere from one hundred to eight hundred men.

Obersturmführer: The rank of first lieutenant in the German SS. Literally: "senior assault leader."

P-47: The P-47 Thunderbolt was one of the main U.S. Army Air Force (USAAF) fighters of World War II. Also known as the Jug, the aircraft was the largest single-engined fighter of its day and was especially effective in the ground-attack missions.

PAN: The Dutch resistance group Partisan Action Netherlands in Eindhoven that was established in 1943 and had nearly a hundred members. Consisting of mostly young, idealistic men and women, PAN operated in the Eindhoven, Netherlands, area.

Panzerfaust: German for a light, portable, antitank grenade launcher. Literally translated as "tank fist," the *panzerfaust* was a lethal and important antitank weapon. The Panzerfaust 30 was the most common version of the *panzerfaust* in September 1944 with a warhead that could penetrate 200mm of armor and a range of thirty meters.

Panzergrenadier: German for mechanized or armored infantry. The term *Panzergrenadier* was adopted in 1942 and applied equally to both the infantry component of Panzer Divisions as well as the new divisions known as Panzergrenadier Divisions. Organized as combined arms formations, *panzergrenadier* units employed infantry, usually mounted in halftracks, and mechanized artillery working closely with tanks. Many *panzergrenadier* units used trucks as German industry was incapable of producing sufficient halftracks for all *panzergrenadier* units. *Panzergrenadiers* were assigned to Panzer-Division. As the war dragged on and attrition ate away at the German army, *panzergrenadier* units more often fought as foot infantry.

PPSh-41 submachine gun: A Russian-made submachine gun. The PPSh-41 (Pistolet-Pulemet Shpagina: in Russian: Пистолет-пулемёт Шпагина) was a simple, durable weapon that was produced in great numbers by the Russians during

World War II. The submachine gun used the 7.62 x 25mm pistol round and could hold either a drum magazine containing seventy-one rounds, or stick magazines containing thirty-five rounds.

Stadia reticle: Targeting reticle used by bazookas and *panzerfaust* antitank weapons that employed a stadiametric range estimation based on the average sizes of armored fighting vehicles.

Sten gun: A British 9mm submachine gun. The Sten was an open-bolt, blowback-operated, selective-fire firearm developed at low cost and very effective at close range. STEN is an acronym, cited as derived from the names of the weapon's chief designers, Major Reginald Shepherd and Harold Turpin, and EN for Enfield. Over four million Sten guns were produced during World War II. The Sten had a side feeding magazine that was a direct copy of the German MP40 submachine gun magazine.

Sturmbannführer: The rank of major in the German SS.

Sturmgeschütz, or StuG: German for assault gun, usually abbreviated StuG. These turretless assault guns provided fire support for infantry, panzer, and *panzergrenadier* units. The StuG was a tank chassis with a gun, usually a long-barreled 75mm, directly mounted on it. It was cheaper and easier to build than a turreted tank and was therefore produced in great numbers. The StuG had a low profile and heavy frontal armor and a crew of four.

Top: U.S. Army slang for first sergeant. The first sergeant is the "top" sergeant of a company.

Typhoon fighter-bomber: The Hawker Typhoon was a British single-seat fighter-bomber, developed in 1941, that was armed with four 20mm cannons and could carry two one-thousand-pound bombs or eight RP3 sixty-pound warhead unguided rockets. The Typhoon became one of the most successful ground-attack aircraft during World War II and was used with great effect along Hell's Highway during Operation Market Garden.

Waffen SS: The Waffen SS, or fighting SS, were a separate army in the German military that had different ranks and was dedicated to furthering the Nazi cause. The Waffen SS was a frontline fighting organization with nearly half a million soldiers by the end of World War II. Most units of the Waffen SS fought with fierce bitterness against the Allies and civilian populations and were responsible for several notorious war crimes. At the Nuremberg Trials in 1945, the Waffen SS was condemned as a criminal organization due to their involvement with the National Socialist German Workers Party (Nazi). Conscripts sworn in after 1943 were exempted from the judgment on the basis of involuntary servitude.

Wehrmacht: German for armed forces, from 1935 to 1945. The Wehrmacht consisted of the Heer (army), the Kriegsmarine (navy), and the Luftwaffe (air force). The Waffen SS was not officially part of the Wehrmacht but was subject to Wehrmacht operational and tactical control.

XXX Corps: The British XXX Corps was an armored (tank heavy) corps in the British army that played a critical role in Operation Market Garden during World War II. XXX Corps was led by Lieutenant General Brian Horrocks. During Operation Market Garden, XXX Corps had the mission to fight its way up a sixty-mile-long narrow road from the Belgium border through the Netherlands from Eindhoven to Nijmegen to Arnhem and link up with the airborne forces that had been dropped at strategic bridge and crossing points along the axis of attack.